A Girl in Three Parts

SUZANNE DANIEL

Alfred A. Knopf

New York

To Mike,

for all he is and all he does

And our children,

Rebecca, James, and Francesca

THIS IS A BORZOI BOOK PUBLISHED BY ALFRED A. KNOPF

This is a work of fiction. Names, characters, places, and incidents either are the product of the author's imagination or are used fictitiously. Any resemblance to actual persons, living or dead, events, or locales is entirely coincidental.

Text copyright © 2019 by Suzanne Daniel
Jacket art copyright © 2020 by Liz Casal

All rights reserved. Published in the United States by Alfred A. Knopf, an imprint of Random House Children's Books, a division of Penguin Random House LLC, New York.
Originally published in paperback in Australia as *Allegra in Three Parts* by Pan Macmillan Australia Pty Ltd, Sydney, in 2019.

Knopf, Borzoi Books, and the colophon are registered trademarks of Penguin Random House LLC.

"I Am Woman" written by Helen Reddy and Ray Burton. © Irving Music, Inc./Buggerlugs Music Co./Rondor Music Australia Pty Ltd. "Open Up Your Heart" written by Graham Wayne Thomas. © Universal Music Publishing Pty Ltd. All rights reserved. International copyrights secured. Reprinted with permission.
PEANUTS © Peanuts Worldwide LLC. Dist. By ANDREWS MCMEEL SYNDICATION. Reprinted with permission. All rights reserved.

Visit us on the Web! GetUnderlined.com

Educators and librarians, for a variety of teaching tools, visit us at RHTeachersLibrarians.com

Library of Congress Cataloging-in-Publication Data is available upon request.
ISBN 978-1-9848-5107-9 (trade) — ISBN 978-1-9848-5108-6 (lib. bdg.) —
ISBN 978-1-9848-5109-3 (ebook)

The text of this book is set in 11-point Caslon 540.
Interior design by Ken Crossland

Printed in the United States of America
April 2020
10 9 8 7 6 5 4 3 2 1

First American Edition

Self-knowledge is no guarantee of happiness, but it is on the side of happiness and can supply the courage to fight for it.

—Simone de Beauvoir

CHAPTER ONE

I AM ALLEGRA ON ONE SIDE AND ALLY DOWN THE OTHER.

And sometimes I split myself in two.

Patricia O'Brien can keep a Hula-Hoop going around her hips for nineteen minutes, and Scott Perkins can ride his bike the entire length of Blair Street with both hands on his knees and a kitten around his neck. And me . . . well . . . my trick is: I can split myself in two. It's not really a trick; it's more my inside-out secret, something I have to do because of Joy and Matilde. They are my grandmothers, and I love them both and they totally love me, in very different ways.

But they can't stand each other, not even for the count of one-apple-pie.

Sister Josepha has chosen me to read the prayer at today's outdoor assembly, our first now that I've moved up to sixth grade after the long summer break. She said she was impressed by my papier-mâché of the Angel Gabriel appearing to the Virgin Mary. Then Kimberly from the Popular Group announced to the class, "It's not even dry!" but here I am, Sister nods and I know exactly what I have to do: deliver the prayer in equal parts to Joy and Matilde.

There's Joy—radiant—in a mauve sun hat on the lunch benches under the mulberry tree. She's sitting next to Patricia O'Brien's mother, who all the sixth-grade boys think is a good sort especially after she showed off her own skills with Patricia's Hula-Hoop after Patricia arrived new to school last term. They're laughing about something hilarious, and Joy's bright face is dancing in tune with Mrs. O'Brien's multi-colored bangles. But the moment I step forward, Joy's head stops dead still and her eyes fasten, fully fixed on me. The prayer is asking the Dear Lord to give us the strength during Lent to resist what we've offered up. And as saintly as Joy looks now, and as prayerful as she may appear, I know she's probably thinking: *Why give up anything, sweetie, when indulgence is so delicious!*

Making Joy focused makes me feel alive.

Matilde is all in fawn at her post near the girls' toilets, alone. She doesn't cook her Hungarian meatballs on meatless Fridays, but I know that she's not a fan of Lent, or of God, for that matter. I think she's pretty mad at him after what happened to her family back during the war. And then there's all the things "that man" did. I don't know who "that man" was exactly, or what he did exactly. I just try to piece together what I can when Matilde's sister visits the first Wednesday of each month, and I cup my ear against the closed door and catch every fourth word when they mix

2

their mother tongue with English. It's like a jigsaw puzzle I've been putting together for as long as I remember. Aunt Helena always leaves looking triumphant, while Matilde looks exhausted and her lips are kind of pale and pinched.

But this morning in the playground, as I deliver the prayer in Matilde's direction, I see her lips relax and form a sort of proud shape and she looks almost S-E-R-E-N-E. . . . That was a word on my spelling list last week.

Making Matilde exhale makes me feel calm.

So at eleven and a half, this is what I know so far: Adults can love you and care for you in different ways that work for them and work for you. It's kind of like the soft drinks delivered to the Lucky Listers across the road, all different flavors but all really good. But while the adults love you in these different ways, sometimes they seem to loathe the differences in each other. They can be mad with their own grown-up children, and those grown-up children can be mad with their parents, even though they're old. But all of them can keep on loving you, as long as you're just a kid, and you pretend not to notice this badness of feeling and you don't tell any of them straight out that you love the others very much, or even that you love all of them the same. But sometimes I really wish it were different.

I live in Number 23 with Matilde. Rick lives there too—sort of—he's in the flat above the garage. Rick's tall and strong and he's my dad, which you would think would make Matilde notice him, but she's got a blind spot when it comes to Rick. She knows he's there because she plates up his dinner and irons his board shorts and ticks her tongue when she hears the horse races coming from the radio inside his flat. Luckily Rick doesn't say that much, so I can usually ignore Matilde ignoring Rick. Occasionally, though, when I see that awful sad look on Rick's face, more banished-bold-boy than dad-sized man, I feel a tightness in the part of my heart that lives behind my throat. And on those days, I am split in three.

Number 23 is sturdy and clean, dark brick on the outside and dark wood inside. Things are always in order because of Matilde, who spends hours dusting, polishing and mending; she never rests, just a couple of sips of black tea downed at the kitchen sink and she keeps going. My uniform is neatly pressed, hanging on the outside of my wardrobe every evening above my shined shoes and packed bag. My fingernails are cleaned every night, and cut once a week and my hair is washed and inspected for nits on Sunday afternoons.

There's no getting out of piano practice with Matilde; she can call a wrong note from the laundry and the wrong tempo while weeding the garden. She hears my spelling words on weeknights and gives me an additional list of her own. In third grade, I was the only kid in the whole school who could spell D-I-A-R-R-H-E-A and that earned me the pick from Sister Josepha's holy card drawer. As I was choosing between *Angels Point the Way* and *Mater Dolorosa,* Kimberly from the Popular Group announced: "Let's call Allegra DIARRHEA PANTS!" She's the meanest girl in our class and definitely disrupts my digestion.

After school it's Matilde's cooking that steadies my stomach and warms my world. When I get to the lane, I know instantly whether it's chicken paprikash, pork sausage or goulash soup for dinner. It's all made from scratch, using the choicest pickings from Matilde's garden and served with hot cheese bread. It's nothing like the chops, peas and instant mashed potatoes the Lucky Listers have most nights, but to me it smells like home and tastes like love.

Matilde's garden is as practical as she is. There are raised vegetable beds with tomatoes, zucchinis, onions and beets—in fact, just about every vegetable I can spell and some I can't. Beyond the six raised beds is a chook pen with three laying hens, which Rick and I have named Scrambled, Boiled and Omelette. He said it's best not to tell Matilde— she'd think naming the chooks is complete nonsense. I sometimes imagine that if the Holocaust came to North Bondi, I could hide in the shed under the bench between the compost bin and the tools, and I could survive for years on the fresh food in Matilde's garden.

Through the brown gate in our side fence and along the path is Number 25. This is where Joy lives, and there's nothing remotely edible in her garden. It's been created, she says, to enliven the senses. On Joy's side, life is in full bloom. Color and scent cocoon me, and my heart always skips to a little trot. Orange and pink bougainvilleas, purple paper daisies, climbing jasmine and our favorite, the fuchsias: Joy is teaching me their names and how to care for each one. Painted rocks border a water-lily pond that is home to a penny tortoise called Simone de Beauvoir. Some nights when Joy gets home from Liberty Club, she discusses issues with Simone de Beauvoir; I can hear her from my bedroom.

It's kind of weird but mostly a funny sort of interesting. Wind chimes hang from all of Joy's frangipani trees that run along our fence line so that on a breezy afternoon we can hear their tunes from Number 23. It gives me little air bubbles down the part of my heart that runs along my spine. But if Matilde hears the chimes from next door, she ticks her tongue and closes all the windows.

■ ■ ■

After a sweltering first week of the first term back at school, it's Sunday, and I'm looking for Joy. I find her in the glasshouse dusting her emotions. Joy, you see, has kept every tear she's ever shed throughout her adult life, all in colored bottles, lined up, dated and labeled. Whenever she feels inclined, we go through the bottles, and she tells me the stories behind each one.

My favorite is ELATION, dated 18 September 1962—the very day I was born. Joy gives it a good dust and a little kiss. There's FORCED CHOICE, dated 25 November 1943. That bottle was filled just after she told the persistent American officer with the navy-blue eyes that she had a responsible Australian fiancé her parents particularly liked who would be returning to Sydney very soon. There's SORROW, dated 2 January 1954, the day her father, my great-grandfather Albert, passed away. This stands beside one I don't really understand called SELF-ACTUALIZATION, which is a purple glass bottle dated 8 March 1973, three-quarters filled after she went to her first Liberty Club meeting.

And then there's a whole row called DEVASTATION, dated 11 August 1965. Joy goes quiet when she dusts DEVASTATION. Her chin drops down and her eyelids quiver like moth wings. Her hands become a little bit shaky and a big bit careful. DEVASTATION doesn't have a story.

"Let's have mint tea," Joy says with a mood-changing grin. I follow her into the kitchen and get everything out. I boil the kettle, lay the tray and pour from the heated pottery teapot. "Ally, you play Mother this time," she says, as though she's never said that before. Joy talks some more about the American officer, his charming smile, his beautiful manners and the jeweled box he so sweetly gifted to her.

"He was completely mad about me, and *boy oh boy*, could that man make me laugh. He could play the harmonica, lift me with one arm and mimic any movie star—foreign accents—the lot! It's so important, Ally, to find a man with heart who provides spark. Responsible is important, of course, but it can be a little dull at times. But spark, my darling— *spark* ignites and illuminates love every day." The mint tea is steaming up her glasses.

After our tea it's time for Joy to get ready for Liberty Club, and I lie on her bed looking at her feather collection as she changes. She's all bottle green and amber velvet, beaded bolero and sequined scarves. I ask if she ever saw the American officer again, and she says, "Good God, no," she was married soon after the war ended and her husband would never "in a month of Sundays" have allowed any contact.

"Although I did sneak off a couple of perfumed letters

and even a photo of your father, Rick, when he was my bonny bouncy baby," she says with a wink.

As Joy is powdering her face, I see her glance at my birthmark, and the flash of an idea appears in her eyes. "Come here, Ally. Let's see if a bit of my matte makeup can help disguise that little birthmark on your wrist. There you go, pet . . . a little pat . . . almost gone . . . perfect. Here, you keep this compact so you can do it yourself." She sweeps me up into her plump arms and I nestle into my favorite place in all the world: the harbor between Joy's mountainous bosoms. As she draws slow circles at the nape of my neck with her long, painted nails and hums "Too-Ra-Loo-Ra-Loo-Ral," I close my eyes and inhale her lavender-scented love.

I could have stayed there with Joy for hours, but she was getting a lift with her friend Whisky Wendy in the V-Dub Beetle and I was getting hungry. There's never any food in Joy's house.

■ ■ ■

Matilde works for Bolton's Fashion House, though she never goes to their house, wherever that is. She is a seamstress and she cuts and pins and sews piecework in our front room at Number 23. Sometimes there's no work so she doesn't get paid, *not a red cent*, but then there's a big rush job that the factory can't handle and the sewing machine goes most of the night. I quite like the sound of that machine, and lying in my bed across the hall, I can make up little rhymes in my mind to match its march and stop-start throb. When the machine halts suddenly, and Matilde sighs, I have to start again.

The next morning Rick wakes me up for school. That doesn't happen very often. When I come into the kitchen, he's there looking awkward like an unwelcome guest. He asks me to take a cup of tea in to Matilde because she's worked through the night.

"Let her think you made it," says Rick gently.

"Why?"

"Well, Al Pal, that way she'll actually enjoy it." Rick passes me Matilde's mug, the one with the pink roses down the handle and the tiny chip on the rim, and I move off carefully toward the front room. "And take her these biscuits," he calls after me. I'm not sure where Rick got the Iced VoVos, certainly not from Matilde's pantry; she wouldn't dream of keeping *shop-bought* biscuits here in Number 23.

Matilde is in her day-before clothes—asleep, with her head on her crossed arms on the cutting table. Quiet as a mouse, I place the tea and biscuits down. She stirs, stretches, and seems pleased to see the tea. But then suddenly she moves the direction of her reach and takes hold of my wrist, firmly.

"What is this?" she asks.

"Tea, I made it myself . . . and biscuits."

"No, this! This on your wrist! This nonsense covering your special mark." Her voice drops and her accent thickens.

What will I say? I don't want to tell her it was Joy's work— she won't like that, not a bit—so I pick at my tunic and tell her I was just playing with makeup at Lucinda Lister's house yesterday afternoon. Her lips pinch in and all but disappear; she sighs through her nostrils and takes her workhorse hands to her temples. There I see her own special mark: a number tattooed on her wrist.

When I was nine I knew enough not to ask Matilde why she always had numbers written on her wrist, so I asked Rick instead. He said that bad people put it there when she was in a concentration camp during the war, but that it was best not to mention this to Matilde. I never do, but this morning I realize something, the way you can at eleven when suddenly you feel nineteen. Matilde thinks my birthmark is a match for hers. I see it too, a red stamp of nature on me in exactly the same place that the dark numbers have been forced onto her. Suddenly I dislike my little birthmark completely. Thank goodness for Joy; I'm going to powder it every morning with that matte makeup.

CHAPTER TWO

IT'S A STINKY-HOT DAY AT SCHOOL. THE MILK BOTTLES HAVE been sitting in the sun by the incinerator since early morning so that by lunch the foil tops come off, releasing a stench that makes all the sixth graders' stomachs somersault. Drinking the milk is compulsory; it's provided by the government. Sister Josepha urges us to think of the starving children in India as we hold our noses and down it reluctantly. Patricia O'Brien whispers that the children in India wouldn't go near it, starving or not. I look around to see who else she'd intended to hear her remark, but there's no one else. I'm at the end of the row. Patricia O'Brien was talking to *me*. She has lively brown eyes, a fine milk mustache and hair that smells of green-apple shampoo. I snort a little giggle and the warm milk comes out my nose and onto my shoes. Patricia O'Brien is giggling too. We're both giggling now. Sister

Josepha is definitely not giggling; her eyebrows are meeting in the middle.

Kimberly from the Popular Group gets hives from warm milk, so hers goes into the fridge that her father donated to the staff room after his business had a bumper year. It's brought to her specially, and she makes a performance of cooling the back of her neck, behind her knees and then all of her pulse points with the chilled bottle before sipping the milk slowly and smugly.

"She makes me feel like chucking, even more than this stinking, off milk," says Patricia O'Brien. She's funny, with glowing brown skin and great with a Hula-Hoop; after six tricky years I might be making a friend who is not under the spell of Kimberly from the Popular Group.

Matilde doesn't understand about the Popular Group, or Kimberly, or why anyone would care about whether they were in with—or out of—the Popular Group at school.

"Just be your own person, Allegra. I'm telling you, hold an independent mind, forget about other people and forge your own way in the world. Kimberly Popular has no power over you." But she does. She really does. She can suck the happiness out of me with a quick look or comment that she knows the whole class will respond to. She can ask sweetly what I have on my sandwich, as though she's actually interested, then snigger, "Liverwurst . . . *Could it be any worse than liverwurst?*"

She can give me a blazing nose-in-the-air glare that makes that part of my heart between my ribs burn with acid.

. . .

I don't want to open my lunch box in front of everyone today.

I'd rather go hungry than bring out Matilde's Hungarian food on the bench behind Kimberly and the Popular Group as they eat their matching grated cheese and Vegemite sandwiches with the crusts cut off.

"Hey, if you're not going to eat your lunch, can I have it?" asks Patricia O'Brien, who's already polished off her soggy jam sandwich wrapped up in a page torn from a magazine.

"Yeah, but not here. I'll give it to you once the second bell rings and we move off the benches," I say quietly.

Patricia happily downs Matilde's liverwurst, pickled onion and chive sandwich in quick gulps and asks if I reckon I'd even know how to spell *liverwurst*.

"Probably," I say.

"I'm hopeless at spelling," she tells me while we're upside down on the monkey bars. "At my old school I used to stick my fingers down my throat every morning on spelling-bee days. Then Mum would think I'd picked up a chunder bug and let me stay home." Patricia is really smart.

Sister Josepha comes in after lunch with a face like a fire truck. She's been playing cricket with the boys during playground duty. Sister is a champ with the bat and can catch most balls and outrun every boy. With all that fabric on her body and around her head, she must be hotter than Hades. She looks like she could do with one of Kimberly's cold milk bottles behind her knees . . . that's if she has any knees.

"Now, class, kindly settle down quickly. We have a lot to get through this afternoon. Yes indeed. Tomorrow morning we have a special visitor, Father Brennan, and he's coming to talk to you about the sacrament of Confirmation that you'll all be making next term. So we're going to have to do tomorrow's spelling bee right now. Could everyone please stand up."

I look over at Patricia. Her fingers are nowhere near her throat, but she suddenly looks really-truly sick. We stand, and the rows near the door and the rows near the windows turn to face each other. I'm looking straight across at Patricia at the end of the first row. Behind her is Kimberly, looking ready with Roslyn, the second-meanest girl in our class and firmly in the Popular Group.

"So let's start with our newest class member, Patricia. Now, dear, please spell . . . *traffic*." Sister is looking at her list, the list we were given on Monday. Patricia's face goes from white to pink to crimson, and she makes a little squeak that isn't quite a person sound and certainly not a letter. It makes me feel long in that part of my heart that gets stretched by someone else's feelings.

"T-R-A-F-F . . . um . . . um . . ." Sixth grade is waiting. Sister looks up. Patricia looks sideways. Kimberly looks at Roslyn, who chortles, and Sister is distracted. It's just enough time for me to catch Patricia's eye and mouth, "I-C."

"I-C," gasps Patricia.

"Well done, Patricia. Keep standing, dear." Sister is moving on around the room, announcing words for us each to spell. Patricia looks unsteady on her legs.

SERVICE, DEFEATED, WHISTLE. We're all still standing.

OXYGEN, TRANSPORTATION, PECULIAR. A few sit down.

MONSTROUS beats Damien White and *WEALTHY* trips up Scott Perkins. Kimberly, I bet, could have spelled that word backward.

Then *VACUUM* sucks out Roslyn. "Bad luck, Roz," whispers the Popular Group.

MYSTERIOUS, SUSPICIOUS, MUSCLE. They're dropping like flies.

MYTH, DOUGH, FAHRENHEIT. And it's back to Patricia. Apart from her there's only Kimberly, Matthew and me left. By some stroke of luck Patricia gets *RECEIVE.*

"R-E-C . . ." Patricia's face is more rose-colored now, and I'm willing her to remember *I before E except after C*—and she does it!

Matthew gets *FOREIGN.* That's a cinch for Matthew. And then Kimberly is asked to spell *EMBARRASS.*

"E-M-B-A-R-R-E-S-S," she pushes out with a hoity-toity grin.

"No, I'm afraid that's not correct, Kimberly," says Sister Josepha. "Sit down, dear. Allegra, please spell *EMBARRASS.*"

Of all the words: "E-M-B-A-R-R-A-S-S." It's easy but it doesn't feel good.

"Good work, Allegra," says Sister, "and because Matthew

did so well this week, and it was Patricia's first St. Brigid's spelling bee, all three of you can come and choose a holy card."

Patricia looks simply relieved more than blessed to have a holy card. I sure don't want to tell her that with her Hula-Hoop skills she could have been heading to the outer rim of the Popular Group. Lining up with me for a holy card has definitely put an end to that. Patricia chooses *Jesus Lost in the Temple*, and as I'm about to make my choice, Sister Josepha ever so slightly pushes forward *Behold Thy Mother Mary* from her splayed selection. It seems to be a message as well as a prize.

•••

Matilde has asked me to pick a ripe cucumber for tonight's sour-cream salad.

I'm searching her vines to find the best one when from over the fence tinkles the tune "When Irish Eyes Are Smiling": Joy likes to play it from time to time on her mother's old music box. After delivering the cucumber to Matilde, I slip through the brown gate and find Joy in her butterfly chair, catching a stream of tears falling from her cheek in a lemon-colored glass bottle she has labeled MOTHER'S ANNIVERSARY.

Simone de Beauvoir is keeping her company in the crook of her arm.

"Ally, my pet . . . ," she says with a switched-on happy face. "Would you believe that today it's fifteen years exactly since my dear mother passed away? Oh, how she would have cherished you!"

"What was your mother's name?" I ask, picking up Simone and settling into Joy's lap.

"Shelagh," says Joy, corking the bottle and pulling me in close. "Shelagh Kathleen . . . She had skin like porcelain and the most beautiful crop of pure white hair."

I reach into my tunic pocket and bring out the *Behold Thy Mother Mary* holy card. Joy studies the card, running her fingers across Mary's face.

"Another holy card," she says. "You're building up quite a collection."

"I got it for spelling," I tell her, but quickly move on to the best news of the week, "and I've made friends with the new girl, Patricia. She's really nice and really funny."

"Nice *and* funny—now that's an excellent combination," says Joy, full of enthusiasm. "Friendship is so *fortifying* for we girls, darling. You must always treasure your female friends."

Putting the holy card back in my pocket, I wait, then I ask: "Joy . . . does *Thy Mother* mean *My Mother?*"

"Well yes, *of sorts*, in an old-fashioned way of speaking," she responds.

"So Mary is sort of my mother . . . ," I say, looking down and wishing that I could *behold* my real mother. But I know that if I dared to share that thought with either of my grandmothers, it would only clamp up Matilde and crush Joy. They might think I'm feeling that with my real mother in heaven, *their* love is not enough down here on earth.

"How about we give Simone's pond a little freshen-up,"

says Joy. "With all this hot weather it could do with a few ice cubes to cool things down." She propels herself up and out of the chair, gathers up the music box and brings down the shutters on any more talk of her mother, thy mother or my mother.

■ ■ ■

Friday afternoons are my favorite time of the week. Once piano practice is done, Matilde lets me go outside and join— well, mostly watch—the neighborhood kids on the street. I can't go past the stop sign on the corner or over the peak of the hill, but sometimes I get to follow the gang into the Lucky Listers' rumpus room, and I feel like I'm almost part of something.

Lucinda Lister had a birthday party last week. She said she would have invited me but she was only allowed eighteen people. Anyway, it was mixed, which means boys and girls together, and sometimes things get *sexy,* so she thought I'd only feel awkward hanging around with nothing to do. I had a hunch that it would definitely be awkward to let on that I have no idea what happens when things get sexy. Lucinda is pretty mature. She just turned thirteen and wears denim hot pants and over-the-knee socks. The Lucky Listers have a swimming pool—*of course*—so Lucinda's blond ponytail is slightly green-tinged. Her dad is dedicated to good pool maintenance, she tells me proudly, so he adds plenty of chlorine every night. She has green eyes to match, and I'm pretty sure she wears a bra.

And just when I thought it was impossible for Lucinda to get any luckier, she and her over-the-knee socks pedal out of the Listers' driveway on a brand-new purple dragster: white streamers flying from the handlebars, a yellow basket on the front, and a sissy bar on the back. She looks astonishing. A mixed party, a swimming pool, a birthday dragster and a green ponytail—Lucinda Lister has everything.

"Jump on, Ally. I'll give you a dinky double."

I don't let my shock at the offer hold her up in any way, and I'm on the back of that bike in a flash. Lucinda takes off at such a rate that her green ponytail swipes my forehead. From behind her back I can see her white-socked knees angling out, driving down, powering up and propelling us forward. It feels like flight . . . like freedom . . . and now past the stop sign . . . almost like danger. If Matilde knew about this, she'd be what she calls *livid*.

But wouldn't Joy find this feeling thrilling!

Lucinda makes a sharp left-hand turn, and we're gliding toward the horizon. Between blocks of flats, the ocean is shimmering in answer to the brilliant blue sky, and the ceiling of possibility seems lifted. Lucinda is in full control and I'm her tingling passenger. The beach is now in view and we're so out of bounds that I may as well be in another country. I never go to the beach. Matilde doesn't allow it. Apparently the Riffraff hang around there, just causing trouble. I don't want trouble, but I wouldn't mind seeing a riff, or a raff, just so I know what they look like.

But when we get to the promenade I see something totally unexpected. I can't believe it. It's Rick! Here at the beach. Could it be possible that my dad, Rick, is a Riffraff in disguise? Maybe that's why Matilde doesn't speak to him. We've stopped now and Lucinda is keeping the bike upright, with both of us on it, by holding on to a pole. She's looking across the beach and I'm looking down, hiding behind her green ponytail and praying to Jesus, Mary and Joseph that Rick doesn't see me and that I don't have to see him causing any trouble.

"Hey, Ally, *look*, there's your dad. I didn't know he was a surfie," says Lucinda, sounding pretty impressed.

"Oh yeah," I say, trying to sound cool but thinking, *I didn't know either.*

Rick is carrying a surfboard on his head and an expression on his face that I've never seen before. Connected but calm. He puts the surfboard into the back of his van, which has ELSOM'S CARPENTRY written on the side in letters that look like pieces of wood, peels off a wetsuit and towels himself dry.

"Aren't you going to say hi to your dad?" says Lucinda.

"Nah, he's probably got Riffraff stuff to do," I say with a vibration in that part of my heart that pulses in warning of danger.

"Cool. Let's follow him, then," announces Lucinda.

I'm thinking this is not such a good idea, but Lucinda Lister has the power of being two years older than me, the power of bike ownership under me and the power of certainty all over me.

Rick drives off and we pedal after him. On our way to the beach we rode on the footpath, but now Lucinda and her hot pants stand up on the pedals, steer onto the road and weave through traffic, doing a remarkable job of keeping up with Rick. She's fanging it and my heart is speeding up too, revving my thoughts to full throttle.

If Matilde knew I was here, on a bike, on the road, I wouldn't be allowed out of the house ever, ever again; only perhaps to go to her funeral. That would be such a sad day. I'll probably have a crushed dress because people are very sick before they die, and Matilde will have fallen behind with the ironing. Maybe I could borrow one of Joy's felt hats and a squirt of her lavender water in case I've forgotten to have a bath. Would Joy even come to Matilde's funeral? Who's going to cook the food when everyone comes back to the house? That's a thing, *apparently*. I heard Matilde's sister telling her that when her neighbor Moira Austin died, the house was full of people after the funeral and the family were such vulgarians that they only served frozen potato gems. Matilde was disgusted. I'd better not disgust Matilde.

"I think I've lost him," pants Lucinda. "He might have gone left at the petrol station. I'll take a shortcut through the park."

"No, no. Not now. Just let him go," I insist with a sudden burst of authority. "I need to get home. I need to learn how to cook."

Lucinda sits down in her seat, puffing. She turns around, still blond, a bit green and very red, and says, "Ally, you really are mental."

CHAPTER THREE

IT'S SATURDAY MORNING AND I'M WITH MATILDE AT JOE'S, THE local greengrocer. Matilde is always particularly tongue-ticky at Joe's. She'd prefer just to grow everything herself, but occasionally her cabbages let her down or she needs a ripe rockmelon, so she has no choice but to stand in line, waiting to be served. She likes the quality of Joe's fruit and vegetables, but she doesn't like the prices and she sure doesn't like Joe, not one bit. Matilde always takes me along with her, to help carry everything home, but mostly so I get to practice selecting the best produce, adding up the total and working out the change. It's also my job to keep a close eye on Joe.

"That Joe," says Matilde. "What a crook. He overweighs his produce and shortchanges his customers."

We get to the front of the queue, and Joe—with a lead pencil behind his enormous ear and a big yellow smile—says: "So how can I help you two *beautiful young ladies* today?"

He has the teeth of a horse and more hair on the backs of his fingers than on the top of his head, but his charm worked a treat with Mrs. Beaumont before us, who, leaning lopsidedly on her walking stick, replied, "Oh, Joe, flattery will get you everywhere." And it worked on Mrs. Tonkin, who chortled out her order through a mouthful of grapes. But it doesn't work on Matilde, not now, not ever. With a straight back and clipped voice she gives her order every time as though she's reading the news.

"Watch closely that the crook doesn't push down the scales while he's weighing our fruit," Matilde instructs me in a loud whisper when she's about to be served. Thank goodness I've never seen Joe push down the scales and *boy*, I hope I never do—I hate to think how Matilde would react. I like Joe; he often gives me free apples.

Today, though, after quickly adding up everything, I do work out that while he owed Matilde eighty-five cents change, he's only put seventy-five cents into her waiting hand.

"Excuse me, Joe—*Mr. Bastoni*—I think you've made a mistake." I'm trying to use my manners for Joe's sake while being firm in front of Matilde. "I think you probably meant to give my grandmother eighty-five cents change."

Joe adds it up again, down the side of the newspaper laid out on the counter, his lips moving in the shape of numbers. He passes me a banana and says, "You, young lady, are one thousand percent correct. You are a very clever girl. When your grandmother says you are old enough, I will give you a job here, as my assistant, in my shop."

"Do not be ridiculous, and keep your banana. My grand-daughter is studying to become a doctor." Matilde looks pea-sized proud of me and pumpkin-sized disgusted with Joe: livid, in fact. We go straight home at a clip with our fruit and veg, Matilde clutching her bag and me swinging mine. Once we get there, Matilde sets me up with a pen and paper in front of the human anatomy chapter of her encyclopedia at her desk in the hall.

"I will be testing you on the circulatory system, Allegra, as soon as I've finished preparing the meatball sauce for the spaetzle noodles . . . *the whole of the circulatory system.*"

■ ■ ■

The weather is cooling and first term is flying: days at school move along with a happier beat now that I have a friend in Patricia O'Brien.

We've finished our math sheets and are ready for soft-ball, but Sister Josepha can't find her key to the sports-equipment room. She's looked everywhere, so instead of picking our teams we're still in the classroom helping her find the key. The whole class is praying out loud:

> *Dear St. Zita, I've lost my key.*
> *Please look around and find it for me.*

"Zita is the patron saint for lost keys and a most inspiring figure, girls and boys, a great reminder for us never to lose

24

the chance to do some good today by waiting to do something better tomorrow." Sister is looking between a pile of geometry sets while we're all searching around and under our desks.

"She was a simple servant girl working for a rich family in Italy. She worked hard, rising early to bake the bread every day for the large household she served, but whenever she had the chance, she slipped away to distribute bread to the poor and the less fortunate." Sister is running her fingers along the bottom of the supply cupboard.

"One day, during a famine, she was so busy that she didn't get back in time to do her usual baking, and the other servants, jealous of her goodness, reported her to their master for neglecting her duties. But, what do you know, when they led the master to the kitchen to investigate, what did they find? Angels—yes, *angels*—there, getting a start on the baking for Zita." Sister is frisking her habit for a third time. "Her feast day was just last week, on the twenty-seventh of April."

"Hey, that's my birthday, and *look* . . . here's the key." Patricia is holding up Sister's silver key like a prize. It had slipped between the boxes of SRA cards.

"Well done, Patricia." Sister is thrilled, but I'm surprised and sort of offended. Not that Patricia found the key but because she hadn't told me it was her birthday. I wonder whether she had a party.

And now it's started to rain—heavily—so the class lets out a moan of collective disappointment that softball is called off and we have to stay cooped up inside the classroom.

"That's enough now. Settle down, girls and boys. I do have a surprise activity for you to do instead." Sister Josepha goes back to her desk, leans in underneath and produces an old wooden box. "All eyes this way . . . *Anthony, this way!*

"This here belonged to my father, and it's very special indeed. He was a telegrapher with the post office for over forty-two years," she says, pulling out a small bronze machine from the box and walking around the room with it so we can all have a look.

"Now, have any of you ever received a telegram?"

Kimberly's hand shoots straight up, which is hardly a surprise to anyone, even Sister Josepha.

"Yes, I have!" she says smugly. "I got two on my tenth birthday, one from my granny in Melbourne and another one from my father. He was traveling overseas for important business, and he sent me a telegram all the way from Hong Kong to *wish me the world on my first double-figures birthday.*"

"Lovely, dear . . . ," says Sister, not quite looking at Kimberly as she moves around the room with the machine. "Now, these days if we want to get a message to someone, we can just call them up on the telephone, even—at great expense—if they are living overseas. But a hundred years ago there were no telephones, and to get a message to someone in, say, London, you had to write a letter, which took three months to arrive by ship. So when the telegraph connected Australia to the rest of the world, it changed everything. Suddenly a message could be got from London to Sydney in seven hours. *Just imagine!*"

Sister passes the small machine for me to hold while she removes two pencils hanging from Anthony's nose.

"Samuel Morse, an American, invented the telegraph. He was the one who worked out that messages could be transmitted across large distances over a wire using electrical pulses. And he also came up with a code. *What a clever man.* Each letter was signaled as a series of dashes and dots, and that's what we call today Morse code."

I pass the machine back to Sister, and she continues on so that everyone has a chance to see it close up. Scott Perkins, sitting next to me, flicks my arm, leans across the aisle, touches Anthony and sniggers, "Allegra germs, no returns."

"I'm watching you, Scott," says Sister, almost like it's just part of her story.

"Now, my father was also very clever, girls and boys, and he was selected to learn Morse code when he was only sixteen, and that's what he did, all his working life. I remember when I was growing up in the small country town of Narrandera, if a customer came into the post office to send a telegram, my dear father had to take down the message and then go into the telegraphy room and use Morse code to send the message to a telegrapher in Sydney, or wherever the nearest post office was to the person who the message was going to. The telegrapher at the other end had to decipher the message, write it down and pass it on to the bicycle boy to ride off and deliver.

"Now it's your chance to be clever too, girls and boys. You can each have a turn using these sheets of the Morse code I've roneoed off to send a message. *Anthony, please, do not tilt your chair!* If you can be sensible, would you like to go first?"

We spend the rest of the afternoon sending messages to each other using Sister Josepha's father's machine. The boys' favorite message is SOS:

```
Save Our Ship
dot dot dot
dash dash dash
dot dot dot
```

But Sister Josepha tells us that she much prefers the other meaning:

```
Save Our Souls
```

■ ■ ■

That night, I hate to admit, I'm dreaming of Scott Perkins. I'm beating him in an arm wrestle. I hear Whisky Wendy cheering me on at the end of my bed. I'm hot. My throat feels dusty, so I get up for a glass of water and realize that Wendy is not in my room, she's not in the hallway, she's nowhere in the house. Maybe I was dreaming her too.

But standing in the kitchen, I hear Wendy again. I creep out to the side fence, and the wind chimes funnel me toward the brown gate. There in Joy's garden is Wendy—backlit by starlight—with a pipe bobbing in the corner of her mouth.

She's holding hands way up high with another Liberty Club lady, and they're dancing in slow motion at the edges of the water-lily pond.

"Is that a little fairy sister I see? Look, Comrade Camille! There at the gate in the fence!"

Wendy takes me by the ribbon at the waist of my nightie and leads me to the mossy patch next to the pond. Holding me by the wrists, she slowly whirls me around and around. Within her smoky cloud I catch glimpses of the stars through the magnolia leaves overhead, and that part of my heart that seeks sense tries to understand the meaning of Wendy's whispered words of being awoken by profound echoes within.

"Always remember, your destiny is outside of you." Wendy is spinning me, spinning me, spinning me.

"Does your heart not echo with the words of Simone de Beauvoir, Ally?" Wendy is asking me, but somehow, it seems, she's not really seeing me.

I've never heard Simone de Beauvoir speak any words at all, but Wendy doesn't wait for my answer. We just keep spinning.

"Do you feel that time is beginning to flow again?"

"Maybe," I say giddily as Wendy winds me down to a slow-motion stop.

And just at that point Simone pops up on the log that crosses her pond. With perfect balance she stands slightly higher on her front legs, stretching her neck long so that her head is tilted in my direction. I know that she is still, but the earth beneath me is turning, and my vision of her is moving.

"I wish that every human life might be pure transparent freedom," says Wendy, ignoring the appearance of the observant penny tortoise.

"I wish Simone could have adventures away from her safe pond and taste pure freedom too," I say, and Simone nods in agreement.

Wendy and her Liberty Club lady friend suddenly seem totally delighted with me. With one dancing in front and the other dancing behind, they lead me to Joy's back porch and, striking the wind chimes, Wendy announces: "A special delivery. Our latest recruit for the Sisterhood!"

Joy is in deep discussion with the Liberty Ladies inside and looks up, surprised to see her granddaughter there at the back door. It's middle-of-the-night late, so it is surprising— even for me—that I'm out of bed at this hour. It may be that Joy is also surprised that Wendy is describing me as a *sister*. Taking Wendy's pipe and putting it in the sink, Joy scoops me in toward her chest and says, "Did our noise wake you, darling?"

"No. I just had a dream that I beat Scott Perkins in an arm wrestle."

A roar of laughter goes up from the Liberty Club ladies. Glasses start clinking, smoke rings are rising, and the sweeties jar is passed from one to the other. Joy is looking proud of me as I sit on her lap and tells me: "Take two sweeties, darling."

A lady in a handkerchief skirt grabs a guitar, and they all follow her, singing . . .

I am woman, hear me roar
In numbers too big to ignore
And I know too much to go back and pretend
'Cause I've heard it all before
And I've been down there on the floor
No one's ever gonna keep me down again

Glasses are filled from a large flagon, and they all erupt . . .

Oh yes, I am wise
But it's wisdom born of pain
Yes, I've paid the price
But look how much I've gained
If I had to, I can do anything
I am strong (strong)
I am invincible
(invincible)
I am woman

With bright eyes and locked arms the Liberty Club ladies are swaying around the sides of Joy's kitchen table. . . .

I am woman, watch me grow
See me standing toe to toe
As I spread my lovin' arms across the land
But I'm still an embryo
With a long, long way to go
Until I make my brother understand

The loving arms are now looping around waists, across shoulders and behind backs, and they seem fortified by the music, the words but mostly each other. . . .

You can bend but never break me
'Cause it only serves to make me
More determined to achieve that final goal
And I come back even stronger
Not a novice any longer
'Cause you've deepened the conviction in my soul

Joy stands me on a chair near the middle of the table as they sing the song over and over. Before long, my mouth knows the words, my soul knows the tune, and that part of my heart that comes directly from Joy feels set to carry the conviction.

Whatever that is.

CHAPTER FOUR

FATHER BRENNAN IS WITH US AGAIN FOR ANOTHER SESSION about the sacrament of Confirmation. He is the sort of man who looks different from every angle. When we all stand and say "Good morning, Father Brennan" and I see him head-on, he looks like he could serve you at Dave's Mixed Business and Milk Bar flipping eggs and working the hot-chips fryer. But once we're seated and I'm looking straight up at him, he is clearly a man of wisdom and answers, who knows all the God-given rules.

This morning I'm sitting off to the side, and from here he seems almost capable of kindness, like you could con-fess to him your very worst sin and he would pretend he'd completely forgotten it the next time he saw you. From this angle I can see Sister Josepha looking at him too, perhaps thinking she could stand on his shoulders and get a leg-up to heaven. I'm wondering what angle God has on Father Brennan, looking down on him through the clouds.

Father tells us that when we make our Confirmation, the Holy Ghost will descend upon us and we will become Soldiers of Christ.

Soldiers! Oh Lord! What sort of soldier will Kimberly become?

The thought of Kimberly with any more ammunition is terrifying. I'm picturing her slipping a hand grenade into my lunch box. Then Father tells us something even more alarming.

"You are to choose a Confirmation sponsor. Remember, God wants you to choose wisely. Someone you feel close to, who cares deeply about your soul. A person you admire— a good role model—someone who will help you grow to be like them in character, faith and fortitude." His brow, chin and voice then drop down and he adds, "I urge you to choose a person who is *full of God's grace*.

"Your sponsor will accompany you on the day of your Confirmation. At the ceremony they will walk with you down the aisle and place their hand on your right shoulder as you kneel before the bishop."

"Can I choose my mum?" asks Mary-Anne Wilson.

"No," says Father. "It can't be one of your parents."

"Can it be my sister's boyfriend?" boasts Roslyn from the Popular Group.

"No," says Father. "Girls are to choose a lady, and boys are to choose a man, a substantial man."

"Can I have two sponsors?" I slip in, hoping to get an answer without too much attention.

"Definitely not. That would be excessive." Father is firm.

Sister Josepha hands out the sheets we have to fill in with questions about the place and date of our baptism, our sponsor's name and the saint's name we are choosing as our Confirmation name.

"You can get your sponsor to help you choose your Confirmation name. No doubt they will know of saints whose stories they think will guide you throughout your life," continues Father.

At lunchtime under the mulberry tree, the sixth-grade girls are full of talk of all the Confirmation names they like and whether the addition of another letter will turn their initials into a word.

"I'm Kimberly Oleander Linton, so if I choose Opal my initials will spell KOOL." The Popular Group is impressed and quickly work through the alphabet, coming up with names and trying out different initials.

"There is no such person as St. Opal," announces Patricia loudly from her seat next to me on the bench behind Kimberly. "Saints have to be real. You can't just make one up so your initials spell a word." Her voice has a Hula-Hoop rhythm as she takes on Kimberly. There's no doubt Matilde would really like Patricia O'Brien even though she's not the best speller. She'd think Patricia is what she wants me to be—what she calls in Hungarian *bátor*—which apparently means *brave*.

35

But right now I'm not feeling brave; instead that part of my heart that sends blood to my ears is pumping hard, and I can feel them heating right up at the thought of what's on its way.

And here it comes: Kimberly is Hula-Hooping right back.

"Really, Patricia O'Brien! Well, I might leave Opal for you. *Patricia Opal O'Brien* . . . then you can be what you are already: P-O-O! Yeah, a big poo, the perfect match for Allegra." This hoop of insult catches me around my neck, spirals down to my waist and cuts me off at the knees, but Patricia is steady and just offers me a Twistie from her moist orange fingers.

The bell rings and we go in for social studies. Sister Josepha is teaching us about Captain Cook "discovering" Australia. She really knows how to shift from boring to enthralling when the boys start to fidget, so she quickly finishes with the botanist Joseph Banks sketching ferns and moves on to describing scurvy in detail.

"When sailors during Captain Cook's day were at sea for months on end, they had to survive on bits of dried-out bread and scraps of old salted meat. There was no fresh fruit or vegetables on board the ships, not so much as a bite, so the crew often got a terrible disease called scurvy. You get it from not eating enough vitamin C.

"Now, if any of you got scurvy, at first it would just make you a bit tired. But as it goes on, festering wounds would form all over your body, then your eyeballs would protrude, your teeth would loosen, wobble in your mouth and finally fall out, and you'd get ghastly corkscrew hair. Eventually you'd just drop dead."

The boys sit forward in their seats.

"But our Captain Cook was so clever, girls and b[oys,] worked out early in his adventures that while he couldn[ʼt] fresh fruit on board his ship for his voyages, he could ta[ke] of sauerkraut, in other words pickled cabbage, and th[ere] enough vitamin C in it to stop his men from getting s[curvy.]"

"Has anyone ever actually tried sauerkraut?" Sist[er] the same look on her face she had when she found th[e rot]ten banana in Mary-Anne Wilson's desk after the holi[days.]

Kimberly glares at me accusingly. I'm too embar[rassed] to put up my hand and luckily I don't, because after a [quick] check around the room Sister goes on to say, "Well, s[auer]kraut is really quite vile, pungent in fact, and when th[e sail]ors turned up their noses, Captain Cook took it away [from] them and only put it out on the tables. Suddenly ever[yone] thought it was a treat.

"So you see, children, telling the crew they couldn't [have] sauerkraut made them actually want it—and conseque[ntly] they all ate it—and what do you know? Not one of Ca[ptain] Cook's crew on the *Endeavor* ever got scurvy."

I'm thinking about Joy's fruitless life, her sweeti[es] and her curly hair, which is actually a little bit corksc[rew.] I'm trying to remember if I've ever seen her eat a piec[e of] fresh fruit and wonder if the colorful drinks she has with [the] Liberty Club ladies have any vitamin C in them. I mi[ght] need to slip her some of Matilde's sauerkraut next time [we] have mint tea.

...

It's late and I'm in bed but so wide awake that it may as well be morning. I can't push this blessed Confirmation thing out of my head. The thought of choosing just one sponsor makes the metronome part of my heart swing back and forth badly out of time. How can I choose between Joy and Matilde? Father Brennan said we have to choose just one role model. Maybe, though I didn't realize it before now, I have two role models. I love Matilde and I love Joy, but do I actually want to grow up to be like them? I can't be like *them* because there is no *them*. . . . There's Joy and there's Matilde, and to be like one is to be totally unlike the other. I don't know if either one is full of God's grace, but I do know that if I make one of my grandmothers happy by choosing her, I'll make the other one seething mad.

...

Rick has given me eighty cents to spend at the Mother's Day stall. He does every year and says the same thing: "Just get yourself a little something you fancy, Al Pal." I like to spend wisely and most years I'm the last at the table; it can be hard to choose just the right gift and card. The pretty-smiley mums who help on the stall are really nice and do up my gifts with extra potpourri sprinkled inside the tissue paper.

I've got the last six years' worth of gifts all wrapped in a box under my bed.

I'm torn between the scented bath bombs and chocolate hazelnut whirls when I spot a silver figurine at the back of

the items for sale. It's a mother angel holding a baby and—Patricia agrees—it's a girl. The writing across her wings says *A Mother's Love Is Forever.*

My heart moves my hand, and I'm holding the figurine gently when Kimberly Linton pipes up with a bark from behind us and says: "Hands off. I was just about to get that!"

"Bad luck, Kimberly. Ally got it before you," says Patricia.

"Well, Patricia Poo O'Brien, *I* actually have a mother to buy for," bites Kimberly. "Not a dead mother. An alive mother!"

My arm goes limp. My blood backs up. My vocal cords constrict.

"She's no angel then, is she!" whips back Patricia with the words I'd use if I could actually find them. "She's probably got BO. Get her some Avon."

Patricia pulls me toward the money-taking mum, and in exchange for my eighty cents the figurine is mine.

For once Kimberly is stopped short, stumped for a comeback, and we leave her with the Blue Grass eau de toilette in her hand and a *you're dead* look in her eye.

CHAPTER FIVE

I'VE ABANDONED THE SAUERKRAUT IDEA ALTOGETHER, OFFI-
cers or no officers. I just don't think Joy would eat it. Instead
I decide to tempt her with something sweet with vitamin C.
It's Saturday afternoon and I find Matilde letting down the
hem of my dressing-gown in the front room. I curl up in the
upholstered chair by the bookcase and flick though *My First
Body Book*, the one that Matilde gave me for my sixth birthday and has tested me on regularly ever since.

"Matilde," I say, my eyes hovering above the skeletal
system while sneaking sideways glances at her for possible
signs of God's grace. "Next time you make your cherry strudel, could you please show me how you do it? You know,
when you put the old bedsheet on the kitchen table?" I
don't tell her why I have a sudden interest in baking; I've
only been an eater before now, not a cooker.

She looks up from her thimble, over the top of her glasses,

and seems pleased. It's a Matilde style of pleased. Joy does big-and-plentiful pleased, but you could miss Matilde's pea-sized pleased altogether if you didn't know to look for the smallest vibrations around the edges of her mouth.

"Well, Allegra, you are almost twelve years old. So yes. *Yes*. Now is a good time for you to learn how to make the strudel. I was about your age when my mother taught me. There is no time like the present," she says, packing away her sewing box with a task-switching face. "But first we need Liszt."

Liszt is not an ingredient. Matilde is talking about Franz Liszt, her favorite Hungarian composer. She sends me to the linen press to get the strudel-making bedsheet while she goes to her old gramophone and puts on a record of the virtuoso who, she has told me so many times while insisting I practice, actually invented the piano recital.

I help Matilde cover the kitchen table with the bedsheet. It smells laundry-powder clean but is stained dark pink in parts from years of Matilde's strudel making. As Liszt's music starts up, I ask Matilde how many strudels she thinks she's made in her whole life.

"That's hard to know precisely but if I would make the guess, definitely more than eight hundred but probably fewer than one thousand," she says, showing me how to sift the flour with the salt and stir in the egg mixture with a little water and oil.

"Good. Now that's done, we listen to Liszt. We really listen, Allegra.

"This is his 'Hungarian Rhapsody Number Two.' In the

1800s he filled concert halls all over Europe and had the genius idea to turn the piano around on the stage so the soundboard faced his audience and they could see his large hands move like magical acrobats. He didn't have the usual webbing connectors between his fingers, so he could cover a much wider span of notes on the keys.

"He is seeking our full attention now. Can you hear that? Give Liszt your full attention, Allegra." I'm listening, hearing, feeling Liszt, and losing myself in his surrounding rhapsody.

"Now, for our strudel we must throw this ball of dough exactly one hundred times from shoulder height against the side of the mixing bowl. You will do it for this your first strudel, Allegra, but wait. We will soon be at five minutes into the rhapsody, and at that point Mr. Franz Liszt will give us the exact tempo we need to make our dough perfect.

"Here it comes. Are you ready? Now, with larghetto, go! Allegra, go now!"

I'm throwing the dough hard. Counting as it hits the side of the bowl. I'm concentrating with all my might, making sure the dough goes from exactly the height of my shoulder and lands in just the right spot. Matilde is keeping tempo with her beater, the baton, and I'm keeping count. She is looking hard at me, and her blue eyes are becoming darker. They start to glisten.

Matilde is my conductor. I look at her between every throw and she keeps me in time, but somewhere between twenty-nine and thirty she starts to blur around the edges.

There is a growing sting under my right shoulder blade. Matilde's movements speed up and her gaze soars. It could be that I'm blurring for her, too. Then I'm no longer seeing Matilde. I'm seeing Franz Liszt. I'm no longer throwing the dough. It's the music raising my arm. The bowl becomes a mile wide—I couldn't miss it if I tried. I'm connecting every single time. The sting under my shoulder blade softens and warms and spreads, I don't need Matilde's direction now, the dough heats my hand, through my arm, up to my throat and down to just above my kneecaps. Eighty-five. Eighty-six. Eighty-seven. I don't want to reach one hundred, not ever. But according to Matilde's count, suddenly, I do.

"That's it, Allegra. One hundred. Done."

And at precisely Matilde's last count, the piano hits its last note and I'm feeling a lot of E words: Exhilarated—Exhausted—Expanded.

Matilde simply snaps back to Practical.

"Now we must roll out the dough until it is one-quarter-inch thick. Sprinkle the bedsheet with the flour and smooth it all around. Use both your hands. I'll put on 'Un Sospiro.'"

Back in the kitchen with the green linen tea towel over her shoulder and little beads of sweat across her brow, Matilde tells me with a stage whisper: "'Un Sospiro' means *A Sigh*. Can you hear Liszt use the piano keys so we sigh with him?"

"Yes, I can hear it, *I really can*," I say, returning her whisper.

"Good. Now we must stretch this dough slowly, moving rhythmically so it covers the whole of the table." I don't

43

know if Matilde realizes it, but she lets out a long throaty sigh.

"Here, Allegra, slip your hands underneath our dough. Put them palm down on the bedsheet, and use the backs of your hands to pull the dough gently to the edges of the table."

Matilde places her hands on top of mine. They are warm and worn. Under the dough, the joints of her fingers let me know they have led a long life full of many experiences.

"Now we move our hands with the motion of Liszt. He is coaxing us to take great care. His music is guiding us so we don't tear the dough."

We are in rhythm with Liszt and in touch with each other. A thought enters that part of my heart that turns facts into feelings: that while over the years Matilde has cooked for me, cleaned for me, sewed for me and read to me, she has very rarely touched me. Doing my hair there was a brush between us. Scrubbing my back there was a sponge between us. But now as we work and thin the dough with our slow dance around the edges of the table, Matilde's hands are on top of mine, and I know that the numbers on her left wrist are sitting directly above my birthmark. I'm glad I didn't powder my birthmark with Joy's matte makeup this morning.

"Our dough must be thin, so thin that we can read the newspaper through it. Now I will lift the dough very gently and you will test it, Allegra."

I fetch the day's paper and choose the comic section, sliding it under the tunnel Matilde has created. And yes, it is actually transparent. I can read Charlie Brown saying, "Life is like an ice-cream cone; you have to lick it one day at a time."

"Now we brush our dough with the melted butter and sprinkle it with breadcrumbs. For the filling we must use only the sour Morello cherries." She is reaching for the top shelf of the pantry, where she stores all her preserved fruit. No one would ever drop dead from scurvy on a ship captained by Matilde.

We spread the cherry filling six inches in from the longest edge of the table and do together what I've seen Matilde do on her own many times before. We lift the bedsheet and roll the strudel.

"Roll it . . . and roll it . . . and roll it," she says, and our strudel becomes one long sausage, which we curl, dust with sugar and place onto Matilde's largest baking tray.

"You know talent is not a gift, Allegra. No, not at all, it is a decision. Liszt worked on his piano for twelve hours every single day. And still he showed the greatest generosity, all through his life. Generosity with his time and generosity with his money. He taught his students without ever asking for one forint. And then when he was a man of advanced years, he established the Royal National Hungarian Academy of Music in Budapest.

"He helped many people, Allegra. He helped the poor, he helped the sick, he helped the victims of disasters and even he helped the small orphans."

The clouds in my heart are clearing. Matilde *must* be full of God's grace.

"Do you think Liszt is your role model, Matilde?" I ask, opening the oven door as she places our strudel on the hot shelf.

"My role model? What sort of question is that? I am my own person, Allegra. I have no business with a role model. Besides, at the end of his life Mr. Franz Liszt became a Franciscan monk. . . . Such nonsense!

"Now shut the door quickly, Allegra. You are letting the warmth out."

■ ■ ■

Lucinda Lister and I are sitting cross-legged playing Spit on my front porch when the man with the gray Plasticine face, who drops off the piecework for Matilde, pulls up and hauls in so many bags of fabric from his trunk to our door that I know it must be another rush job. Matilde will be at her sewing machine nonstop until the work's done, so now's my chance to take the strudel to Joy. I whip through the game and thrash Lucinda so thoroughly that she leaves in a huff, forgetting she's left her dragster against the front wall of Number 23.

Slipping through the side gate to Number 25, I hear the sound of Whisky Wendy's husky voice. The back door, with its colored glass panels of kookaburras sitting on a leafy branch, which Joy normally keeps wide open, is only half ajar. Through it I can see all the usual Liberty Club ladies, but there are no colorful drinks, no sweeties jar, and certainly no music. Only mint tea and a bottle of disinfectant. There is a new lady, though, and she is the one talking now. She sounds very sad. Not missing-someone sad, but scared sad.

"It started as early as our honeymoon—at Surfers Paradise—almost overnight. I confided in my mother soon after we got home, but she told me that I just had to toughen up. *Can you believe that!* She told me, her own daughter, to be a proper wife. Not to make a fuss. Even now my mother says that I just need to try harder and avoid doing things that make him angry, but that means I'm walking on bloody eggshells all the time, and that in itself seems to set him off."

Joy has her hand on the lady's shoulder. All the other ladies have cranky-sad faces, and the lady talking about her mother has one eye closed and all puffy and bruised; it looks like a big fat dark-blue silkworm is sleeping across the lid. The bottom of her chin is sewn up with the same blanket stitch that Matilde does around the edges of my face washers. I'm wondering if Joy's matte makeup is enough to cover up this terrible sight.

"A few months ago he got laid off at work. That's when the drinking started up first thing in the morning instead of after work. Twice, without any warning, he just exploded like a madman and pinned me up against the wall with the broom handle across my throat. I let out such a bloody scream that the neighbors called the cops. Both times they came to the door, but both times he just told them we'd had a bit of a tiff and everything was good now; he said he was just trying to calm me down. They just pushed off up the path, and the second time I heard one of them say: 'Seems to be just a night full of domestics.'"

I feel that part of my heart that pipes air into my stomach gurgle with hot and cold froth.

"I did think about leaving him, a couple of times, I did," the lady continues. "But he keeps such tight control on the money and I've got nothing, no savings, not even access to a bank account. I've got nowhere to go. Mum would be too embarrassed if I went home to her place—and there's Mandy, I've got to think about her. I made some inquiries about somewhere else we could live, just till I got on my feet, but I was told that women and children don't qualify for emergency housing if the matrimonial home is still intact."

I'd better not interrupt Liberty Club, and I don't really want to hear any more, so I crouch down quiet as a mouse to leave the Tupperware container of strudel on Joy's back porch.

Then I get an almighty kick, hard, in the left heel.

"I'm allowed to play with this tortoise." A strange little girl startles me from behind. She has hair the same color as the scared-sad lady inside and is wearing dirty yellow pajamas even though it's well after lunchtime.

"Who are you?" I ask. I've never seen a child in Joy's garden.

"Mandy. My mummy is inside and her is Dee and my daddy is Ron but we runned away from him."

The little girl has Simone de Beauvoir upside down in the palm of her hand. Simone is wriggling as the little grubby fingers are tightening dangerously around her neck. Joy would need a very big glass bottle to catch all the tears she would cry if anything bad happened to Simone de Beauvoir.

"Why did you run away from your dad?" I flip Simone de Beauvoir right side up and tap her twice on the shell to let her know it's me.

"Daddy kept hitting Mummy even when she's fallen down and she was crying on the bathmat. I hided under my bunks with Kevin and when Daddy fell asleep on the couch me and Mummy sneaked out. Then we had to run our very fastest and we couldn't bring Kevin."

"Is Kevin your brother?" I ask.

"No!" she says, giggling. "Kevin is my cat. He had to stay at home because he wouldn't like the hospital. I didn't like the hospital but I was brave. They put needles into Mummy's face."

I just want to leave the strudel and go.

But Joy must have heard my voice, because swinging the back door wide open, she says, "Ally! Darling! You found little Mandy, how nice. Would you like to play with her in the garden while I talk to her mummy?"

I tell Joy, "Not really," holding back that *Mandy actually gave me a kick from behind and she was holding Simone de Beauvoir upside down, way too tight. And anyway, why is she wearing pajamas when it's after lunchtime?*

Joy gives my elbow a little squeeze and is suddenly very happy to see the Tupperware container. "What do we have here, Ally? Look at this, Mandy, darling!" Joy's right hand, the one that she uses to draw circles with her fingernails at the nape of my neck, is playing with one of Mandy's knotty pigtails. Mandy is still holding Simone de Beauvoir way too tight, and Joy is just ignoring it. Joy would never ignore me holding Simone that way.

"I made you cherry strudel," I say. "It's got vitamin C in it and I specially made it, just for you, Joy, so you won't get scurvy."

I don't want Joy sharing my cherry strudel with Mandy.

"Cherry strudel! Oh, how clever, Ally!" Joy opens the lid and does a sniffy-beamy face. Mandy looks up, copies Joy and does a sniffy-beamy face too. She looks like such a faker. My heart closes my jaw hard and tells me that I don't want to share anything with Mandy, especially Joy.

■ ■ ■

I've just walked Lucinda's dragster to the Lucky Listers' place across the road, and as I'm heading back to Number 23, I see Joy beckoning me from the cane lounge on her front veranda next door. My feet don't feel their usual skippy selves as I move toward Joy, but then I see she has a dusting of icing sugar on the collar of her orange blouse, and I'm thinking she might have eaten some of my cherry strudel.

"Ally, darling. That was, *without a doubt*, the most delicious strudel that has ever graced my lips. I was completely and utterly exhausted when everyone left this afternoon, but after two little bites of your vitamin C–packed cherry strudel, I perked up completely."

Sister Josepha did tell us that the first sign of scurvy was being tired, so maybe I got the cherry strudel to Joy just in time.

"I'm fully restored now and it's all thanks to you, my darling Ally." Joy gathers me in toward her chest, and her fingernails get to work on my neck.

"Now, how does this sound? I thought before it gets dark, you and I might have a little adventure. Simone de Beauvoir is not quite herself after the events of today, and since she's a penny tortoise and can't have your cherry strudel to perk her up, I thought some fresh tadpoles might do the trick instead. What do you say? Go tell Matilde you'll be with me for a while, and we'll sneak to the creek next to the golf course and catch a tadpole feast for Simone."

I'm back in the harbor between Joy's bosoms and my heart loosens a little as I push a deep breath out of my lungs. Because even though Mandy was in Joy's garden today, I am the only one with a berth in her chest. Besides, Joy doesn't have a colored glass bottle of the tears she shed on the day Mandy was born labeled ELATION.

. . .

We set off to the golf course with a net and a bucket. I follow Joy to the edge of the creek, and when we arrive she points out piles of transparent black-spotted jelly lying on the mud.

"Ally, look down here, these are tadpole eggs. Aren't they beautiful? If you look closely, you'll see itty-bitty tadpoles inside each one of these tiny jelly balls.

"Now, darling, you take the net and wade just a little way out from here. I'll watch as you scoop up a delicious feast for Simone de Beauvoir. She'll be so grateful."

Joy waits by the bank in her red tartan gumboots.

"You know, Ally, standing here reminds me of funny old Commander Jacobs," she says, looking across the creek as though she can see him in the distance. "He was rather fond of Simone de Beauvoir. He arrived one day with these smart gumboots for me, saying he knew the perfect spot to catch tadpoles for Simone. But of course, being British, he called the boots 'wellies' and the tadpoles 'pollywogs.' Oh, he was a hoot!"

"What happened to Commander Jacobs, Joy?" I ask, realizing I haven't seen him visiting Number 25 for a while. He used to let me try his monocle and taught me how to play chess.

"Oh, I sent him packing, back to London. Home to his wife, where he belongs."

With each scoop I make through the murky water, the net emerges with at least a dozen wriggling black tadpoles. I wade back and forth through the reeds, emptying the tadpoles into the bucket. Simone will hopefully be fully restored when we tip this load into her pond.

"How long would it take for these tadpoles to turn into fully grown frogs?" I ask.

"Well, that depends on their environment, darling," says Joy. "If they live in the right conditions with everything they need, the right food, the right current and the right weather, it might take only a couple of months. But if food becomes scarce, or the current goes against them, or the weather perhaps closes in, it could take considerably longer. And of course, sadly, predators will eat some of them, so they won't ever grow to become frogs at all.

"It's a bit like children, Ally. Put them in the right environment and they thrive. They're hopping about in no time. But if you don't protect them and give them what they need, especially love and affection, they'll never grow legs to stand on their own two feet. That's why I had to help little Mandy, darling. I do hope you understand."

"But how do you even know Mandy?" I ask.

"Well . . . through our Liberty Club. We're more than just sweeties and song, pet. We're the Sisterhood. We're the champions of women and children who live in fear."

"But what are they living in fear of?" I've changed the swing of the net in the water so that now I'm letting out as many tadpoles as I'm catching.

"Not every daddy is like yours, Ally. Some daddies are drunks. Some have tempers, and some are cruel and violent. Instead of looking after their families, they actually hurt them."

That's so sad . . . *dads hurting their families*. Rick might be a Riffraff, but I know he would never hurt me.

"But what can Liberty Club do?" I'm moving the net differently now, trying to avoid catching any tadpoles at all.

"Well, as it turns out, quite a bit, darling. We're letting women know that they don't have to put up with it. We're raising consciousness. And we're trying to set up a safe house where women and children can go if they need to leave their own homes in a hurry to escape being beaten."

My arms stop moving and the net sinks to the murky creek bottom.

"Is your house going to be the safe house?"

"Good God no, darling, not my house. I'm just doing the little I can to help. We're trying to establish a special house called a refuge. Just imagine if you were so frightened you had to run away from your home in the deep of the night wearing only your pajamas."

Joy looks in the bucket and empties half of the tadpoles back into the creek. "Let's give these little ones a chance to become frogs."

On the way home I'm carrying the net and the half-full bucket. I'm picturing Mandy as a tadpole with little frog legs starting to bud, and I'm wondering if, with Joy's help, she'll get out of those dirty yellow pajamas and hop around on her own two feet.

Joy is ahead of me, swinging her arms. Her corkscrew hair seems loosened as she whistles "I Am Woman" into the dusk. The moon is rising, and the part of my heart that sends signals to the hairs on the back of my neck is telling me that Joy is saved from scurvy and she is at least half full of God's grace.

CHAPTER SIX

THE BUS IS BUZZING WITH CLAPPING-GAME GIRLS AND PEA-shooting boys as we head to the Blue Mountains for the sixth-grade camping trip. Last week was full of tears in the playground, all caused by Kimberly Linton, of course. She kept changing her mind about which *pick-me* girl it would be from the Popular Group who would get to share her tent.

First Roslyn was the chosen one, but then she tipped Kimberly out in a game of tag, so she was dumped for Bernadette—who, without having any idea why, was dumped for Karen.

We each got to nominate one person we'd like to share with, and just as I was working up to asking Patricia, she actually *picked me* first. That was the best-ever day in my whole entire life.

Sister is out in the front with a large stick, leading us into the bush in pairs to walk the Valley of the Waters track. The Popular Group is on slippery footing, with Kimberly still quite twitchy and switchy. I drop behind with Patricia and fall into step with her green-apple scent and her light-footed tread. Patricia has this uncanny way of somehow reading my thoughts and resetting them to a happier rhythm. She's picked up that I'm working hard not to absorb Kimberly's peppery mist.

"Breathe the bush right down into your lungs, Ally. Go on; take it in with big deep breaths. It clears your head and blocks off any badness floating around out there." We stop among the green foliage and together breathe in the blue haze.

"And hey, Al, just watch that stupid lot ahead—the soothing smell of the oil from the eucalyptus trees will sort them out in no time and stop their bickering before too long."

Patricia is spot on. Ten minutes later and the Popular Group is singing "Kookaburra Sits in the Old Gum Tree," a bit out of tune but at least all together.

A little farther along the track, Patricia stops and pulls down a woody shrub toward her chest. She leans forward and sucks the ends of the spikes on its yellow flower head.

"What are you *doing*?" I ask, thinking she really shouldn't be putting this prickly plant anywhere near her mouth.

"It's okay . . . these banksias are chocker-block full of nectar. It's good, really sweet. Here, have a go."

I look around quickly and join her in sucking the ends of the spikes, nervous that Sister might see and give us both a demerit. Patricia is right again; the liquid flowing over my tongue is actually quite delicious.

"You know what, you can soak these flowers in water and make them into a sweet drink," she tells me as we move farther along the track. "It tastes heaps better than that Tang orange powder stuff you get at the shops, and it doesn't cost a cent."

"Really?" I had a cup of Tang once in the Listers' rumpus room; it's hard to imagine anything tasting better than that.

"Hey, stop here a minute, Ally. Look . . . up there . . . there are geebung berries growing on that tree. Here, can you see that? You can eat those berries. Not now, they're still green, but when they're ripe they'll fall on the ground and you can collect them and eat them up. Now, they've got *plenty* of vitamin C.

"I like that Sister Josepha, I like her a lot, but sometimes the things she teaches us are pretty stupid. If Captain Cook or that Captain Phillip fella had watched what my people ate, and copied them, they wouldn't have had to worry about scurvy, and they wouldn't have had to eat that stinking sauerkraut stuff either.

"And look here." Patricia is peeling back the bark of the berry tree. "If anyone gets an insect bite, you can make a bush Band-Aid from the red stuff under here. It stops the sting, and it's just as good as the antiseptic you get from the chemist shop."

"How do you know all this stuff?" I ask Patricia, amazed by what's under *her* bark.

"From my nana. Nobody could ever know more about the bush than my nana."

"Does your nana live with you?"

"Nah, she moved on."

"Oh right . . . moved on," I say. Whatever that means.

It's nighttime, and Patricia and I have pulled our sleeping bags close together so we can talk in our tent without being caught out. After a while there are no sounds coming from any of the other tents, so we know we're the last ones in sixth grade still awake. I can see the outline of Patricia's face and the white triangles at the edges of her eyes. Whispering to each other inside this moonlit canvas makes everything we say feel like an important secret.

"Where did your nana move on to? Is she living with some of your other relations?" I ask softly. I'd really like to meet this woman.

"Here, Ally, I'll show you where she is." Patricia pops up, puts her head through the slash in the tent, makes room for mine and beckons me toward her.

"Can you see that dark patch up there, near the Southern Cross?" she says, turning my head gently and pointing up to the stars. "That's the emu. See, can you make out its head, the dark bit? Now follow across and you'll see its body and farther down . . . see . . . there are its legs. Then over to its left is the great river of light. That's the Milky Way, and right up where the brightest cluster is glowing, that's where my nana's campfire is. She moved on to be with her mob." Patricia goes quiet for a bit.

"We used to live with Nana up in Armidale, Mum and

58

me, but then she died. Mum says the diabetes got her in the end. But Nana told me, on the sly, just before she went, that the great canoe would come for her in the dead of night and take her to join her mob's campfire. She sent a shooting star down soon after she went, and that let me know that she'd got there safely."

For a long while we sit in our sleeping bags with our heads poking out of the tent. With the whisper-close talk and clear sight of all the burning campfires in the sky, that part of my heart that powers my thermostat warms right up. I never realized before that having a best friend could bring up the core temperature of a person.

Patricia drifts off to sleep, but I stay awake. Stargazing.

I'm searching the night sky for a shooting star to behold. To perhaps . . . *Behold My Mother.*

. . .

There's no buzz on the bus on the trip home from camp. Everyone is exhausted. No pea-shooting or even much talking. Most of the sixth grade's heads start nodding off. Except for mine. My head is taken up again with the round-and-round question of who I should choose to be my Confirmation sponsor.

I arrive home to find Rick hosing down his van in the driveway that runs along the other side of Number 23. I ask if I can help him with the windows. He throws me an old cloth nappy and the glass cleaner and I set to work. When I'm almost done, Rick lifts me up so I can reach the top of the windscreen. His hair smells like still-warm hot chips.

Rick doesn't put many words into the world. He says we have two ears and one mouth and that we should talk less and listen more. Today I want Rick to listen, but I also want him to talk. I really want Rick to tell me who *he* thinks I should choose to be my Confirmation sponsor.

"I love Matilde very much and I love Joy a lot, and I think they're both sort of full of God's grace, but I don't know which one is actually my role model. Is it Joy or is it Matilde?" I'm doing big circles with the nappy, making sure to polish all the salty haze off Rick's windscreen.

"Sometimes I think it's Joy, but then she does something a bit mental, and that makes me think it has to be Matilde. And then, when I'm thinking it's Matilde, she gets that cranky cleaning face and she ticks her tongue, so Rick, I just don't know who to choose."

"You're overworking this, Al Pal." Rick sits me down on the low brick fence and moves in close. He squirts the glass cleaner at a bull ant making its way toward my bare toes until it changes direction.

"It's pretty simple, really. Joy is Catholic and Matilde was Jewish. You have to choose Joy."

"Joy! But Matilde will be so sad if I choose Joy. I don't want to make Matilde sad."

"It's not really your choice, Al. It won't be you making Matilde sad. I think you'll find that Father Brennan won't let you have Matilde. She's not a Catholic, she wasn't baptized, she wasn't confirmed, so she can't really be your sponsor. Church rules."

"Oh . . . okay . . . church rules. So you think it's gotta be Joy." Rick nods. My heart releases the muscles around my shoulders, easing them down and forward.

"Can you please tell Matilde for me, Rick?"

"It's best if you do that, Al Pal. But I tell you what, I'll stand right beside you when you do."

We go inside, and Rick boils the kettle and I set to making Matilde toast. I lay the tray the way I do at Joy's place, and I'm about to take it in to Matilde at her sewing table when she appears in the kitchen doorway.

"So first you are baking the cherry strudel and now you are making the tea tray. You are becoming very able indeed, Allegra."

Matilde looks pea-sized proud, like she thinks she's my role model and that I'm growing up to be *able* just like her. I know I have to get out fast what I need to tell her, and I glance at Rick, who slides a little closer toward me along the bench. My lips start moving and I hear the words they say to Matilde: "I have to choose a sponsor for my Confirmation when I'll become a Soldier of Christ and Father Brennan says the sponsor has to be my role model who is full of God's grace and even though you're quite a bit full of God's grace, because Joy is Catholic and you were Jewish, I'm choosing Joy. But I've made you honey toast."

Matilde looks down at the tea and honey toast. Her right hand moves across to her left arm and she slowly rubs her thumb across the numbers on her wrist. She leaves the kitchen without looking at me or looking at Rick or touching the tray, and she goes back to the front room and her sewing table.

After a while Matilde's Singer starts to pulsate, and my birthmark begins to throb.

■ ■ ■

Joy is in the glasshouse, breaking up boiled lettuce to feed to Simone de Beauvoir. It's been four days since Matilde didn't eat my honey toast, and my birthmark has finally settled down. It's time to ask Joy to be my Confirmation sponsor. Besides, Sister Josepha has reminded me twice that she needs my forms returned.

Joy is "tickled pink" that I have chosen her. She holds a small crimson glass bottle against her rosy cheekbone to catch the pooling tears at the corner of her right eye, and she tells me all about her own Confirmation day, "oh, so many moons ago."

"I remember it as if it were yesterday. I wore a beautiful white dress made of broderie anglaise that my mother bought for me at Veronique's, *and she paid a pretty penny, too.* We matched it with a shoulder-length white veil handmade especially by our neighbor, Mrs. Dunmore. It was a shame I had to wear the veil, really. My older sister, Joan, did my hair in the luscious wavy style that was all the fashion back then, but the veil covered the back of my hairdo completely. I was almost thirteen, rather petite and particularly pretty. I had a tiny waist, dainty wrists and the ankles of a ballerina.

"That was the first time I noticed Douglas Fernon noticing me. All the girls loved Douglas. He was tall and fair with a strong jawline and a counterclockwise cowlick. Oh yes—dear Douglas—he *was* a handsome boy, but just a bit too holy for my liking." Joy gives me a little wink with her dry left eye.

"We thought he'd enter the priesthood, but he ended up entering the police force. Similar work, I suppose."

"What was your Confirmation name?" I ask.

"I almost chose Rose, my most favorite bloom, but then I read about St. Thérèse, who was also called The Little Flower, and I thought, *Why not cover them all?*"

At least Joy wasn't just picking a name so her initials spelled a word.

"I do remember that after church we had a special breakfast, and my mother served tiny butterfly cakes with plum jam. I didn't touch mine, it was way too beautiful."

I can hear Matilde calling me from Number 23 for dinner.

Joy tells me to just ignore that for the minute, and she takes me by the hand to her bedroom. Still holding the glass bottle to her eye, she goes through a number of trinket boxes on her dressing table until she fishes out a tarnished silver medal that she pins to my T-shirt.

"My favorite aunt, Katherine, gave me this medal on *my* Confirmation day. She was my sponsor and a most glorious woman. Sadly, poor Katherine died a terrible death from tuberculosis only eighteen months later." The glass bottle is filling fast.

"You can keep my medal, darling, and you might like to wear it on your own special day. Now, off you trot for dinner, and keep that medal safe."

I'm almost out the door when Joy says: "And Ally, pet, thank you for asking me. I couldn't be more thrilled." Her face looks backlit with moonlight as she wipes her cheek and places a tiny cork in the glass bottle.

Usually when I make Joy happy the right side of my heart pumps little pulses that send thinned blood to my head, sharpening color and sweetening sound. But today, even though Joy is tickled pink, I know that Matilde is bruised blue, and the left side of my heart is pumping hardened blood to the back of my throat. All color looks muddier and sound seems duller.

I realize something for the first time, the way you can at eleven and three-quarters when suddenly you feel twenty-two. Joy and Matilde make up my right side and my left side. But now I've put that out of balance and I don't know how I can feel right again when I'm leaving one of them feeling wronged.

CHAPTER SEVEN

KIMBERLY MANAGES TO KEEP THE POPULAR GROUP CONstantly impressed. Today it's her new take on lunch that draws mini-gasps from all the girls jostling to sit next to her. Dipping deliberately into an Esky cooler, she produces a devon-and-tomato-sauce sandwich prepared like a gift in rainbow-colored wax paper. And if that's not enough, she follows through with still-frozen orange segments and chilled chocolate crackles. I'm sitting a few benches behind with Patricia, and we're trying to ignore the performance. But then it gets worse.

"My mother says she wants me to shine on my Confirmation day, so she's taking me late-night shopping in town tonight, and we're going to buy the most beautiful dress there is. She's spoken about it with Daddy, and he said *he doesn't even care how much it costs.*"

Patricia is rolling her eyes into her plain SAO biscuits.

She tells me quietly that she's just going to wear her school uniform next Sunday because her dad is on another bender and has stopped giving her mum any housekeeping money. I nod, although I'm not really sure what a bender is, and I tell her not to worry because I'll be wearing my uniform too. That's a good thing, because having chosen Joy as my sponsor, I didn't feel right about expecting Matilde to make me a new dress, and besides, solidarity with Patricia feels way more important than any outfit right now.

■■■

It must be busy in heaven this morning as the Holy Ghost limbers up to descend on all of sixth grade and turn us into Soldiers of Christ on our Confirmation day.

With Joy's help I've chosen my name. Well, she chose it, really, following a message she got from her long-dead aunt Katherine. Apparently after Liberty Club last Monday evening, while watering her maidenhair fern near the magnolia tree, Joy appealed to her glorious aunt for a suitable Confirmation name for me, and Katherine whispered on the wind that it simply must be Liberata. Joy absolutely loved the sound of that, and now there's a small violet-colored bottle of tears in her glasshouse labeled LIBERATA.

When Sister Josepha told me that Liberata was actually the patron saint of women trying to escape difficult marriages, and that her prayers to be freed from a persistent suitor were answered when the twelve-year-old Liberata sprouted a luxuriant beard, I wasn't so sure she was the saint for me. But with the delay in choosing my sponsor, and returning my forms so late, I was running out of time, and any better ideas.

Then in bed on Tuesday night, while listening to Matilde adding up numbers with her pinwheel calculator, I worked out that even though I don't really want to be *like* St. Liberata—and sure don't want to have to escape a difficult marriage, or grow a beard—if I at least go with her name, mine would become Allegra Belinda Liberata Elsom, and my initials would spell ABLE. So, this is my inside-out secret way of keeping things balanced, making Matilde proud and choosing her too. I can't tell Matilde about this, of course; she's still acting a bit tongue-ticky and bruised. Both of us are avoiding any mention at all of this Confirmation business.

And I sure won't be telling Patricia, because she'd never share her Twisties with me again if she knew I had chosen a name that makes my initials spell a word.

I haven't sighted Matilde this morning, but I heard her machine going all night. She's left my breakfast set for me with a note to see her before I get dressed. While I'm finishing off her rice pudding and poached pears, Rick comes to the back porch and asks me to go next door and let Joy know that we'll be leaving for the church at nine-thirty.

"Tell Joy she can sit with you in the back of the van," says Rick.

I'm starting to understand the meaning of things when adults speak their leaving-out-words language. What Rick is actually telling Joy, even though he never really speaks to her, is that she can get a lift with us to the church and she doesn't even need to look at Matilde.

At Number 25 Joy is on the phone. Her hair and makeup are done, but she's standing in her mint-green silk kimono with red cherry blossoms along the edge, listening with careful eyes to whoever is speaking. Then she says: "No, no, it's best if you leave before he gets home. Go back to the first plan and wait at your place." She hangs up, does a slow whirl and takes me by both hands.

"My luscious little Liberata! So today is the big day."

Joy has a switched-on happy face, but her neck is flushed and her hands are cold. She goes for her matte makeup and hurriedly covers my birthmark while I tell her we're leaving for church at nine-thirty and Rick is really stoked that she's my sponsor and says that on the way there he'd love for her to sit in the back of the van with me.

"Ally, darling, how about the three of you go ahead. It would be nice for Matilde to sit next to you on the way to the church. I'll just meet you there."

That's certainly a surprise; I've never known Joy to think of what would be nice for Matilde before. "But Joy, how will you get there?"

"Wendy will bring me in her V-Dub. We have a little something we need to do beforehand; she'll drop me there afterward. Don't worry, darling, I'll be there in plenty of time."

Joy mustn't want to even breathe the same air as Matilde. If she can't sit in the same van, how is she going to sit in the same row at the church? I wonder if there is a patron saint for kids with grandmothers who can't stand each other.

I head back to Number 23 to get ready. The clock in the hall says it's ten past eight, and I remember that Matilde wanted to see me before I get dressed. Her bedroom door is all but shut, and for the first time ever I see Matilde lying down when the sun is up. She is dressed in church clothes, but her eyes are closed.

"Matilde, are you okay?" I ask softly.

"Yes, yes. I'm perfectly fine, Allegra. Did you eat your breakfast?"

"I did, I ate it all up, it was delicious. Thank you, Matilde. Rick says that we're leaving at nine-thirty—oh, and that he'd love for you to sit in the van right next to me. I'm going to go and get into my uniform now."

"Wait, before you do that, Allegra, look behind the door."

There on a hanger is a beautiful blue dress. It is the exact same color—Oriental Blue—that I have loved ever since I first saw Kimberly's complete set of seventy-two Derwent watercolor pencils when she displayed them, one by one, for show-and-tell in second class. It has a cream ruffle on each side of the bodice from the neck to the waist and cream piping around the cuffs. It is way more beautiful than anything you could find late-night shopping, even if your dad didn't care how much it cost.

"I thought you were working on a rush job, Matilde."

Matilde gets up, laces her shoes and straightens her skirt.

"Well, I was, but that can wait for now." She helps me into the dress.

"Ah, good. Yes. This is perfect—it fits you like a glove. Go and take a quick look."

I see myself in the mirror at the end of the corridor, and for the first time ever, I think . . . maybe . . . I might be pretty. Maybe I'll have dainty wrists and the ankles of a ballerina, and boys with counterclockwise cowlicks will admire me. Today I might have the weirdest Confirmation name, but I'm sure I'll have the best dress.

"The blue matches your eyes precisely," says Matilde, standing behind me and tying the sash.

I see in the mirror that my eyes and Matilde's are actually the same color. Both sets are looking at me now as though I'm a reflection of her. Then, while doing up the buttons on the left cuff, Matilde sees the matte makeup covering my birthmark and snaps: "Don't admire yourself for too long, Allegra. Vanity is the domain of fools."

My heart drops down a few floors . . . and I remember Patricia O'Brien. If I wear this dress, she'll be the only one in all of sixth grade in the school uniform. Kimberly and the Popular Group will crucify her. My temples start to thrum. I can't let Patricia be made fun of by the Popular Group. But Matilde has been up all night making this Oriental Blue dress with the ruffles, cuffs, piping and sash especially for me.

She put off her rush job. I'm in it now. I have no choice. I have to wear it.

CHAPTER EIGHT

Mrs. Perkins with a holy tilt sitting at the organ is respiring gently; "Breathe on Me, O Breath of God." We're seven rows from the altar, arranged alphabetically, behind the Egans and in front of the Ervings. I'm sitting next to Matilde, and Rick is on her other side with something of a space between them. I slide along and leave the spot next to the aisle for Joy.

I'm half proud of my Oriental Blue dress, wanting Kimberly and the Popular Group to notice the ruffles, cuffs and piping—but I'm half ashamed of it too, hoping that Patricia doesn't think me a Judas, or worse still, a Kimberly.

Roslyn arrives, all pleased and prancing in purple crushed velvet. She spots me and looks longer than usual, clearly impressed with my dress but not with who's wearing it. She sits in the same row but across the aisle from us and shares a joke with her sponsor.

And then in flounces Kimberly, flanked by her proud parents. She's wearing all manner of lemon—head to toe. Her dress is soft lemon hail-spot tulle. Her perfectly tied hair ribbon is mid-lemon satin, and her shoes are deep lemon patent leather. Even her socks are cream touching on lemon. I hate to admit it, but she does look *KOOL*.

If Patricia were next to me now, she'd whisper, "She looks sour!"

I scan the rows behind me but can't see Patricia.

And there's no sign of Joy, either.

The organ pipes up and begins pumping out "Spirit of God in the Clear Running Water."

We all stand. Father Brennan begins his procession, followed by twitching altar boys in long white robes, their dirty sneakers poking out from under the hem with each step.

Then, after the third verse, the bishop appears at the church entrance, backlit by God.

The bishop is big and gold and red and wears a pointy hat. He's carrying a rod that is hooked at one end like a shepherd's crook. His eyes are raised so he's not noticing any of us, or our dresses. He's looking straight ahead at Jesus on the crucifix above the altar as he proceeds steadily down the aisle.

But where's Joy?

Mrs. Perkins's tilt starts to sway, and the organ plays louder. The congregation responds with raised voices, singing of their lonely and hungry hearts that are watching and waiting.

I'm watching.

I'm waiting.

I'm watching and waiting for Joy to appear. My heart *is* lonely—and a little bit cranky.

Come on, Joy.

If she just walks in now, that's okay. We're still standing. All eyes are on the bishop, so she could slide in unnoticed.

Where are you, Joy?

The bishop has finished welcoming us and tells us to sit. It's too late for Joy to slide in unnoticed now. Hopefully she will know to come through the side door rather than walk the full length of the aisle. Not that she'd mind the attention.

There are readings and offerings, more hymns and a creed. But still no Joy.

And now the renewal of baptismal promises. The bishop asks the candidates for Confirmation and their sponsors to stand. Rick squirms, rolling his head around on his neck. Throughout the church, sponsors are beaming, proud as punch, ready to support those who have chosen them. Matilde's head and neck are dead still, but I can hear her tongue ticking.

I stand on my own.

With the group—and my out-loud voice—I reject Satan and all his works and all his empty promises. In my heart, my inside voice mutters, *I know how Satan must feel; I am what rejection looks like.*

From across the aisle, Roslyn no longer sees my Oriental Blue dress, or its ruffles, cuffs and piping. She sees me standing on my own, exposed. I may as well be standing here in the nude. That part of my heart that dresses my pride is stripped bare.

I'm cold.

Mrs. Perkins takes up her post at the organ again, and the church is filled with "The Lord's My Shepherd." Sister Josepha is slowly walking backward down the aisle. As she approaches each row, she nods and a child moves forward to the altar with their sponsor by their side. They kneel reverently in front of the bishop. The sponsor places their hand on the child's right shoulder as the bishop asks for the Confirmation name and turns them into the latest chuffed Soldier of Christ.

Sister Josepha has come to the end of the D rows. Rick is rubbing his fists along his thighs toward his knees, back and forth. Matilde turns around, and for the first time ever in my whole entire life she is looking for Joy. She inhales deeply through her nostrils and exhales with a small noise from the back of her throat.

I'm standing Joyless.

Sister has arrived at my row.

"Allegra, where is your grandmother?" she says. Then, glancing at Matilde, she specifies, "Your other grandmother?"

"She's been caught up with Whisky Wendy," I whisper, realizing that mightn't sound like someone full of God's grace.

"Whisky Wendy? . . . *Oh* . . . I see," she says.

"Mrs. Kaldor, would you like to accompany Allegra to the bishop?" Sister clearly has absolutely no idea.

"She can't," I say in a rush. "She's Jewish!"

"So was Jesus Christ, dear."

Sister steps aside and ushers Matilde and me into the aisle, but instead of continuing backward she moves forward, walking behind us.

I'm breaking church rules, and I can't believe I'm doing it with a Jew and a nun.

I arrive at the altar, and kneeling in front of the bishop, I try to look extra holy to make up for what's going on behind me. Sister takes Matilde's left wrist and places it on my right shoulder, then steadies it there with her own hand.

The bishop's eyes widen—slightly—but only after Sister tells him my Confirmation name.

"Liberata," he announces, making the sign of the cross with the oil of chrism on my head. "Be sealed with the Holy Ghost."

On the way back to our row, I'm at least partly dressed again. No one appears to care much that we've broken church rules and a Jew was my sponsor. In fact, the only person who seems to notice Matilde at all is Mr. Linton, Kimberly's father, who weirdly gives a small but definite nod in her direction as we take our seats again.

Moving into Joy's empty spot by the aisle, I'm just too spitting mad at her to feel anything near full of God's grace. I reach across to hold Matilde's hand, but it's not available; she's moved it to clutch her left wrist. Instead, I take my own right hand to my left wrist and start rubbing away the matte makeup.

I wait for Patricia to walk down the aisle, but she never does. Maybe she was worried about being mocked by the

Popular Group for wearing her school uniform to the Confirmation and stuck her fingers down her throat?

• • •

Patricia must be really-truly sick, because it's four days now since the Confirmation, and there's been no sight of her at school. I miss the broad smile and fresh smell of my only friend and spend lunchtime reading alone on the benches under the mulberry tree.

I haven't seen Joy, either. When we got home from the church, I rushed through the brown gate, expecting to find her back at Number 25, full of remorse, filling up glass bottles labeled NEVER SO SORRY with a forgivable reason for letting me down. But her house was silent, empty and completely Joyless, and there wasn't a single clue as to where she might be. So I left and bolted the gate from our side—loudly—with an *eemmff*.

If she's slunk back home since, she certainly hasn't hovered on her front veranda to catch my eye, or beckoned me in with her wind chimes.

There's no point asking Matilde why Joy didn't turn up at the church. They never share the details of their lives with each other. And anyway, as angry as Matilde might be at Joy for upsetting me, I suspect she's kind of glad for herself that after I made her sad by choosing Joy, *that other grandmother* only went and let me down. Matilde's not saying that, at least not with her words, but sometimes her thoughts escape in little wafts into the room, and I can't help but breathe them in when she's rolling her pastry and mincing the meat.

And now, six days on, my *mad at Joy* is being eclipsed by *worried about Joy*. She's never been away for this long before, not without telling me.

"Where exactly did Joy go in Wendy's V-Dub Beetle, when she was meant to come and meet us at the church?" I ask Rick, finding him fixing the dripping tap by the back door. "I never thought she'd let me down like that."

"She didn't mean to let you down, Al," says Rick, looking through his toolbox. "Let's just say she had an important job to do."

"More important than being my sponsor?"

"No, I didn't say that." Rick wipes his brow with his sleeve. "She intended to get there on time, but things didn't go quite to plan—and, well, she needed to take a break afterward. She'll be back before long."

But how long?

Without Joy next door, that part of my heart that revolves around three separate suns is spinning off course and knocked out of orbit.

■ ■ ■

The following Monday Sister Josepha writes in big yellow letters on the blackboard: *The Gold Rush*. Dusting her hands and creating a chalk cloud, she says that we should all choose a partner because we'll be pairing up to make a goldfields village out of matchsticks. The Popular Group pounces on Kimberly, and the rest of the girls look around hungrily for the scraps. I'm going to wait for Patricia to get back. I'll just get going on it alone for both of us until then.

"Can I be your partner, Allegra?" asks Mary-Anne Wilson.

"I'm already partners with Patricia."

"But you can't be partners with Patricia. She's left. She's moved to a different school."

"No she hasn't." I know Patricia wouldn't just leave without telling me. "You're making that up."

"No I'm not. You can ask Sister."

And so I do, approaching Sister by the board.

And afterward I wish I hadn't.

Patricia and her mother had to move suddenly . . . *yes* . . . that's true. They've gone interstate, Queensland, or was it Tasmania? No particular reason was given . . . the school got a message at the end of last week . . . there was no time for Patricia to collect her belongings. These things happen sometimes. . . .

"But would you like to keep the plaster-of-Paris mold Patricia made of her hand?"

The nightlight-in-the-dark-alley part of my heart flickers, dims and shuts down. Giddy sick rises up in my throat as I feel my way back down the wavering aisle between the desks, holding Patricia O'Brien's hand tightly by the chalky thumb.

I pass Kimberly and she makes like she's coughing into her closed fist, muttering only loud enough for me to hear: "Sucks for you. The abo's gone walkabout."

Everyone else has paired up, so now I'm stuck with Mary-Anne Wilson, the girl with bits of dried cereal on her tunic who eats Perkins paste . . . Every. Single. Day. And now Mary-Anne's looking satisfied! Satisfied that she knew before I did that Patricia has left me for a new school. And satisfied that I'm stuck with her as a partner. I know I should be kind, I know I should be full of God's grace, but Mary-Anne Wilson is smelly and annoying and completely useless at gluing matchsticks straight.

And so I'm left to endure the last term of St. Brigid's as I began.

Friendless.

CHAPTER NINE

THERE'S A BIG RUSH JOB. THE BIGGEST RUSH JOB EVER. SO BIG that Rick and I have eaten Matilde's leftover beef and cabbage casserole for dinner three nights in a row.

Matilde only leaves her sewing machine to take hurried bent-over steps to her ironing table and back again. The stop-start throb is filling the house so that every brick is humming, floorboard vibrating and lampshade murmuring, and my jawbone is buzzing—late into the night and every hour of every day. I don't like the sound of that machine anymore. I fall asleep to it in the dark and wake to it in the early light of the morning. I'm feeling headachy and exhausted.

This afternoon I take tea to Matilde.

Tea I make without Rick's help.

Tea I lay on the tray in Matilde's favorite mug with hot honey toast.

Matilde does eat my honey toast now. Actually, it's all she eats. And sometimes she almost forgets to take the pins out from her pinched-in lips before she mindlessly washes down small nibbles of toast with gulps of warm tea.

Rick says it's the looming summer season that's caused the rush job. But Matilde tells me, when I bring in the tray, that she's sorry it will be the same casserole again tonight but there was a mistake at the factory with the sample sizes and if she doesn't finish eighteen perfect pieces by Tuesday, she won't be paid a red cent for this job or for the last three she's done for Bolton's Fashion House.

"Why don't you just be *bátor* and tell them that's plain unfair, Matilde?" I'm holding out my palm for the pins.

"Mr. Linton doesn't factor in fair, Allegra. There are very many outworkers besides me who would do this work for far less than what is fair."

"*Linton!* . . . Mr. Linton?" I'm starting to piece things together. "The Mr. Linton you saw at the church?"

Suddenly the weird nod Kimberly's father gave Matilde on my Confirmation day makes sense.

"Yes, yes, that is Mr. Linton. The bully from Bolton's Fashion House."

"Matilde, that man is Kimberly from the Popular Group's father! She is the meanest girl in our whole school. She is *horrible*. She's the one you told me just to ignore."

I'm picturing Kimberly cooling herself with the milk delivered from her father's bumper-year fridge. And now I know that that very man is a bully and not paying Matilde a red cent for the work she's done.

I'm remembering Kimberly sniggering with the Popular Group when Patricia struggled with her spelling words. I'm feeling the flush of shame from Kimberly taunting me in front of the Popular Group because of what I have in my lunch box.

I'm sucked out by Kimberly saying *Sucks for you. The abo's gone walkabout.*

I'm burning at the hot sting of Kimberly announcing at the Mother's Day stall that she has an *alive* mother to buy for.

Not a dead mother.

Not a dead mother.

Not a dead mother like me.

I'm still holding Matilde's pins in my left palm. I pick up one with my right hand, rolling it between my fingers and thumb, until it starts to scrape across the birthmark on my wrist.

Not a dead mother like me.

"Just tell him, Matilde. Just tell him he *has* to be fair."

"Allegra, calm yourself! I need this work. Without Bolton's Fashion House there is no chicken paprikash, there is no goulash soup. There will be no electricity, no hot water. There is not even this house, our home here, at Number 23.

"Do you know what a mortgage is, Allegra? Well, because your grandfather cared for the gambling more than his family, I have been left to pay a very big one all on my own.

"This work pays for your piano lessons, your swim-squad training, and it will pay for your university education so that you can become a doctor and be respected and never have to put up with this or the Bully Boltons of this world." Matilde is pushing her foot hard on the throttle of her sewing machine.

"I don't need those piano lessons, or squad training, and I don't even want to go to university. I hate Kimberly and now I hate her father. He can't be mean to you. She's so mean to *me*, Matilde. He can't be mean to *you*." It's then I notice that blood is dripping from my pulse point onto the fabric falling at the ground around Matilde's feet.

"Allegra, what are you doing with the pins? Allegra! You are bleeding all over my fabric. Allegra!" Matilde's voice is as loud as it goes. "Allegra, my God, *Allegra!*"

The back screen door slams and there's Rick.

I run to him and he scoops me up in the corridor. His chest is strong with a thin layer of gentleness wrapped in a soft T-shirt that soaks up my tears. He takes me to the bathroom and runs cool water over my wrist. He applies pressure with his big thumb, and when it stops bleeding, he peels a Band-Aid, saying: "Put on your togs, Al Pal—we're going for a drive."

...

I'm alone with Rick in his van. It's not often that it's just Rick and me, and we haven't even told Matilde we have left. I have an after-tears headache, and my body memory tells me I've had one like this before, but my mind memory thinks it must have been a very long time ago, at least before I started kindergarten.

We don't speak. We just drive. My eyes are stinging. My wrist is throbbing. We both just look straight ahead. The sun is getting low behind us and the ocean is a silvery stretch before us. We are driving the same route I rode on the back of Lucinda's bike that day we went to the beach and discovered that Rick was a Riffraff. I roll down the window, and the salty breeze settles my catch-up gasps so they become deeper, steadier, breaths.

It's a relief to be with Rick, alone.

Away from Matilde and her pins.

Away from Joy's hollow chimes.

I don't care if Rick is a Riffraff; he's my dad, and right now it feels like that counts. Rick stops the van in the car park that looks out over the beach. He studies the waves for a while, for what feels like a stretched-out while. Then he goes to the back of the van and arrives next to my door with a surfboard under his arm.

"Okay, Al Pal, let's have a paddle."

The tide is a long way out, and a glassy film of water on the sand reflects the last shimmer of the day. Silhouettes of surfers with long shadows carry boards toward the water, screechy seagulls barracking them in. We walk out together to where small waves are breaking, and Rick lifts me up onto the front of his board. I lie on my tummy, and he tucks in behind me and starts paddling steadily. The waves come to meet us, licking my arms, my chest, my legs and the small of my back. The water is cooling me down even on the inside. We keep moving out to where the waves are growing. They start breaking over my face. The water is washing away the sting, the throb and the headache. And soon we are beyond the white foam with just clear green water between us and the horizon. The water is a long stretch of endlessness.

Suddenly Rick turns the board to face the beach and paddles with purpose. He paddles hard, he paddles fast. I can feel the muscles under his arms brushing my ankles. There's a silver-lipped wall growing behind us. Rick gets us into its curve, and from there the ocean's power takes over and we are carried forward. Sound is suspended. Time is suspended. We are suspended.

And we take off. Rick and I are on a wave together. We fly.

Everything lifts inside me, and that part of my heart pulled down by gravity swiftly elevates so that it's hovering above me. We catch more waves like this: maybe eleven, maybe twelve, it could be thirteen. It's the best feeling in the world. And a whole lot of opposites seem to collide: it's cool but warm, fast but slow, scary but safe.

Finally the setting sun beckons down its glow. We're the last ones in the water, and it's only Rick's suggestion of hot chips that stops me begging to catch "just three more waves."

Sitting on the sand, still damp, wrapped in one towel, we take turns to dip our hands into a warm parcel of hot chips.

"This is a good place, Al. Waves are great at washing away the stuff you don't need. And you know, sometimes they kind of give you answers."

Rick passes me an extra-long chip. I wonder if I should tell him that I did see him here once before, but instead—surprising myself—I say: "Why did my mother have to die, Rick?"

It's Rick's turn for a chip but he doesn't take one.

"Sadly, sometimes, these things happen, Al," he says in a quiet voice. "But hey, you have me. And you have your two grandmothers. . . . What have they told you about your mum?"

"Nothing. They don't talk about her, except Joy says that she's watching over me from heaven. I tried asking Matilde about my mum a long time ago, but her face set like cement. She suddenly got busy with a bunch of urgent chores. I knew not to ask again."

Rick looks across the water for quite a long time. "Okay then. I won't fob you off. What would you like to know?"

"How did she die? Was she sick?"

"You could say that, Al Pal."

Now I miss my turn at the chips. "Did she love me?"

"Yeah, she did. She did love you, Al, *a lot*. She loved you like a lioness. She was so stoked to have a baby girl."

"Were you stoked to have a baby girl?"

Rick turns his head to the side, away from the waves, and looks straight at me. "You bet, Al Pal, and I've been stoked to be your dad ever since."

"Well, why aren't you in charge, Rick? You know, like a normal dad. Why does Matilde get to make all the big decisions? And Joy the leftover ones? You don't get to make hardly any. We don't even really live together."

"There's a bit of history there, Al." Rick looks down at

the sand and after a while he says, "When your mum died, I kind of fell in a hole, you know. . . . I wasn't really coping. I wasn't looking after myself too well, and Matilde and Joy took the view that I wasn't up to looking after you all the time. So they stepped in, and I kind of . . . got pushed out."

"I don't want to make you feel bad, Rick." I really don't.

"Nah, you never make me feel bad, Al." He leans in so that our heads are touching. "I can't say I blame Joy and Matilde for taking over back then. It probably was the right thing to do. But when I picked up and got back to work, sorted myself out . . . things just seemed stuck, being done a certain way. *We* were all stuck . . . and it's just continued like that ever since. I don't have to tell you that your grandmothers are both pretty strong forces, especially when it comes to you."

"Am I like her at all, my mother?"

"More and more, Al. The look of you, the way you see the world and that big heart of yours. Your mum was always trying to make things right for everyone around her, just like you do, especially the people she loved."

"Did she do stuff with me?"

"Doing stuff with you was her favorite thing. See that rock pool?" Rick is pointing over to our left. "She'd swim around there for hours with you on her back, even before you could walk. I can picture your chubby arms clinging around her long neck, your beaming smile matching hers. She would dive down under the water and you'd go too . . . chortling as you surfaced and caught your breath. You had complete faith, just seemed to know she'd keep you safe."

Rick is describing one of my dreams.

One that I've had forever.

One where I see my mother's back, shoulders and arms but I can never quite see her face.

Do the waters within me remember being underwater with her?

"Did she love you?" I ask.

My dad picks up a fistful of sand and lets the grains fall slowly onto my toes.

"Well, that was a bit more complicated. But yeah, on a good day, she loved me." His rib cage is expanding next to mine.

"I reckon she would have loved you every day, Rick."

Rick pulls the towel tight around us so that I'm nuzzled in under his arm. We sit like that for a long time. He throws a chip to a seagull, and before long we're surrounded by squawking birds, and even though it's nighttime and tomorrow is a school day, Rick seems in no hurry to get me home to Number 23.

CHAPTER TEN

OUR ESSAY "A DAY IN THE LIFE OF A GOLD PROSPECTOR" IS due today. Sister has to rush to the office to get the whistle before playground duty, so she asks that when the lunch bell rings, we each leave our work on her desk. I'm putting some finishing touches on mine and I look up to find I'm the last one left in the classroom. I place my essay on the top of the pile. And there, poking out near the bottom, is a border of Oriental Blue and Primrose Yellow that could only be the finicky work of Kimberly Linton. Her handwriting is curly, her headings are artistic and her drawings are detailed and three-dimensional. It's a guaranteed A-plus.

And now it's a scrunched-up ball in my pocket.

I open my lunch box in full view of the entire sixth grade and enjoy my liverwurst sandwich more than usual while watching Kimberly a few benches away relating a story with a happily angled head and no sense of what might be coming her way. I tingle at the thought of what's in my pocket. I want Kimberly to be puzzled, doubted, punished. For once I want to crush Kimberly Linton with all her performing and perfection and popularity, just long enough to make her pay. Make her pay for what she did to Patricia in a few short terms, make her pay for what she's done to me for seven long years and make her pay for what her father is doing to Matilde.

We have free reading in the afternoon, and Sister is at her desk marking our essays.

"Scott Perkins, I don't have an essay from you." Sister doesn't sound one bit surprised.

With eyes fixed on his *Wheels* magazine Scott mumbles: "I accidentally left it in my dad's car."

"Well, make sure you bring it to me first thing in the morning. That's another demerit, Scott. You're just one away from a week of picking up papers. And, Kimberly, dear, I can't seem to find yours either." Sister's voice softens.

Kimberly loosens her hold on her Nancy Drew novel. "But I definitely put it on your desk, Sister Josepha."

"Well, it doesn't appear to be here. Would you like to come up and point it out to me?"

Kimberly flicks confidently through the pile. She grows a little flushed and confused. She goes back to her desk, lifts the lid and searches under the Cuisenaire rods, the label maker and the souvenir ruler collection. She rifles through her schoolbag hanging on one of the hooks at the back of the classroom and goes back to Sister's desk, now looking in the bin underneath. Tears are starting to pool in the bottom half of her aquamarine eyes. Roslyn is away sick from school, so Kimberly looks to the next rung down of the Popular Group for backup.

"Karen, you saw me put it on the desk, didn't you?"

"I definitely did, Kimberly. . . . Well, *actually* . . . I was at piano, but you deadset would have handed it in."

"See, Karen is my witness. And my dad is too—he helped me write it."

"All right, Kimberly, sit down. If you can't bring it to me by the end of class today, you'll have to do it again and bring it in tomorrow." Sister goes back to her marking.

"But I can't do it again tonight," bursts out Kimberly. "I won't have time. We're going to the drive-in for my sister's birthday." Her neck is blotchy red, and a couple of the boys are starting to smirk. Without Roslyn here today the scaffolding of the Popular Group is a bit shaky, and they're not sure where to look or how to reinforce Kimberly.

"Well, it's up to you, dear, but I'll be writing your reports next week, and this essay is worth sixty percent of your social studies mark."

"You can't make me do it again. I've already done it. My parents will complain to Father Brennan and the Department of Education. They'll complain to the Pope," Kimberly lashes out.

"Calm yourself, Kimberly, unless you want to go straight to three demerits." Sister reins her in.

I keep my head low, reading the same line of *Watership*

Down over and over. A circuit in my heart releases a little electric charge at the sight of Kimberly, who usually fires out, getting so fired up before being shot down.

The risk. The reward. The thrill.

And it's all happening because of something I've done.

I know it's probably bad and certainly not full of God's grace, but right now it's clearing all my pipes.

■ ■ ■

Matilde has finished her rush job, so her Singer has quietened for now. She's back to her cooking and cleaning and gardening but isn't saying all that much to me. Although she does have an almost-conversation one night with Rick out on the back porch, quite a while after I've gone to bed. I can't hear every word, but I do make out that they're talking about Joy and how long "she'll be there," how long "she'll be staying away with her friend Wendy."

Joy must have gone on a holiday with Whisky Wendy.

So that's the important thing Rick said she had to do?

The break she needed was a holiday!

Why didn't Joy just tell me?

That part of my heart that counts on my grandmother being reliable feels sore and inflamed.

Before school I slip into Number 25 with some lettuce for Simone de Beauvoir. Even though I'm still pretty mad at Joy, I know she would just die if Simone didn't live. The penny tortoise is on the lookout for Joy. When I stand at the edge of the water-lily pond, she pops up hopefully, and while I know Simone and I are definitely friends, and she's very pleased that I have brought her the lettuce, I see her lower her head just slightly in disappointment when she realizes it's me and not Joy coming to feed her.

While I'm there I water the bougainvillea, the paper daisies, the jasmine and fuchsias. Through Joy's back window I can see the sweeties jar still opened on the table and the dirty dishes all still piled around the sink. Matilde would never leave dishes in the sink before she went on holiday. Then again, Matilde would never in a million years even think of going on a holiday.

CHAPTER ELEVEN

WE'RE DOING MATH BEFORE LUNCH, AND SISTER JOSEPHA asks if anyone managed to do the extra challenge with the homework. I worked it out last night, but I'm sure not going to own up to it. Sister waits by the board. For a long time she waits, and she gets her waity face, popping the chalk with precision from one palm to the other. Not even Matthew puts up his hand.

"Allegra, dear, what about you? Can you show us how to graph the image of the rectangle after a rotation of 35 degrees counterclockwise around the origin?"

Of course I can, but why always me! Doesn't Sister know how picked on I am each time she singles me out to give the right answer? But you can't say no to Sister Josepha.

Even before I get to the board, the sniggering starts. It seems louder than usual. I'm up to the third rotation, face to the board, and the Popular Group is erupting. Kimberly is laughing louder than anyone else. Turning around briefly, I see her pointing at my back from her desk. Sister tells her sternly, "Be quiet!" and, coming in close to me at the board, says gently: "Allegra, let's step outside for a minute together."

In the corridor outside the classroom she half whispers: "Dear, it seems that you have become a woman."

"A what?"

"A woman, dear. You have become a *woman*. It seems that you have started your monthlies."

The bell rings for lunch, and Sister escorts me to sick bay and gives me a floral pack to take to the bathroom and "sort myself out." I'm horrified by what I find. And it's on the back of my uniform as well. I'm going to stay in the bathroom all day. All week. All term if I have to. I can never go back into that classroom again.

"Allegra, can I help you in any way?" Sister is hovering outside the cubicle. "I have a clean uniform for you, dear." This is getting worse by the minute. And now I can hear that other girls are coming into the toilets.

Sister passes me the uniform over the top of the door. It's crushed and smells of used tea towel and is definitely too tight across the chest, but I have no choice but to wear it. I feel hot and teary and wobbly.

After a while Sister tells me that it's time to open the door. I slink out. Sister takes me by the hand—patting it a few times—and, walking past the office, she tells the secretary that we're going to the convent and if she's not back by the end of lunch, please send the sixth grade next door into Miss Hunter's room.

The convent is across the road from the school. It's where the nuns live, and I've never been even close to going inside before. Nobody has, except for Thomas O'Malley, who went there in third grade because his mum is cousins with Sister Claire. He told us afterward that they had a platter of Holy Communion hosts topped with devon for dinner and that he fed the leftovers to a three-headed horse called Holy Trinity that the nuns keep out the back. Thomas's nickname is Tall Tale Tom.

I follow Sister into the convent kitchen. She pours me a glass of milk and puts a couple of Shortbread Creams onto a plate. We move into the lounge room, and she tells me I can sit on the tapestry couch by the television set. Even though it's a convent, it almost seems like normal house, except there's a soapy clean smell, lace doilies galore and pictures of Jesus looking loving and sad, pointing to his red heart, hanging above every doorway.

"Now, Allegra," says Sister. "Do you fancy a game of Chinese checkers?"

I'd probably prefer a bit of telly, but I guess that Chinese checkers is better than the science lesson I'd usually be doing in class on a Friday afternoon.

Sister clears the table, sets up the board and asks if I'd like to be yellow or green. After just a few moves I can see that she's quite the champ at Chinese checkers. She beats me quick smart in the first two games, but I manage to win by a whisker in the third and am well ahead in the fourth. Actually, Chinese checkers is a pretty good game.

I'm picking my path across the board when Sister says without looking up, "Allegra, what happened today is perfectly normal. Yes indeed, natural, in fact. It's called menstruation, and it happens to all healthy girls at some point, and it will even happen to Kimberly." She jumps three of my marbles and continues, "I'll send you off today with a note to give to your grandmother. She'll explain everything and help you with what you need."

I have read about menstruation in Matilde's biology books, but I never guessed it could lead to something embarrassing on the back of my uniform.

"That's it. Well done, dear," says Sister. "You've got all your marbles home. Would you like another Shortbread Cream?"

I take the note home to Number 23. Matilde reads it and I'm looking at her, waiting for her to explain everything and help me with what I need like Sister Josepha said she would. Instead she studies me briefly, pea-sized displeased, and swiftly slaps me across my face.

"Remember that the life of a woman is one full of pain and restraint, Allegra. Wait in your room while I go to the pharmacy. And keep away from my rising dough."

I'm completely confused. The slap wasn't that hard, but Matilde has never hit me before, and I have no idea what her rising dough has got to do with anything.

When she gets back, she places a package at the end of my bed. I go to the bathroom and sort myself out for the second time today and come out for my dinner: a big bowl of still-pink-inside chicken livers. Everything about today is disgusting.

If only I could *Behold My Mother.* She could hold me, and make everything right.

. . .

"I have a *terrrrible* earache, Matilde," I tell her, coming out late for breakfast on Monday morning after deciding an earache is something she can't see, measure with a thermometer or test with the palm of her hand. I just can't face going to school today, not after what happened in front of everyone at the end of last week.

"A clove of garlic will remedy that in no time, Allegra," announces Matilde, smashing one with the back of her carving knife. "Is it your left or right ear?"

"Ah . . . left," I say, expecting she's going to make me eat the garlic . . . *raw.*

"You will notice a difference by the time you are dressed for school," she says with a healer's confidence, coming over my shoulder while I'm hunched at the table moving my food around the plate. But instead of putting the garlic in my mouth, she puts it in my ear.

"I'll give you a couple of peeled cloves to keep in your pocket so you can change them during the day. Now hurry up and get ready—you don't want to be late."

I don't hurry. Instead I do a whole lot of D words. I Dawdle, Delay and Drag the chain. I *do* want to be late. So late that it's *too late* to go to school at all. But Matilde is right on top of me and insists on walking me there so she can set a making-up-time pace. There's no missing school with Matilde around.

Arriving at St. Brigid's gate, I stop and it just bursts out of me. "I *can't* go in, Matilde, I can't. They were all laughing at me . . . Kimberly Linton worst of all. And now that Patricia's gone, I don't have any friends. . . ."

"You have your *good self*, Allegra, and that is life's most dependable companion. Now, draw on your dignity and hold your head high. And here—put these cloves in your pocket. . . . I suspect your earache is cured, but the garlic will repel that Kimberly Popular."

It repels everyone, except for Mary-Anne Wilson. She probably can't smell me over her own scuzzy smell.

"Can you be partners with me for art this afternoon? Allegra . . . *please?*" Mary-Anne asks like someone too used to being turned down. "I don't even mind about the mess on your tunic last week. It just means you're mature."

She is looking at me hopefully, almost kindly and per- haps even knowingly, like she might be seeing something the Popular Group doesn't: something other than mature.

"Yeah . . . okay. I'll be your partner, Mary-Anne," I say, feeling worn down. I take the squashed garlic out of my ear and put it into the bin. Her face lights up, and I can't shake her for the rest of the day. It doesn't take much to make Mary-Anne Wilson happy; in fact, it's kind of contagious, and after a while my *good self* feels slightly better than terrible. And while Mary-Anne was no good at sticking matchsticks straight, it turns out she's actually not bad at mixing colors and painting Blue Mountains landscapes. Not bad at all.

...

Sister Josepha asks me to stay back and help her wash out the paintbrushes after school. Once I finish drying them all, she calls me to her desk and says she has something to give me. I'm terrified that she has solved the mystery of Kimberly's missing essay; I probably deserve a detention . . . suspension . . . maybe expulsion.

But when Sister opens the desk drawer, I see Patricia's writing on the front of a letter, a letter addressed to me at St. Brigid's School.

I can barely wait to read it but work hard at accepting it casually from Sister, just like I would if I got a letter every second day. Once under the mulberry tree, I open it quickly and try to understand all the things Patricia has to tell me.

I read it again, more slowly, because my eyes went all fuzzy the first time:

> Dear Ally,
>
> I didn't have a chance to say good bye to you and to tell you that I have been to 8 schools but no one was ever such a good friend to me as you are. You are fun and smart and you've got guts Ally. But mostly you are loyal!
>
> But this is no suprise because Mum says you've got good genes. Joy is cool and copped a blow for me. Fake

dad was on a bender, he's not my real dad, and he blew up when we tried to leave and he found us hiding at the naybours. He threw the boiling hot kettle at me but Joy stood in the way and she saved me but she got the hot water all accross her face. I felt real bad Ally. I still do. It looked like it hurt her alot. Tell Joy I say hello and tell her I say sorry and tell her I say thankyou Joy.

We are in Armidale now but we might move around a bit so its hard to give you our adress but Mum is going to keep in touch with Joy so may be we can be pen pals so give a letter to Joy and she can send it to the right place.

I hope you like high school when you go and that we can do a trip around Australia together one day like we talked about in a flower power hippy van with curtens.

Give Kimberly and all the popular group a bite on the bum from me.

Love from your best-ever friend,
Patricia

Something that tastes like metal pushes down any happiness I might feel about hearing from Patricia, because right now I just need to see Joy. I need to know where she is. I need to know that her face is not boiling hot, that her eyes aren't burnt closed, that her voice can still hum, her arms can still hug and that her bosom is still my safe harbor.

I run and don't stop until I get to our lane. At Number 23 Rick is reversing his van out of the driveway. I stand blocking his way.

"Where's Joy?"

Rick sees me, cuts the engine and jumps out of the van.

"Tell me, Rick, where is she? I know she's not on a holiday." I'm panting, and as my words come out I realize I'm crying, too. "I know she's been burnt. Where is she?"

"It's okay, Al Pal. Calm down. Joy's going to be fine."

"But tell me where she is."

"She's safe and sound at Wendy's."

"Take me there. Take me to Wendy's house—*please, Rick!* I need to see Joy."

Twenty minutes later, Whisky Wendy opens the door of a house that smells completely different from Number 23 and looks nothing like the convent. She tells us to just step around the holes in the floor as we weave our way behind her down a dark corridor. There's a room at the end with cane furniture, a fishbowl, a desk with a typewriter and posters on the walls. I read a few quickly as I walk past.

"What does 'From Adam's Rib to Women's Lib' mean, Rick?"

"Buggered if I know, Al." Rick's head is down and he's not stopping to read anything.

Wendy beckons us outside into the backyard, where some little kids on dinkies are making their way around trotting toddlers in nappies. Some women sitting on mismatched chairs on the back veranda are holding cups of tea and smoking cigarettes, chatting to each other while keeping half an eye on the children. One of them dashes out to scoop a child off a tricycle and onto her hip as soon as she spots Rick.

We follow Wendy past the women and children through to the end of the yard, where we come to what looks like old horse stables. She tells us to wait at the door and she'll check if Joy is up to having visitors.

Visitors . . . Wendy sure does describe me in weird ways. A few weeks ago I was a *sister;* now I'm a *visitor.* I don't think she realizes who I am to Joy and what Joy is to me.

And then there is my Joy. Altered. Moving slowly. No matte makeup. But her eyes are smiling and her arms are open.

I don't want to look too long at Joy's red-and-brown face, so I bury mine, eyes closed, into my berth in her harbor. She hums "Too-Ra-Loo-Ra-Loo-Ral" gently into the top of my head. And I exhale. But with my next deep inhale, longing for lavender, it's not the scent of Joy that hits the back of my throat but more the smell of something Matilde would use to clean the bathroom floor. That part of my heart that grabs feelings before they escape takes hold and tells me not to let Joy see what I'm seeing or sense what I'm smelling.

"Ally, darling, I didn't want you to see me with this silly burnt face. I really didn't want to frighten you." Joy leans lightly on my arm to walk across to an old velvet lounge. We sit together. Her voice sounds a little bit different. "I'm so sorry I couldn't be at your Confirmation, darling. Was it a wonderful, magical day?"

"Your face doesn't frighten me, Joy." I'm staring down at

yellowed sponge through a hole in the lounge. "And I know why you couldn't be at my Confirmation. Patricia wrote me a letter and she told me that you copped a blow for her." I'm starting to understand what a blow does to a person.

"How is dear little Patricia? And her mother? Did she say where they are now?"

I pull Patricia's letter from my uniform pocket and Joy reads over it with a chin-up smile.

"Well, that's good news indeed. . . . Armidale . . . they should be safe there. And won't it be fun for you to have a pen pal, Ally?"

I nod, but I'm not thinking so much about being pen pals with Patricia right now.

"Does your face hurt a lot, Joy?" It stings mine to see Joy's looking so bad.

"No, darling, not anymore. Wendy is quite the Florence Nightingale, and every other minute she's been applying gel from her aloe vera plant that she keeps cool in the fridge. She's taking very good care of me."

"We can take care of you, Joy, at home, at Number 25." I look over to Rick, who's standing silently by the door. I want him to back me up. Let Joy know that she should be with her family. And a few moments later, after a couple of nods from me—he does—sort of, calling Joy by a name that I knew she was, but I've never heard him use before.

"Yeah, Mum, come on home. Al will look after you."

■ ■ ■

Everything is quivering in Joy's garden this afternoon as we bring her home. As we walk down the side of Number 25, the breeze freshens and the frangipanis fan their leaves in Joy's direction. The backyard orchestra of string macramé, tambourine branches and woodwind foliage responds, and the wind chimes sway, warming up their soprano, tenor and alto tones. Joy's eyes lift and her pace quickens. She approaches the water-lily pond, sending forward a low hum. Simone de Beauvoir pops up and, dropping the reeds from her mouth, she swims to the painted rocks at the edge closest to Joy, almost trembling. I leave them in tune under the magnolia tree, Simone nesting in Joy's lap and Joy resting in her butterfly chair doing a slow head count of all the paper daisies. I lay the tray inside for mint tea, and Rick disappears next door to his flat above the garage. He's driven us back so his job is done.

Wendy has sent me home with the aloe vera plant and instructions on how it should be applied. After we finish our tea, I sit in front of Joy and do gentle little circles with the pads of my fingers around her crisping face. I tell her all the news of the neighborhood, all the news from St. Brigid's—and—after a pause, all the news about my body.

"I got my monthlies while you were away, Joy." I pull back slightly, ready, in case she's about to slap me across the face like Matilde did. I'm hoping she'll instead explain everything the way Sister Josepha said Matilde would, but didn't.

"Oh, Ally, darling, your very first moon time and—*what a*

shame—I wasn't here to celebrate!" Joy looks disappointed at first, but then, clutching my shoulders, she says in a rush, "Never mind, I'll make it up to you. Yes, I will. My little Liberata, I can barely believe it! You're in the tent now."

I have no idea what Joy is talking about.

• • •

The eve of my birthday has always belonged to Joy.

We eat Neapolitan ice cream from her mother's cut-crystal bowl, then bring out the little glass bottles and dust Joy's emotions, talking about her life as it was when she was the age that I'm turning. And tomorrow I'm turning twelve. Before I set off to Joy's at sundown, Matilde serves me an extra-large helping of matzo-ball soup, which she says is "to keep the wolf on the other side of the door because some people have no idea how to nourish a child." Matilde doesn't know about the Neapolitan ice cream.

Strangely, when I get to the brown gate to Number 25, for the very first time in my whole entire life, it's locked closed from Joy's side of the fence. I pull hard, trying to open it. I knock. I knock louder. I call out to Joy. There's no answer. But then a heart-shaped note appears from underneath the gate. It says: *Come to the front veranda.*

And so I do.

A sprinkling of red rose petals is carving a path to Joy's open front door. The house lights are down, but there's a beckoning glow at the end of the corridor. I step forward—gingerly—wondering: *Is there a Liberty Club meeting tonight that's made Joy forget all about my birthday?*

Then from behind the chaise lounge Whisky Wendy and Comrade Camille appear, floating barefooted toward me without speaking. They place a garland of crimson flowers on my head and red beads around my neck. They lead me through the dimmed house toward Joy's back garden and the sound of a single strumming guitar. The music becomes clearer, and I recognize the tune. . . . It's Van Morrison's "Moondance."

At the end of a red-ribbon aisle, looking larger than usual in a purple kaftan, is my grandmother Joy. The Liberty Club ladies are singing softly about magic, moonlight and blush.

Joy is illuminated, from above and within, standing proud under the magnolia tree, which is hosting tiny lit lanterns and swathes of deep red organza. The Liberty Club ladies close in from all corners of the garden, still singing "Moondance" and holding small candles. They form a circle around me. Instead of being an observer at the edge of their gathering, I'm suddenly central, surrounded and almost alight. Simone, who it seems was in on the secret, is popped up and poised and watching from her painted rocks; she is wearing a ruby-red choker.

And then Joy with her healing pink face steps forward and announces: "Welcome, Liberata, to this sacred circle of women. This circle that surrounds you is continuous, open, collaborative and never broken."

She reads like a performer from a linen-covered book:

Ally, our sister
My cherished granddaughter
Your first moon time is here
And we are here with you

Consider your body a beautiful garden
Nourish it and it will nourish you
It is a glory of nature, a sacred grove
Take pleasure in it and it will pleasure you

Your body has matured and blossomed
And your womb can now bring forth new life
Embrace your lunar cycle
Delight in its rhythm, wisdom and light

And remember the power is yours
So only open the gates to your garden
And share its beauty, mystery and offerings
With those who deserve and treasure your love

At Joy's invitation the ladies go around the circle, happily sharing icky stories about their very first *moon times*. I want to block my ears.

Maidens and cramps; goddesses and lifeblood; cycles and thresholds.

Surely they're not expecting me to join in with a story of my own?

I want to run at the fence and hurdle right out of here.

"I was the youngest of three girls and always felt left

out from the older girls' secrets. I couldn't wait to start my period, and when it finally came, I was allowed to enter their club. We celebrated with a trip to the milk bar for a double-choc malted. I still have a sweet card my sister Fay wrote to me. We truly became *sisters* that day."

This lady's voice is upbeat and bouncy, and I'm trying hard to look up from my feet.

"We were on summer holidays when my aunt Flo visited me for the first time," pipes up another. "I had to lie on a beach towel on the sand and pretend I had a headache when everyone else was having fun in the water. Finally my older cousin twigged to what was going on and told all my other cousins, including the boys. I could have throttled her at first, but they all seemed to have a new respect for me after that. Thank God for tampons—no more pads and belts and sitting on the sand!"

If only Matilde could call me home with an urgent voice.

And now it's someone called Dinah's turn. She doesn't seem as faked-up happy as the others.

"I was so shocked when my usually loving mother greeted my first moon-time news with a slap straight across the face. It wasn't terribly hard, but she was normally quite tender, so for her it was really out of character."

It was out of character for Matilde to slap me too. I wonder if she's ever met Dinah's mother?

"Years later, with tears in my eyes, I asked her why on earth she'd done this to me, and she said, completely unapologetically, that it was just an old Jewish custom to slap sense into a newly fertile girl. What a brutal tradition—it only humiliated me. There's no way I'll be slapping my daughters."

Joy has an expression that suggests there's no way she'll be doing that to me either, but right now, quite honestly, I'd prefer another slap to being in the center of this awful circle. That part of my heart that draws blood from the tips of my fingers, between my toes, under my liver and around my esophagus is sending it all up the front of my neck to my face. And it's pulsing: *This is weird—this is weird—this is weird.*

Joy asks me to walk forward down the red-ribbon aisle and join her under the magnolia tree, which she says is a symbol of fertility and life force. She takes a feather and circles me, reciting:

> *May mother earth always support you.*
> *May the divine feminine nourish you.*
> *May the sun warm you and the moon guide you.*
> *And may you, our sister Liberata, grow wings that*
> * help you soar.*

The Liberty Club ladies are beaming, clapping and hooting and are clearly feeling a whole lot of E words: Elated—Ecstatic—Euphoric.

I'm feeling two . . . Extremely Embarrassed.

CHAPTER TWELVE

Every freaky-deaky detail about last night's Moon-dance is looping like a Hula-Hoop around the coils of my mind. I used up so much energy trying to look at ease for Joy's sake that this morning I'm heavy-boned exhausted.

And I'm confused: Is my first moon time a cause for celebration or is it a time to be pea-sized displeased? If I had a pretty-smiley mum, she would no doubt tell me and help sort me out.

"Still in bed, Allegra . . . lazing-bones-sleeping-head," says Matilde, appearing at my door. "Are you too big now to bounce up excited that it's your birthday?"

I can't tell Matilde why I'm so tired; it would just make her tick her tongue and think that Joy was completely cracked. At least I now know what Matilde's slap was about, even if I'm still not sure why I had to keep away from her rising dough.

I pad out to the kitchen and find that Matilde has made my favorite cream-cheese-and-walnut crepe. She always makes it on my birthday. It's warm, sweet and filling. I fork it in while Matilde cleans up the kitchen behind me. Some days her food works like medicine, strengthening my skeleton with the right dose of no-nonsense nourishment.

"Today, Allegra, you are turning twelve years old, and so I have something for you." Matilde places an envelope on the kitchen table in front of me and walks outside to empty the teapot under the lemon tree.

I open it and find two tickets inside. They are tickets to the ballet. A ballet at the Sydney Opera House, a ballet called *Onegin*, and the tickets are for the matinee performance today!

Kimberly from the Popular Group takes private ballet classes and brings in trophies and medals that she wins at eisteddfods. Sometimes she comes to school wearing a netted bun and still-there makeup from a concert she's performed in the night before. At least once a week she uses the handrail outside the tuckshop to practice her *grand battements* while the St. Brigid's kids are queuing for their Cobbers and Sunnyboy iceblocks. None of her high kicks impress me—I usually turn away—but I couldn't help but be just a bit enthralled when for news in fourth grade she described going to see the ballet *Romeo and Juliet* at the Sydney Opera House just after it opened. She had a Polaroid photo taken on the steps wearing a velvet cape and her own pointe shoes. She walked it around the classroom; we could all *look but not touch*.

And now, *I'm* going to the Sydney Opera House, to see a real ballet, *today.*

Through the open back door I catch a glimpse of Matilde sneaking a peek at me as she scrapes the tea leaves from the pot around the base of the tree. I run out, throw my arms around her waist and hug her hard. She feels softer with all the trapped air squeezed out.

"Are we really going to the Opera House, Matilde? *Really?* Going today to the ballet? How did you get the tickets?"

"Never mind how I got the tickets, Allegra; there is much to do before we set off."

I follow Matilde back inside as she rattles off the list, which includes times tables and piano practice and hair washing that need to be done before midday. I fly through it all and at Matilde's instruction put on my Confirmation dress and meet her at the front door at noon. She's holding her small brown handbag and looks neat and ready in her fawn skirt with a seed pearl brooch pinned at the top of her cream blouse.

Climbing up to the Opera House is about the most exciting ascent I can imagine. The steps are wide and shallow, and Matilde tells me that just like the Spanish Steps in Rome, they are made to match perfectly the gait of a horse. There are no horses about, only dressed-up ladies of all different shapes, a handful of men and a sprinkling of girls about my age. We follow the crowd to the foyer, where Matilde buys a program and, my second surprise of the day, a box of malt balls.

We keep climbing until we get to the last door, which

displays the number that is printed on our tickets, and after I bump past a lineup of knees, tread on a couple of shoes and knock over a few handbags, we take our seats. The lights go down, and the audience greets the arrival of the conductor with a round of enthusiastic applause. I follow Matilde's lead and clap along, even though from what I can tell he hasn't done anything yet.

The curtain goes up and for the next couple of hours music, movement and feelings take me to a different continent, another time and, without warning, a sudden set of plans for my future: I'm imagining my life as a ballerina.

"Can you see the muscles in Tatiana's legs working, Allegra?" whispers Matilde. "Look at her sculptured power. She is every bit as strong as Eugene and Prince Gremin. And when you think of the flexibility and endurance required of her, she is in fact even stronger than the male dancers."

On the bus on the way home Matilde tells me that *Onegin* is definitely the most important ballet "because it does not fill a young girl's head with the happy-ever-afters. Tatiana falls in love with Onegin, an arrogant aristocrat who has no love for her, but then after she has married another man, he appears again, trying to win her affection. She is a strong and sensible woman and sends Onegin packing. You must learn from Tatiana, Allegra. Never be swept away by a man, aristocrat or otherwise. Make your decisions with your head; never put your trust in your young heart. It will only misguide you."

"I think I want to *be* Tatiana, Matilde," I say, feeling inspired. "Is it too late for me to start learning ballet?"

"Don't be delusional, Allegra," Matilde snips. "Ballet is

for you to watch and appreciate; it is not for you to do. You will be too busy being a doctor to dance. You will earn good money of your own, which, if you manage it well, you can use to buy the good seats at the ballet, close to the front and center stage, without having to climb all those impossible stairs."

"And I'm going to bring you with me," I say. I don't know about this doctor business, but I do want to make Matilde proud. Her expression softens, and I wonder if it might even be possible to one day make Matilde happy.

I'm relieved that this grandmother celebrated my birthday by taking me to watch something magical from the safety of the dark rather than making me the embarrassed center of attention surrounded by all that confronting light.

...

My mind has been twirling and whirling ever since last week's ballet, and I've been privately practicing pirouettes on my way down the lane.

Arriving home from school this afternoon, I find Matilde sitting at our kitchen table drinking black tea with another lady, who she introduces to me as Mrs. Kowalski. Matilde mostly keeps to herself, and I've never known her to have a friend over for tea before. It would be nice for my grandmother to have a friend; then she could perhaps even learn to have fun. Only they don't seem to be talking to each other in a way that sounds at all friendly.

Matilde quickly serves me a small plate of last night's

stuffed cabbage leaves and tells me to take it into my room and get a start on my homework. Usually I have my afternoon tea in the kitchen with her, so this is something pretty unusual. I'm curious. I really want to know what Matilde and Mrs. Kowalski are talking about. I half close the door to my room, count to one-hundred-apple-pie, then sneak out the front door and around the side of the house and sit down low underneath the kitchen window, where I can hear every word.

"We are not just on strike at the factory for the equal pay, Matilde. We are also on strike for the right to have *more rights*," says Mrs. Kowalski. "We want the right to more than just one lousy tea break. We want the right to go to the toilet when we *need* to go to the toilet. The way things are, all the women at the factory are only allowed two toilet breaks during the whole of the day, and if we take more than just the three minutes, then the pig-of-a-man supervisor bangs on the door and drags us back to the floor. Once he even dragged one of our women out by the hair who was in the beginnings of losing a child. I tell you, that Bolton's Fashion House is more like a prison than a place of work.

"We need your support, Matilde. We need all the out-workers to support us. If you do the extra piecework for Bolton's at home, then the workers at the factory will lose the power that the strike will give us, and then we will all lose this important battle. We need to stand together, Matilde, united. I am Polish, you are Hungarian, but we have both endured unspeakable suffering to get to this country.

We are the survivors. We need to stand up and be strong."
Mrs. Kowalski is sounding every bit as strong as Matilde.

"I have no problem with being strong, Rutka. No problem at all," Matilde replies. "But I also need to eat. I need to pay my mortgage and I need to care for my granddaughter. You saw the girl—she is still young. I cannot leave her alone for a job outside this house. She has no mother. What else can I do?"

"It won't be forever, Matilde. Just until we have won our rights. You have no idea what we have to put up with at that factory. There is also the crazy unfair bonus scheme. It is compulsory, but we do not know what are the rules. We do not even know how much extra work we need to do to qualify, and last month two of our girls got the sack because they didn't meet it, but they didn't know what *it* was.

"And also, we all have to put in money from our own pay for the boss's birthday. We have to put up with his terrible conditions, his abuse, and then—can you believe it?— buy him a big present and wish him *many happy returns*. I don't see you doing that from the comfort of working in your home, Matilde."

"I am paying in other ways, Rutka. If there is no work, then I have no pay at all, *not a red cent*. And if I refuse the work now, I will never get the work again. This I cannot do. On my shoulders I carry everything here, *everything*. The child's father makes little contribution; his focus is too much on the horse races. He too has the *Játszik* sickness. But my granddaughter, she is a clever girl . . . *a very clever girl* . . .

just like her mother, so I must also save for her future studies at the university. I am sorry. I cannot help you." I hear Matilde push her chair out from the table in a way that I know means the conversation is finished.

I scurry back to my room just in time to hear Mrs. Kowalski leave through the front door.

I wonder just how sick Rick is exactly.

Did he catch this "*Játszik* sickness" from my dead mother?

Sometimes when I get information from secretly listening in to the adults, it feels as though growing up is not so much about getter taller or smarter or stronger, but about the happy shell of being a kid being chipped away from around me one chink at a time.

CHAPTER THIRTEEN

THE MAN WITH THE GRAY PLASTICINE FACE HAS BROUGHT BAG after bag of blue fabric, and Matilde is working with it every second of every minute of every hour of every day. Her hands and her neck and her face are all turning blue. She's barely washing, sleeping or eating.

So for tonight I decide to take over the cooking. Rick reckons that's an excellent idea and gives me five dollars to buy some ingredients.

It would be nice to make Matilde her goulash or fisherman's soup, but I'd like to keep my dinner a surprise, so I don't want to disturb her for instructions or a recipe. I walk to Dave's Mixed Business and Milk Bar one street away and am wondering what I should buy when Mrs. Lister breezes in through the plastic door streamers looking every bit as colorful as a packet of Fruit Tingles. She's wearing a green crocheted pantsuit and orange platform heels, and her big blond hair is center-parted with flicks and wings. She's curvy and tall and shares a joke with Dave on her way to the freezer. I hover by the magazine stand, holding an open *TV Week*, watching her closely for inspiration.

"That's dinner sorted, then," she says, placing a box of fish fingers down on the counter with a bag of frozen mixed veg. "Oh, and Dave, a packet of Benson and Hedges, thanks, darl."

I can only see the back of Mrs. Lister's head, but it's not hard to imagine her giving Dave an open-mouthed wink.

"Right you are, Tracy, love," says Dave, looking like he'd give her the world if he could.

I copy Tracy Love's purchase exactly—except for the Benson and Hedges—and leave excited that for once we'll be having the same tea as the Lucky Listers across the road.

Back at home I follow the instructions on the box and the bag and take the tray in to Matilde early, before she's even had a chance to think about dinner. She's definitely surprised to see the meal I've prepared and shows no signs of noticing that the boiled-up frozen mixed veg has made the fish fingers slightly soggy, and their undersides are just a bit singed.

"So now, Allegra, what are you bringing to me here on the tray? Well, this is certainly more than tea and honey toast." Matilde's pea-sized pleased is almost lost among the rolls of blue fabric, pincushions and pinking shears, the thimbles, tape measures and tracing paper.

She stops for a few minutes while I watch her stand at her cutting table and eat almost all of the dinner I've made for her. She thanks me with a nod and gets back to her machine, dabbing the corners of her mouth with her hankie.

I eat mine alone in the kitchen, thinking I should enjoy it more than I do.

It's my job to take Rick's dinner up to him each night, and I feel proud that for the first time the dinner is one I've prepared. As I walk up the stairs to his flat, I can hear the radio; it's always on. Rick does like to listen to those horse races. Maybe it takes his mind off his *Játszik* sickness. I've given him extra mixed veg to help keep up his strength and two more fish fingers than I gave to Matilde.

I study Rick closely as he eats. He doesn't look sick, not in the slightest, but then I remember Cathy McNally's father, who traveled all over the state selling lawn-mower parts. He looked strong in an apron spinning the chocolate wheel hard at the school fete last September, and less than three weeks later he died in his sleep in a motel near Terrigal.

And there's nothing wrong with Rick's appetite, either; he loves the fish fingers and mixed veg. "Gotta say that was a welcome change, Al Pal," he says after downing the last bite. "Did you cook it all by yourself?"

"Yep. It wasn't really that hard—I just read the instructions on the packet and the box."

"You're a champ, Al. Reckon Matilde would appreciate you taking care of the dinner when she's so busy." He hands his empty plate back to me. "I'm catching a few waves first thing tomorrow—want to come?"

"Sure!" I'm deadset keen. I like it being just Rick and me, and that's easier to pull off when Matilde's distracted with her piecework. Besides, I want to keep an eye on my dad now that I know that he's got the *Játszik* sickness.

Whatever that is.

...

I wake in the half-light before sunrise to Rick tapping at my window: he's here to take me on what he calls Dawn Patrol. After he polished off his fish fingers last night he went on to explain, wiping singed crumbs from his chin, that when the wind and the tide are right, he likes to get to the beach at dawn because that's when the temperature of the water equals the temperature of the earth's surface and the sun starts to wake up the waves.

A few weeks ago when I first lay on Rick's board, it was late in the day, and the sun was setting on our backs. But this morning as we paddle out to meet the beams of sunrise, I'm tucked in behind my dad and a shaft of light is streaming through the parting clouds, moving us toward a glistening target that keeps moving forward just in front of Rick's head.

"Can you see God's rays, Al Pal? They're coming from the point in the sky where the sun radiates."

I've never heard Rick mention God before. In fact, I've only ever seen him inside a church twice, once on my First Communion day and recently on my Confirmation day, and both times he looked like his collar was choking him. But Rick's different out here in the vastness and the beauty and the waves, with the near-silence and cool-calm.

I feel different too.

Rick tells me that the dusk and the dawn bring smooth waters and offshore winds. Blowing from the beachside and out toward the ocean, the offshore winds help the waves keep their curved shape by blowing steadily up their face.

We are the first to break through the unridden swell and to drop down onto the other side.

We lie silently on the board.

Rick tells me to swap places with him so that now it's me at the front of the board and him at the back.

We wait.

Rick's strong arms start to move through the water, turning us around to face the beach. Suddenly his arms pick up pace and rhythm, and he paddles with power.

And then we are actually riding a wave: buoyed by the water but floating on air.

I feel a shift of weight on the board behind me and turn around to see Rick standing up.

"Kneel, Al! Kneel up!"

I kneel.

"Now stand. I'm right here behind you. Just pop up!"

My heart pushes my thighs toward my toes, my knees to my chest, my shoulders forward and up, and my head toward the sky.

I can't believe it. I'm standing up.

Rick is *woohoo*ing behind me, but I'm holding in all the salty air that's filled my lungs and I don't have anything extra to push out a sound.

We are weightless. At one with the wave and the water and the movement of each other, Rick and me, father and daughter, powered by the ocean, in the middle of nature, with God's rays on our backs and our goal straight ahead.

And then—without warning—I am wet.

I am shocked.

Shocked that I stood, shocked that I fell, shocked to be left behind as Rick and the board move on toward the beach.

Kicking my feet hard, my toes brushing the seaweed and sand beneath them, I break through the surface and I'm about to swim in when I see that Rick is now paddling back out to me.

"You okay?" he calls.

"Yeah, I'm okay," I splutter, clearing the salty foam from my nose.

"You stood, Al, what a champ. You stood up!"

"But then I just fell off."

"You've got to expect to wipe out, Al Pal. You stand and you fall. Jump back on and we'll do it again."

■ ■ ■

Dawn Patrol has become our special thing. Each morning I slip out quietly and meet Rick by the van. I wipe crusts of sleep from my eyes as we set off for the beach. Once past Dave's Mixed Business and Milk Bar, Rick pumps up his

Beach Boys *Surfin' Safari* tape, and when I look across the bench seat at my dad's face, I can see by the smile lines at the sides of his eyes that he likes having me there, singing out loud.

Matilde is so busy with piece after piece that she doesn't seem to notice that I'm gone before breakfast. I've taken to having showers in the mornings instead of baths at night, so maybe that's why she doesn't suspect anything when I eat my boiled eggs and cold cuts in the kitchen with wet hair.

But then after eight days the rush job is done and Matilde's attention returns suddenly and is once again fully focused on me.

"Ah, bugger," says Rick as we turn in to the driveway and see Matilde waiting at the end near the garage.

"And where exactly have you been?" Matilde's voice cuts sharp as her scissors as she approaches my side of the van.

I slither out through the van door in my swimmers, still damp, barefooted, with my hair salty, sandy and knotted. That part of my heart that shifts gears releases the clutch abruptly on my floaty exercised-exhaustion and pedals up energy-sucking dread. Now Matilde will think that her only granddaughter is a Riffraff.

Rick—head down—busies himself taking the towels out of the back of the van, then the board, and sets to hosing it down on the grass. Why doesn't he tell Matilde where we've been, where *he's* taken me? Why doesn't he tell Matilde that he's my dad and he can take me for a Dawn Patrol surf anytime he wants?

Rick's not sticking up for himself.

He's not sticking up for me.

"Go inside, Allegra. Immediately! And get ready for school." Matilde is livid. She's not looking at Rick, not even for one-apple-pie.

I don't want Matilde to ignore Rick anymore. He's my dad, and when Matilde ignores him, it feels like I shouldn't like him one bit for her sake, but I should love him extra hard to make it up for his sake. Their unspoken words bounce off each of them but chisel deep into me.

I come into the kitchen after my shower.

"You are not to go to the beach, Allegra. Ever again! Do you hear my words and understand what I say to you?" Matilde is preparing my breakfast swiftly with bigger movements than usual.

"But why, Matilde? It's so much fun at the beach. I didn't go there by myself, or even with other kids. I went there with Rick, my very own father. He looks after me and he's teaching me how to ride the waves on his surfboard."

Matilde stops cutting the mortadella.

"He took you on his surfboard! What sort of *father* is that? What sort of girl are you? Where will that lead you in your life? I will tell you, Allegra, I will tell you right now. It will lead you straight to trouble with the worst . . . of the worst . . . *of the worst sort!*"

Matilde is holding the knife in front of her chest and the blade is shaking, directing shards of light from the kitchen window across my face. The knife looks as though it's coming to life. Matilde's voice is almost louder than when I dripped blood over her fabric, and her neck is a network of raised curtain cords. I just don't understand why this anger is inside her, bursting into the room, and heading toward me. It makes my core tremble. And now *I've* caught the anger. But it changes shape inside me and shifts to *bátor* and propels my legs to run straight out the back door, down the side path, through the brown gate, past Simone de Beauvoir and into Joy's kitchen.

It's seven-forty-five and Joy isn't up. Her blinds are drawn and her kettle is cold. I try to slow myself down in the corridor so I don't startle her, but today I can't wait until she wakes. I jump onto her warm bed, burrow under her eiderdown and nuzzle into my harbor. Joy pulls her silk sleep mask up to her hairline and says with surprise: "Ally! Oh, this is a good-morning surprise! Ally . . . *pet* . . . are you crying?"

Even though Matilde has made me scared and angry and full of *bátor*, I don't want to give Joy another reason to have eyes that don't see Matilde and ears that don't hear her and a mouth that never sends words her way. I want Joy to stick up for me, but I don't want her to have a showdown with Matilde. I want Joy to tell Matilde that Rick was once her bonny bouncy baby boy and that he is my dad and he can take me to the beach and teach me to ride waves any time he wants. Matilde might love me with chicken paprikash and Oriental Blue dresses and piano lessons, weeding and mending, but she's not the boss of the whole world and she should stop making that part of my heart that carries her heaviness throb so hard that it pounds and pains inside my rib cage.

But then I realize something else. Joy, in a lavender mist with a switched-on happy face, kind of does that to my heart sometimes too.

So I say nothing and just let Joy's fingernails work their magic at the back of my neck.

CHAPTER FOURTEEN

IF RICK IS STILL DOING DAWN PATROL, HE'S DOING IT ALONE, or at least without me.

He might be my dad, but Matilde's still in charge and things are stuck that way more than ever before.

And now Matilde has a new and all-consuming focus.

Sister Josepha has put me forward to sit the Selective High Schools' exam. This came just in time, saving Matilde from thinking that I am a complete Riffraff headed for the worst of the worst of the worst. And now she's more interested than ever in my education, telling me that "this is critical, Allegra, the very opportunity you need to become a doctor," and she has drawn up a study schedule for before and after school, the weekends, and is testing me herself each night before bed.

The exam is tomorrow, and tonight I can't sleep. My mind is full of graphs and charts, dates and timelines and all sorts of rules for arithmetic and grammar. My neatly pressed uniform is hanging on my wardrobe door, with my shined shoes underneath and my bag packed ready for the morning. And now I am dreaming . . . awake dreaming not asleep dreaming. . . . I'm dreaming that this is not the work of Matilde but of my pretty-smiley mum, who tucks me in tight with a warm hug and tells me, *Don't worry about the selective schools' exam, honey. Just do your best and all will be fine, whatever the result. I am already proud of you.*

■ ■ ■

Today the sixth-grade class is saying goodbye to our time at St. Brigid's School.

For weeks after lunch we've been practicing the songs that Sister Josepha has selected and the *just one* song we were allowed to choose for ourselves, as our class farewell to the rest of the school. The choice of song was actually my idea and, amazingly, everyone agreed. Even Kimberly from the Popular Group didn't object.

The classroom is buzzing this afternoon in the lead-up to our performance tonight, the sausage sizzle afterward and the fact that we've all outgrown our just-making-it-to-the-end uniforms and will be going off in different directions to different high schools next year. That part of my heart that catches excitement from particles in the air is simmering. But some of the bubbles are popping and dropping and fizzing with the uncertainty of what lies on the other side of our long summer holiday.

And now our big moment arrives.

We file out one by one to the clapping crowd. Sister Claire is tapping fifth-grade boys with her pointer and telling them not to wolf-whistle as we assemble in our rows, forming a ready choir of thirty-four along the steps in the playground to the left of the tuckshop.

Rick is the first one of my family I spot. He hasn't come to anything much at St. Brigid's before, but today he is leaning against the large gum tree and gives me a slow wave. I wave back at him from our step-stage, using just my eyebrows and a down-low gesture with my hand.

And there on the other side of the playground is Matilde. She's been to everything at St. Brigid's, and now she's standing at her post near the girls' toilets, all dressed in fawn, for the very last time.

Sister Josepha moves in close to us with a conductor ruler and beckons all eyes to look straight ahead and only on her. I'm scanning the crowd for Joy. She's been to most things at St. Brigid's, except of course my Confirmation day. And there she is on the benches under the mulberry tree with someone who looks very much like Patricia O'Brien's mother. And that lady is sitting next to someone who looks very much like . . . *and actually is . . . Patricia O'Brien!*

The dropping bubbles shoot back up through my windpipe and into my throat, giving me direction and volume so that I send every word of "They'll Know We Are Christians by Our Love" toward Patricia O'Brien, and I don't take my gaze off her throughout "I Am the Bread of Life" or "Blessed Are the Peacemakers." And when we break into "My Sweet

Lord," written by George Harrison, selected and conducted by Sister Josepha and her rocking ruler, Patricia is beaming and jumps to her feet. She's leading the crowd so that everyone joins her in arms-up swaying: everyone, that is, except for Father Brennan and Matilde. Although Matilde's arms are firmly by her side and she's fixed like a statue, she does have a slightly relaxed look around the edges of her mouth.

And now it's time for Kimberly to step forward and announce our choice of song.

"As our farewell to St. Brigid's, *I have chosen* for sixth grade to perform for you 'The Pushbike Song.'"

Sister Josepha, facing the rest of us, probably doesn't mean to, but she rolls her eyes ever so slightly. But I just don't care anymore about Kimberly Linton, because Sister knows I chose "The Pushbike Song," the whole sixth grade knows I chose "The Pushbike Song," and I know I chose "The Pushbike Song." And at long last, as I'm about to leave St. Brigid's after seven tricky years, I'm exchanging a look that says everything, and is understood completely, by my best-ever friend, Patricia O'Brien.

And finally it feels like Kimberly Popular has no power over me.

■ ■ ■

Patricia tells me, between bites of charcoaled sausage covered in tomato sauce and wrapped in white bread, that she's down from Armidale until just before Christmas. She and her mother are staying in Glebe. That's quite a long way from North Bondi, I tell her, *I know*, because Rick and I had to drive to Glebe to collect Joy after her face was burnt.

I don't bother walking around the playground to have my uniform signed by all the kids in the class but instead hang upside down on the monkey bars for the very last time with Patricia. With our hair swinging just above the bitumen, hers blowing whiffs of green-apple shampoo, we start hatching a plan to spend as much time together as we can now that she's in Sydney and school has broken up for the year.

"I could ask my mum if you can come and stay with us in Glebe, have a sleepover. There's lots of room there."

"Nah, I wouldn't be allowed. Matilde would never let me do that."

"Well then . . . we'll just have to run away together . . . don't you reckon? Maybe we can go bush, to the Blue Mountains. We liked it up there." Even though I know Patricia is definitely *bátor* and she could probably keep us alive for months in the bush, I also know she's not really serious. Patricia is a perfect mix of the best ideas, laugh-out-loud funny and dependable sensible.

"Yeah, we can definitely do that when we get the hippy van after we finish high school," I say, feeling pressure behind my eyes building against gravity. "Hey, I *could* ask Matilde if you can stay the night at our place." I'm trying to sound like that's actually an option, even though on the inside, still upside down, I doubt it will work. But with the rush of blood to my head, I decide to give it a go. I tell Patricia to wait under the mulberry tree while I try my luck with

Matilde. I find my fawn grandmother standing next to Sister Josepha, having what looks to be a serious conversation.

"Ah, Allegra," says Sister as I walk toward them, wondering what they are talking about, "I was just telling your grandmother the good news I received yesterday afternoon. . . . You, my dear girl, did very well in the selective exam, yes indeed. You have been accepted into Sydney Girls High. What do you think of that? The only student from St. Brigid's to do so in more than five years. Isn't it marvelous! Your grandmother is *very* proud of you, and rightly so. And I have to say I am, too. Well done, dear!"

My timing couldn't be better, although Matilde doesn't see the point of a sleepover: "Why would you want her to stay for the whole night when you will just be asleep, Allegra?"

And I have to beg her: "Because it will be so much fun, Matilde, and we can see each other last thing before we go to sleep and first thing in the morning, and we can do things together all day." She does seem to be listening to my plea.

"Matilde, *pleeease!* Patricia's my best-ever friend and soon she'll be going back to Armidale and I don't know when I'll ever get to see her *ever* again."

"Patricia is a delightful young girl, Mrs. Kaldor. She is a worthy friend for Allegra," says Sister Josepha in her nunly way, which is a statement and an instruction all at once, even, it seems, to a Jew. And guess what, *it does the trick*. Matilde is selective-school pleased with me and reluctantly agrees to inviting Patricia O'Brien to stay with us overnight at Number 23.

It's the best-ever ending to my last-ever day at St. Brigid's Primary School.

■ ■ ■

Patricia arrives the next day just before lunch with a little bunch of gardenias tied at the stems for Matilde and a big bag of Twisties for me. Even though Matilde acts like she's not much interested in our sleepover visitor, I can see that she has gone to extra trouble with her cooking, because she serves us her chicken schnitzel with herbed mashed potatoes and pan-fried cabbage for lunch, which Patricia wolfs down in happy quick gulps.

"That was delicious! Thanks, Mrs. Kaldor. Reckon it's some of the best tucker I've ever had. How do you get the crumbs to stick on the chicken like that?"

"It's simply a matter of coating the chicken with best-quality flour and whisked egg and then crumbing it swiftly and lightly. It is critical that you let the chicken sit in the fridge for a couple of hours before you fry it in a hot pan with a tablespoon of butter and a good slurp of virgin olive oil. Do you care for another piece?"

"If that's okay with you," says Patricia.

"I would not offer it to you if it was not *okay* with me," Matilde replies deliberately, but her eyes start to soften when Patricia smiles up broadly as though Matilde has just shared a warmhearted joke.

"This cabbage is so good, Mrs. Kaldor. Did you get it from Joe the Robber?"

Matilde throws up one hand, looking pea-sized pleased, and announces to Patricia: "No, he would never have a cabbage that fresh. It is from my vegetable garden."

"Really, you grew that cabbage yourself? Do you grow anything else?"

"Allegra will take you out and show you my vegetable garden once you have finished your lunch." I knew Matilde would like Patricia, even though she's not the best speller.

"Your nana is cool," says Patricia, crunching down on a red pepper while we're walking between the garden beds.

"Yeah, I suppose, but sometimes she can be pretty scary."

"But she grows all this stuff and she cooks you all that good tucker. And look at your house: everything is neat and clean and nice inside. She's not scary, Ally; reckon she's just busy."

. . .

We slip through the brown gate and find Joy sitting in her butterfly chair under the magnolia tree, reading from her Liberty Club linen notebook with Simone on her lap. Joy looks up, delighted to see Patricia, and Patricia is clearly pleased to see that Joy's face is healed, and is pretty stoked to finally meet Simone de Beauvoir.

"Can I hold her?" asks Patricia.

"Certainly, pet," responds Joy. "I was just discussing with Simone de Beauvoir some of her own wisdom."

Joy gently passes the penny tortoise to Patricia and shares with us out loud, "De Beauvoir summed up the female condition so well when she said: 'her wings are cut and then she is blamed for not knowing how to fly.' That's it exactly! And yet she still urges us to be loved . . . be admired . . . be necessary . . . be somebody."

Patricia is looking somewhat uncertain; she is studying Simone for evidence of wisdom, a voicebox and maybe cut wings.

"And here . . . just listen to this, girls," Joy continues. "'One's life has value so long as one attributes value to the life of others, by means of love, friendship and compassion.'" Joy closes her eyes and pauses for a moment before adding, "So even in the face of robbed choice and curbed freedom, Simone still speaks of love as the greatest principle."

"Does Simone really speak to Joy?" Patricia asks me with an incredulous whisper.

"She seems to speak to all the Liberty Club ladies," I say, then realize that it might sound kind of strange.

■ ■ ■

Patricia has been staying for four nights now; she loves it here at Number 23. She says her tummy has never been so warmed-up full, and she tells Matilde that she should open her own restaurant and call it Tildie's Tucker.

"You could have a sign out the front and set up long tables out the back in between the garden beds. Me and Ally could be waitresses, and afterward we could do all the washing up."

Matilde dismisses this suggestion with a wave of her

tea towel, but I can tell that she thinks Patricia is a bit of a trick. Each morning we ask if Patricia can stay *just one more night*, and while my best-ever friend never seems surprised when we ring her mum and she says yes, I *am* surprised that Matilde keeps agreeing.

Maybe Patricia is right: maybe Matilde is kind of cool and I just never noticed before now.

Patricia and I find a new rhythm. Having long days together, which roll on through the evening and into the night without a looming close, stretches everything out. Our games go on longer, our jokes seem funnier and our ideas bounce off one another's, becoming bigger and bolder. Our edges start to blend in the way two hues do when they combine to make a new color. And if I had to name it . . . it'd be our take on the color of sunshine.

"Do you like Bing Crosby?" I ask Patricia as we set up a game of Mouse Trap on the front porch.

"I've never met him," she replies.

"I haven't either. He's actually a famous person—he lives over in America. But tomorrow you'll get to hear him when Joy puts up her Christmas tree at Number 25. I always help her on December eighteenth—every year without fail—and we play Bing Crosby on her tape deck and listen to him telling the story of *The Small One* while we put on all the tinsel and decorations and arrange the nativity scene. You can help us if you like."

"Yeah, that'd be cool. I would really like to do that . . . we had a Christmas tree once. Is Matilde going to go in and help too?"

"Nah. She doesn't go anywhere near Joy's place."

Patricia looks up from the cheese wheel as though this needs further explaining, so it seems that I have no option other than to spell it out: "My grandmothers can't stand each other. They don't even speak." I'm surprised that Patricia hadn't picked up on this before now; she's usually pretty sharp.

"*Ohhh,*" she says. "Is there bad blood between them? That's no good—bad blood—it happens sometimes. . . ." She moves her mouse along the path. "But *you* get on with both of them. From what I can see, they love you real hard. I reckon they'd both kill for you, Ally."

"Yeah, I suppose, but it's too much being put into just one person, and the way they love me . . . well, it kind of flows into me in a weird way. Sometimes I wish they could just love me less and take what's left over and put it into liking each other a little bit more."

"You're trapped in their bad blood. You should tell them, Ally, tell them that. They're both cool—maybe they'll take it onboard and make their peace with each other," Patricia says.

"I don't think so. It's been like that forever," I say.

"Well, what about Rick? He could sit them down and have a yarn."

"Rick! They don't listen to *him*. And he doesn't really talk to them, either."

"Jeez, Ally, all three of them. Looks like you're trapped inside a bad-blood triangle."

• • •

And now the man with the gray Plasticine face arrives with even more bags of fabric than ever before. I overhear him tell Matilde that "those stupid sows at Bolton's are all on strike and bringing the business to its knees." It's up to Matilde and the other outworkers to fill the orders by the end of the week or Bolton's will shut down forever and that will be it. There'll be no work for Matilde—or anyone else—ever again.

The cooking stops and the machine starts up, and Patricia can't seem to believe it. "Your nana can do anything," she says, watching Matilde across the hall from the end of my bed once we're bunked down for the night, head to toe.

"Yeah, she's pretty *able*. I think she wants me to be *able* like her."

"That'd be all right. It's good to learn stuff from your nana. Wish I still had my nana to teach me stuff." Patricia rolls slowly onto her back and, with her hands behind her head, looks up at the ceiling. Her whispered words are touching on wounded, but I'm being pulled out by the undertow of sleep, and my tongue feels too big for my mouth and too floppy to respond. I'll console her about her no-more nana tomorrow.

After four nights of head-to-toe I can't stay awake a minute longer.

■■■

The moon is lighting up the turned-down summer quilt at the end of my bed where Patricia was lying before I went off to sleep. She's not there. Maybe she's gone to the bathroom. I wait for sixty-apple-pie, but she doesn't come back. I hope she wasn't missing her mum suddenly and made off to Glebe in the middle of the night.

Or perhaps she's gone over to Joy's house. Patricia still thinks Joy is a champ for taking a blow for her when her fake dad threw that kettle of boiling water. But I can see from my window that Joy's place is nothing but darkness.

I'll check the bathroom.

Matilde's machine is still going, only it's not sounding as urgent as it usually does in the dead of the night in the middle of a rush job.

Padding out of my bedroom, I can see from the hall clock that it's twenty past three. And there in the front room in the soft glow of the lamp, sitting at her Singer, is Matilde. Her glasses have slid down the sweat gleam on the bridge of her nose, her foot is pressing rhythmically to the floor and her metronome head is keeping time with the recording of Liszt's *Years of Pilgrimage* playing on her old gramophone. While anchored at her machine here at Number 23, Matilde is traveling through Geneva, Bologna and Rome.

And the mystery is solved.

Patricia is there too, in her shortie pajamas, working silently at the ironing table. She looks content to be *able*, and Matilde looks pea-sized pleased to have Patricia pressing and hanging her perfect pieces.

I watch on, half hiding behind the side of the doorframe. Matilde and Patricia look up briefly as though waiting for their next instruction, and without seeing me, they exchange a glance with each other before returning in time to their separate tasks within the same score. It's not a look past, or a look through, but a shared thing. I've never seen two people I love share a look like that before. I step forward out of the darkness of the corridor, but still they don't see me. They are watching someone else who has gathered the light.

He is tall and he is thin. Straight-nosed, strong-jawed, with a small pale face and a beautiful high shining forehead. His mop of thick hair moves with the music covering—then uncovering—his directive expressions.

I've seen him before. When I was throwing the dough.

It's Franz Liszt. And he's here in the front room.

His arms are carving through the air. His torso bends way back, then moves fully forward, as though he's fanning the flames of a fire. He is waving his baton, bringing Matilde's foot-pedal presses into unison with Patricia's bow strokes of the hot iron.

He is conducting a two-step between the body and soul of my grandmother and my best-ever friend.

They are in time and in tune.

That part of my heart that has always craved to join the dots between the people I love is pressing down lightly, drawing a line between Patricia and Matilde: a line that is following the fire-tipped baton of Franz Liszt. But then the invisible ink starts to sting because I wonder why Matilde has never allowed *me* to stay up in the dead of the night to help her at the ironing table.

Liszt suddenly turns sharply and looks straight at me.

I draw a deep breath; he might be about to bring me in. But his left index finger shoots out and directs me toward the door. I realize that these perfect pieces don't have *me* in them tonight.

I slip back to my room and climb into my empty bed.

CHAPTER FIFTEEN

PATRICIA IS HELPING ME FEED THE CHOOKS AND WATER THE veggies because Matilde is still crouched over her Singer and pedaling hard to finish the rush job before Monday. She's been wearing mostly the same clothes and the same look around her lips, jaw and brow for three solid days. I wonder if she'll ever stand up straight again.

The man with the gray Plasticine face comes by late every day to check on Matilde's progress. He tells her that if she wants to be paid anything at all, she'd better "speed it up, pick up the pace, and just get the friggin' job done." Patricia says he sounds like a train screeching on its tracks: "Metal on metal grinding . . . I hate that sound. We used to live next to the train station when we were living with Mum's boyfriend Ozzy in Muswellbrook, and I had to sleep with it going all through the night."

We're winding up the hose in the soaked garden when Joy chimes me in from her place next door.

"What's that noise?" asks Patricia.

"Oh, they're Joy's wind chimes—she must want me for something. Lately she's taken to blowing the chimes with her fireplace bellows whenever she wants me to come over to her at Number 25."

"That's a lovely sound," says Patricia. "I wouldn't mind sleeping to that."

Popping through the brown gate, we see Joy on the other side, waiting with the bellows in her hands and a rosy flush across her cheeks.

"There you are, my darlings! Are you having the most scrumptious time together?"

We agree that we are, and Joy invites us inside for sweeties and lemon myrtle tea.

I pick the best leaves off Joy's lemon myrtle tree, and while I'm heating the teapot, Joy says to Patricia: "I was at Wendy's today, pet, and your mother sent some things home with me to give to you. She thought you might need some fresh clothes and your shampoo."

Patricia seems to take that in her stride, but I am completely confused.

Why was Patricia's mother at Whisky Wendy's? And why would Patricia's clothes be at Whisky Wendy's house? I think about it on and off for the rest of the day.

Settling in for another night of head-to-toe, I ask Patricia: "When you said you were staying in Glebe, did you mean you were staying at Whisky Wendy's place?"

"Well, yeah, at Wendy's place. Where did you think we were staying?"

I hadn't really thought about it, I tell her.

"When we got off the train from Armidale, we didn't have anywhere else to stay, so we just headed to Wendy's and bunked down there."

"Is she your other nana?" I ask, puzzled. I didn't even know that Patricia knew Wendy.

"Nah, I don't have another nana," Patricia says, as though there are obvious things I simply don't get. "Wendy's just friends with my mum; she's friends with lots of people. Mum calls her a good stick. She lets women—and their kids—stay at her place, especially if they have to get away quick smart and have nowhere to go.

"Yeah, she's great, Wendy, and she's pretty gutsy too for someone who's old." Patricia is arranging the sheet on the bed so that we have the same amount at both ends.

"This all-frazzled-up woman arrived in the middle of the night, the first night we were there, and her two little kids. You should have seen them: they were both covered in chicken pox. They slept in the room with us, on a mattress on the floor. Both of them were itching and whimpering all through the night. Wendy was up putting aloe vera gel on their sores when their dad came banging on the door, *drunk as a skunk.*

"Through the blind, Wendy told him to bugger off. She had a cricket bat in her hand, and I tell you what, she looked ready to swing it. He was completely gutless, just yelled out some swear words and staggered off up the path."

I've never seen a drunk-as-a-skunk man before, or kids

covered in chicken pox, or a gutsy old lady telling someone
to bugger off. It keeps me awake for a while, but eventually
I drift off to sleep dreaming of Wendy caring for kids with
her cooled aloe vera gel and keeping watch at the window,
cricket bat at the ready.

···

"Hey, do you want to go to St. Brigid's now that it's empty?"
says Patricia with a burst of enthusiasm while packing away
the Monopoly board. "We can carve our initials high into a
branch of the mulberry tree."

Patricia's suggestions always seem clever and completely
compulsory. I hadn't thought about what the school might
be like all emptied out, without the jiggling energy of the
kids and the responding restraint of the teachers. I wouldn't
mind seeing that—with Patricia—now that we've both left
St. Brigid's and before she goes back to Armidale.

There are no cold cuts in the kitchen, so we collect some
eggs and I cook them with little soldiers of buttered toast,
and that impresses Patricia no end. We make enough noise
in the backyard with a hiding game to reassure Matilde,
who is busy at her machine, that we're occupied. Then after
two-hundred-apple-pie we sneak down the side path and
set off to make our mark on the mulberry tree.

Patricia scrambles up the trunk first. She grabs at
branches just beyond reach with one hand, then the other,
then the first again, until the sight of her is almost lost in

the white-green leaves of the mulberry tree. She's impossibly high. I think I'll just watch her from down here on the ground.

"Come on, Ally, join me up here at the top. It's a great view." Patricia's voice is encouraging. "Don't be scared—you're *able*, remember? You stood up on that surfboard and you rode those waves . . . you can climb a bloody tree."

But I am scared. Stuck-to-the-ground scared.

"Ally, I'm telling you, if you can ride a wave, you can climb a tree."

And so with Patricia calling me up, telling me I can do it, her confidence that doing one brave thing means that I can do another becomes my mantra.

If I can ride a wave, I can climb a tree, climb a tree, climb a tree

Ride a wave, climb a tree

Climb a tree

A little way into my climb the branches begin to cooperate, and after a few reaches they take shape to form a spiral staircase. They aren't so much taking me away from the ground now as bringing me up toward the sky.

If I can ride a wave, I can climb a tree, climb a tree, climb a tree

Patricia's legs are dangling above my head, looking loose and free.

Mine are trembling beneath me but somehow managing to find their footing.

If I can ride a wave, I can climb a tree, climb a tree, climb a tree

"Keep on coming, Ally, you're almost there."

My saliva is frothy and foamy and slightly metallic.

If I can ride a wave I can climb a tree, climb a tree, climb a tree

And I arrive. . . .

I'm here. . . .

I'm at the top of the mulberry tree with Patricia.

"You made it, Ally! I knew you could do it."

We sit straddling the same branch, and Patricia holds me by the tips of my elbow wings: two friends roosting.

We look down on the lunch benches below and the barely-there hopscotch chalk markings on the asphalt like astronauts with a new view of the world.

Patricia produces a key from her pocket, a key she tells me is from the old flat that she and her mum had to run away from when her fake dad went on that last bender. She starts carving our initials into the bark so that the mulberry tree will never forget us.

"Do you have a middle name, Ally?"

"Yep, I do. It's Belinda."

"Hey, that's a cool name . . . Belinda. Yeah, I like it— Belinda really suits you. Mine is Faith."

PFO + ABE is scratched into the tree, sealing memories of the friendship we forged at St. Brigid's and grafting us to one another forever.

Patricia leaves out L for Liberata, my Confirmation name, but I don't mention that. Since she missed the day altogether, she probably doesn't have a Confirmation name. Anyway, it looks better balanced with three letters each.

"It's cool up here," she says, breathing in.

"Yeah . . . it is . . . *cool*." I breathe out. And now, feeling steadier, I get an idea.

"Let's take some of these mulberry leaves back for Joy's silkworms," I say, snapping off twigs and sticking the woody ends into my waistband. "You'll really like Joy's silkworms—she breeds them to feed to Simone de Beauvoir." Patricia's immediately on board and starts snapping too.

■ ■ ■

Back at Number 23 I take a tray of tea and honey toast in to Matilde at her Singer. It keeps her energy up and her curiosity down about what we might be up to. Afterward Patricia and I slip over to Number 25 so I can show her the silkworms in Joy's glasshouse. It's early afternoon and stinking hot, so Joy is sure to be having a rest on her chaise longue under the fan in the front room.

Inside the glasshouse to the left of the door is a lineup of shoeboxes with holes in their lids; all are full of wriggling silkworms. The worms are about to become fatter and juicier after their feast of mulberry leaves. Simone de Beauvoir will be well fed, and Joy will be delighted.

"What are these?" Patricia asks, looking curiously at the neat rows of little glass bottles on the shelves above the bench.

"Oh, they're Joy's emotions," I tell her, realizing for the first time that that sounds a bit weird.

"Her emotions? What do you mean her *emotions*?"

"Well, Joy feels things, you know, down deep, she feels

150

things *in her bones* and *in her waters,* and so she does quite a bit of crying." Patricia is looking completely fascinated so I keep going. "She cries when she's sad, but also when she's really happy. Sometimes she cries when she sees something astonishing or just because she realizes something for the very first time. And when she cries, she catches the tears running down her cheek with these little glass bottles . . . see, like this." I take a fresh bottle from Joy's carved storage chest and press it against my cheek below the corner of my eye.

"Then she corks the bottle and labels it and keeps them all here in the glasshouse. She's done it forever. I help her go through them and dust them every now and again, and always on my birthday."

"Jeez, Ally, your nanas are really the chalk and the cheese."

"What's that mean?"

"Well, they're both really cool, I like them both—a lot—but they are deadset totally different. Joy's done enough bloody crying here in these little glass bottles to fill an entire ocean, but I can't imagine that Matilde would *ever* cry. Even if you cut off her leg, she wouldn't cry. She'd be too busy getting up and getting on with things."

Patricia is right. She says things out loud that I've known forever inside.

"And what's in that one down there?" Patricia asks, pointing at the cupboard beneath the sink where Joy prepares the lettuces for Simone.

"I don't know. We've never gone through that cupboard."

"It's a bit sticky." Patricia is pulling hard at the small handle. "It seems stuck closed," she says, getting out her key. Working at the door, Patricia leans in, using all her strength to lever it open with the key. I'm not so sure she should be trying to get into that cupboard, but suddenly the door flies open and hits the wall next to it with a bang.

"Look, there's a whole lot more glass bottles down here . . . behind these rags. I don't think she's been dusting these ones; they're filthy dirty."

Patricia starts bringing them out, one at a time, carefully placing them on the bench.

We count them out loud, thirty-two altogether. All the same size and all with similar labels. But they're grimy and smudged and difficult to read. I join Patricia in spitting at them, and we wipe away the dust with the bottoms of our shorts. Now we can see that they all say the same thing.

BLAMED FOR BELINDA

Patricia stops speaking.

I stop breathing.

That part of my heart that wishes you can un-see something so you can keep on not knowing makes me want to put all the bottles back—*quickly*—and shut the cupboard door and stick it stuck forever.

"Was your mum called Belinda?" whispers Patricia. "Ally?" She brings her forehead gently against mine. "You can tell me. Was that her name?"

"I think so," I squeeze out with held-in old air.

CHAPTER SIXTEEN

PATRICIA HAS GONE BACK TO ARMIDALE, RICK HAS GONE surfing up the coast, and with Christmas behind us I have little to do but wait out the long January days before I start at my new school. Everything is nudging on different, and that part of my heart that pumps out *me* is feeling slightly offbeat. At some point, hard to pin down precisely, between the October long weekend last year and New Year's Day just gone, even the tilt of our street seems to have changed.

The neighborhood kids have moved from playing table tennis in the Lucky Listers' rumpus room and Marco Polo in their pool to hanging out as a gang in their garage, sometimes with the door open but mostly with it closed and the sound of Deep Purple vibrating its wooden panels and hot silver handle. There's plenty of space in the garage now because Mr. Lister's station wagon is never parked there anymore. The Lucky Listers' front lawn has grown prickly weeds, and their pool has gone a murky green-brown color.

On the occasions I used to make it into the Listers' rumpus room on Fridays after school, I never felt altogether comfortable there. But, if I flattened out into the thin space between an outline and a shadow, no one asked me to leave. And it felt better being there and watching than just wishing I were there and wondering. Now I'm pretty sure that Lucinda, her older brother Mark and the teenagers they hang around with wouldn't want me with them in the garage in any shape or form. But today as I'm walking home from Dave's Mixed Business and Milk Bar with table salt and vinegar for Matilde's pickling, the garage door is open, and Lucinda waves at me and invites me in. Even though the two-year age gap separating us has remained the same, the gulf between us has opened up to become a mile wide.

The garage door goes down behind me, and Lucinda studies me closely and lights up a cigarette. She has a holiday job at Miss Fashion so she has money, and with that money—she tells me—she buys Alpine Lights. With the Alpine Lights she does the drawback, the dragon and double smoke rings while pimply Geoff Alderman, who lives a few streets away, announces each one as though it were a gymnastic display. After the smoke rings she chews gum—with big, slow rhythmic movements—freshening her breath and keeping all the boys in the garage focused on her mouth. Lucinda, it seems, knows the power of her pout and the clout of her curves.

"So, Ally, I hear you got into Sydney Girls High," she exhales.

I tell her I did.

"Yeah, well . . . good for you . . . I didn't know you were brainy!" Lucinda is looking at her chipped painted finger-nails between drags. "You know that's where I go."

I tell her I do, that I've seen her in the uniform and ac-tually I didn't know she was brainy either. That seems to prickle the gang but not to bother Lucinda.

"So I'll be there too, but I won't be able to talk to you at school, or look at you, because, you know, I'll be a third former and you'll be a First-Form Dropkick. You should just act like I'm invisible to you. But if there's anything you need to know before you start, if the garage door's up, you can come in. I'll sort you out." Lucinda is blowing smoke from her nose to the side of my left ear.

I say, "Yeah, that's all right, I get it, I won't go anywhere near you at school, or look at you either. And by the way, thanks." Lucinda gestures to Geoff, who pushes up the ga-rage door.

I back out, trying to look like I don't need sorting out even though I'm not wearing a tube top, puka shells or a pair of velvet slaps on my feet like all the other girls smok-ing with Lucinda in the garage. Clutching the bag with the table salt and vinegar, I head home to Number 23, hoping that Matilde doesn't get a whiff of the Alpine Lights. If she ever thought I'd been smoking, she'd most certainly set me on fire.

Coming up our path, I realize I should have asked Lucinda if she had any old uniforms that she'd outgrown. When the list arrived last week with everything I needed for high school, Matilde shook her head and ticked her tongue, horrified at the cost of the two school tunics, blouses, blazer and the sports uniform and bloomers. She said she refused to pay such *ridiculous prices* and that instead she'll be running up all of mine on her machine.

I'll be starting high school invisible to Lucinda, badly needing sorting out and looking completely homemade.

■ ■ ■

The twenty-eighth of January 1975 is finally here, and I'm ready for my first-ever day at Sydney Girls High School.

Sort of.

Joy has spent the past week filling an orange glass bottle labeled ADJUSTING TO CHANGE that she's given to me in a small velvet box. And there's another aqua-blue one—LAUNCHING LIBERATA—that she's placed on the shelf with the rest of her emotions.

Outwardly I'm all set to go—early, thanks to Matilde's planning and packing, sewing and scheduling.

Inwardly I'm not so sure. What if I get lost at the big high school campus or behave like a First-Form Dropkick—without even realizing? What if I don't have anyone to sit with in class or make any friends? Suddenly I'm wishing I was going back to St. Brigid's: the Popular Group was mean and annoying, but at least I knew what to expect every day.

During the holidays Matilde showed me the way to the bus stop. The bus takes the girls directly to their gate and the boys to theirs. So at least I'm feeling okay about that first part of the trip. But now, as I head out the door, Matilde is closing it behind us and insisting on coming too: "Just to make sure you aren't confused about where to get on, Allegra."

I wasn't confused in the slightest, but I'm certainly embarrassed now, especially because Lucinda Lister is walking only slightly ahead. Luckily we had that conversation in her garage about the importance of being invisible.

The bus pulls up with piles of kids hanging out all the windows, hollering, wolf-whistling and waving to their waiting friends. One boy squirts a water pistol out the back door at a bunch of ducking girls, who giggle as they get on.

"Bye, Matilde," I say hurriedly. No one else has a grandmother around.

Boarding the bus, I quickly work out that the younger kids are all up front and the older ones have claimed the back half of the seats. I'm looking for a spot that's free and appropriate when my heart suddenly snap-freezes. I hear Matilde behind me: "Keep moving, Allegra; there are empty seats for us farther down."

I'm not imagining it. Matilde has actually got onto the bus. *The high school bus.* There are forty cool kids, my grandmother, her brown handbag and me . . . the biggest First-Form Dropkick in the entire history of Sydney Girls High before I've even walked through the school gates.

A girl about my age is sitting alone with a black case that

is taking up the seat next to the window. Matilde gestures and the girl slides across, lifting the case onto her lap to make room for the old lady I'm pretending I don't know.

"Here, Allegra. Opposite, here is an empty seat. Sit down safely before the bus moves off." Unfortunately it must be clear to everyone that the old lady certainly knows me.

"This is Allegra, my granddaughter. It is her first day at the selective school."

Then, leaning over, she confides to the girl, as though she were another grandmother, "She has the nervous stomach."

The girl looks across at me and says to us both, "I'm Annabel . . . *Renshaw*. It's my first day too. My stomach is fine."

"And what instrument do you have there in that case?" asks Matilde, pea-sized impressed.

"Oh, this one is a viola. But I also play the flute."

"The viola *and* the flute. This is good. I will change seats with Allegra so you can sit next to her. She plays the piano . . . *very well*."

Annabel Renshaw seems relaxed about that. I'm not relaxed. I move but cannot speak. Apart from the nervous stomach, I now have the threaded throat, the shamed shins and the blushing brain.

A few stops along, Matilde announces: "I must leave you now, Allegra. Have a productive day with your studies. Goodbye, Annabel." She gets off the bus and walks back in the direction of home.

"I thought your grandmother must be a teacher at the school when she first got on the bus," says Annabel.

"Nah, she just thinks she's my secret bodyguard," I manage to say.

To my relief Annabel laughs, out loud, in a sharing-a-joke way, not a mean way. Then she starts chatting so steadily that my stomach settles slightly and my humiliation is soothed.

■ ■ ■

High school is better than I expected, and by the end of the second week, I get word from Patricia.

> Dear Ally,
>
> How are you???? I'm in the library and meant to be working on my essay for english about Charlotte's Web which is a stupid kid's book about a pig that talks to a spider and the spider is trying to save the pig and writes stupid mesages in her web. I'm in the lowest english class so the books i have to read are litel kids books and I don't even feel like I'm in high school. You probbly read this bloody book when you were about 6. Any way I'm not working on the essay, becuase im writing to you and becuase a pig talking to a spider is dumb and I don't know why when they think you are stupid they make you feel more stupid by making you read these stupid books.
>
> Apart from all that my high school is pretty good and the best part is I get to do dress making with Mrs. Oaks on wensday afternoons for my electave. We are making a poncho and when we're finished we'll make a circuler skirt. They have this room with a whole row of sowing

machines and we get to use them and can work on them at lunch time if we want to finish something off.

Even though I'm still hopeles at reading and spelling I got into the second top class in maths and Miss Sutherwaites told me after I got 82 percent in our last test, that another mark like that and I might find myself in the top class. Pretty good hey????

Mums got a job at the gas station so I walk there after school and do my maths homework until she nocks off. Dez who owns the place said that when I turn 14 I can get a job there too, I think he likes mum. Actualy I know he likes Mum. So before then I've been babysitting for our neighber when she gets a mygrain which is not that much but I get 50 cents an hour witch I put in the hippy van tin. The kids are a real handful but I do drawing with them and tell them stories and let them ride on my back and that settles them down a bit.

How do you like your high school???? I bet you're in all the top classes.

Have you made friends yet with anybody????

There is a cool chick here named Deb. She's funny and she has her own horse that she keeps at her cousen's farm. She said I could come out with her one day and she'll teach me how to ride that horse, some of the other kids in my class are ok too.

Guess what??????? Mum says that we are going to come to Sydney again maybe at Easter so then me and you could get to see each other. Maybee you could sleep over at Wendys with me this time???? So Ally do

something that makes your Nana proud so she
says yes!!!
　　Theirs the bell so I have to go to PE.
　See ya!
　　　　　　From your best friend,
　　　　　　Patricia

I miss Patricia badly. The girls at my new school wouldn't be interested in sewing or babysitting or working in a gas station. Annabel Renshaw writes short stories in her spare time, mostly science fiction with female protagonists who save the planet. I've read over some of them and they do seem pretty good. She plays her viola in a mixed-youth orchestra group and wants to be a barrister, whatever that is. She tells me that her father is a barrister—*one of the best at the bar*—and that her mother—*like any spirited woman*—is a women's libber.

"There's more to life than waiting on your husband," says Annabel toward the end of geography. "Mum and her friends are big fans of Germaine Greer. I found a copy of her book stuffed under the lounge cushion after one of their coffee mornings."

And with one thick eyebrow raised, as though she's about to classify me, Annabel asks: "So, Legs, are *you* a women's libber?"

Thankfully, the bell rings.

Joy doesn't wait on her husband—probably because she doesn't have one. And even if she did, it's more likely that he'd be waiting on her. I think she could be *a spirited woman,* so this afternoon while making the mint tea at Number 25 I decide to ask Joy if she's a women's libber. I'm hoping there might be a hint of what a women's libber is, exactly, wrapped up in her answer.

"Well, yes . . . *yes* . . . I'm proud to say that I am, Ally." Joy's voice drops half an octave like she's taking an oath. "It surprises even me, but as it turns out, I am . . . *I am a women's libber.*" She reaches across the corner of the kitchen table and pours the mint tea between our two pottery mugs. Joy doesn't usually pour the tea.

"What actually makes someone a women's libber?" I ask, sipping my tea.

Joy settles in, the way she does when she's about to go through her emotions: "Life has a way of shaping you, darling," she says. "You're born into certain circumstances, which you just accept—blindly at first—and often for quite some time, but then things happen that prompt you to start to think and, *God forbid*, start to question.

"And when you're finally given the chance to connect the dots with the experiences of other women, you realize that you're not the only one thinking these thoughts or questioning the world in this way."

Maybe Joy thinks she's answering my question, but I'm still pretty hazy about what being a women's libber actually involves.

"When I was growing up, I simply accepted that men were in charge: in charge of society and *in charge of me.* My father was a decent enough man, quite loving really, but he was very much the head of the house and he told us what to do, where to go and what to be . . . well, actually . . . more precisely . . . *what not to be.* My poor dutiful mother just accepted it as the way of the world, and my dear sister Joan was very pretty, but not what you'd call exactly bright." Joy gives me a small wink.

"*But I* . . . I always wanted more, and I secretly dreamed that marriage would be a delicious escape from the rule of my father. When in fact"—she cools her tea with a steady blow through Just Plum–colored lips—"I only exchanged one form of control for another, with the new twist of also being told what to think!"

"What happened to your husband, Joy?" I ask, unleashing my wondering about Rick's dad, *my grandfather.*

"Well . . . Frank started out as a good solid fellow, pet, but he was never *my* choice for a husband. My father was so taken with his job and his family that he encouraged—well, more accurately, *insisted on*—our engagement being announced before Frank left for the war. But unfortunately he came back a broken man before it ended. . . ." Joy looks slightly sad, but surprisingly, no tears are flowing.

So I venture to ask, "Did he ever hurt you, Joy?"

"Not physically, thank God, but when a man is a wreck he's bound to sabotage the lives of those around him. He was incapable of love, simply incapable: giving or receiving it. And he constantly made me feel the fool, which I put up with for a long while in exchange for the bills being paid. But as time went on, he became impossible to please: unbearable, controlling and completely unlikeable. The cancer didn't help things, of course, but really, he was as good as finished before it took hold." Joy adjusts her long wooden beads.

"I don't *dislike* men generally, darling. . . . *Oh no,* I wouldn't say that at all. I've rather liked a number of them over the years." She takes a long sip and appears to be remembering the ones she has liked *over the years* and all the reasons she liked them.

"Men can be tremendous fun, and some are generous and kind and use their strength in positive ways. Some actually respect women's minds," she says, pushing up the gray curls on the left side of her neck with a cupped hand.

"But I've come to realize, especially in this last year, that many of them are not that way. And even if they never lay a hand on the women in their lives, they all seem to want to lay down the law . . . they want to control women, and quite frankly, I'm *jack* of that, pet, and I'm not the only one."

Joy pulls a book from the drawer at the end of the table. It has a woman's torso on the cover, hanging from a bar, all hollowed out without any arms or legs.

"I was invited to join Liberty Club by my old school chum Helen Hayes. She gathered us together as a consciousness-raising group after her divorce when she went back to university to finish her arts degree. She'd read *The Female Eunuch* in Women and Philosophy, and she urged us all to do the same. You can read it too, pet—when you're a bit older," Joy says, patting the book. "I thought at first that the group would be a good way to broaden my horizons: you know, new friendships, interesting conversations, a night out, really. I certainly wasn't thinking about empowerment, darling." I want to ask Joy what *empowerment* is exactly, but she's on a roll, barely stopping to take a breath.

"And when we got down to it and I started to hear the other women's stories, I realized that I too had been oppressed . . . *all my life.*"

"What does *oppressed* mean?" I manage to slip in.

"Well, for me it meant not being able to make my own decisions or direct my own life in any way at all: I was always under the control of a man. I was made to feel inadequate, hopeless and dependent. But after talking to other women it became clear that I wasn't bad *or mad* for feeling resentful about this. A lot of them were feeling the same.

"Then Wendy joined Liberty Club, and she brought with her a new and urgent perspective. She's witnessed so many women—young and old and at every point in between—not just oppressed but living with constant violence, victims of crushing brutality. The scales were lifted from my eyes, darling. I had what you could call an awakening. I realized that through the Sisterhood we had to change the agenda.

"The brave Suffragettes won women the vote early this century, and some property rights too, but that's not enough. We need to do more. Women's isolated problems and individual miseries are rarely isolated, or individual. So, darling"—Joy leans forward and places her hand on mine—"the most important thing to understand about women's liberation is . . . *the personal is political.*"

If that's the most important thing to understand, I'd better let my grandmother know: "I don't really understand that bit at all, Joy."

She pauses, then goes on to explain, "Women have always blamed themselves for their unhappy circumstances, pet, when in fact their diminished lives are not the outcome of their individual choices but are part of systematic oppression: men are holding all the power in society, *and holding it over women*. We need to challenge this. And we need to press on and campaign for other rights, too: equal opportunity, equal pay and childcare to make it all possible." Joy's voice is marching now. "We need to overturn this age-old notion of women being inferior to men. Put an end to this servitude. It's only through true equality that women will ever be in control of their lives and free of violence."

I'm thinking of the Liberty Club meetings I overhear on warm nights through my open window, when bubbles of energy and feathers of conversation float into my room. I'm picturing the ladies with their notepads and pens, cigarettes and flagons of wine, their music and linked arms and sometimes their dancing. I'm remembering the little girl in the dirty yellow pajamas in Joy's garden kicking me hard in the back of my heel and telling me about her father hitting her mother on the bathroom floor, and Joy's crisping burnt face after she copped a blow from Patricia's fake dad who went mad with boiling water after another bender.

That part of my heart that stores jigsaw pieces in not-sure-where-they-go categories is placing them down now, one piece after another after another. A picture is starting to take shape.

There's no more tea in the pot and Joy gets up, I think at first to reboil the kettle, but she goes to her medicine cabinet in the cupboard above the fridge and gets out a little glass bottle.

"I'm interested in change mostly because of *you*, Ally. Yes, my little Liberata, you! I want you to be able to decide your own course and steer your own ship and be in control of your own life. I want you to live in a world where you are empowered to be the very essence of yourself and to live that essence and feel free to express that essence. I want you to have opportunities and to work in fields that excite you and to have your own purse, to achieve financial freedom. To love and be loved, but mostly to be valued as a whole person full of potential." Joy is catching the large tears falling from her left eye as they roll to the high point of her cheekbone. I don't fully understand why, but my eyes are starting to water too. That seems to encourage Joy's tears further. She brings her arm around my back to my face, holds her glass bottle against my cheek and catches a few fresh drops of tears from me.

So it seems that Joy is definitely a spirited woman *and* a women's libber and that I might have something to do with it.

Matilde is calling out for me from Number 23. It's almost six o'clock and time to go in for dinner: it's paprikas krumpli tonight. I leave Joy busy dating and labeling the new colored-glass bottle containing her old and my young tears: SEALING SISTERHOOD.

CHAPTER SEVENTEEN

Matilde has made a gift on her Singer for Sister Josepha. I think it's to thank her for teaching me the stuff for that exam that got me into Sydney Girls High. She passes me the gift, wrapped in brown paper, with instructions to drop it off at the convent tomorrow on my way home from school.

"If you are invited to go in, do not stay long, Allegra," she says. "You do not want to impose." She hasn't told me what the gift is, and I haven't asked. What could you possibly give to a nun?

"Oh, Allegra, what a lovely surprise," says Sister Josepha when she opens the convent front door. "Come in, come in. Tell me all about how things are going at your new school."

Back again in the convent with Sister on the tapestry couch, eating Shortbread Creams, everything looks pretty much the same as last time, only there's a new picture of

Jesus on top of the television set. But in this one he's not pointing at his red heart or carrying a cross or holding out his bloody nailed hands. He looks kind of cool, like someone you could bump into at Bondi Beach.

"Are you enjoying the challenge of Sydney Girls High, Allegra?" asks Sister.

"Yes I am, thank you, Sister," I say, thinking that the Jesus on top of the telly could be a surfie.

"And what would you say is your favorite subject?" she asks.

"I kind of like them all," I respond, thinking that maybe the new Jesus could be a pop star, or even a Riffraff. "Science is good. English is probably my best one."

"Any thoughts on what you'd like to do when you leave school?" she says, catching my eye looking at Jesus.

"Matilde really wants me to be a doctor . . . but I'm not so sure I could do that."

"Allegra, I'm sure you *could* do that," says Sister. "Or anything else you put your mind to. You have been blessed with a wonderful intellect. What's important, dear, is that you choose for yourself what you want to do."

"But I need to choose something that will make Matilde proud, and something that pleases Joy. Matilde wants me to be a success; you know, so I can earn good money. I think she wants me to have a job that people respect."

"It's a funny thing, Allegra," says Sister, offering me another Shortbread Cream. "People think respect comes from success, fame or fortune, when in fact the most admired quality at the end of the day is kindness. Because

169

kindness, dear—*kindness*—is the best indicator of a person's well-being. Yes indeed, kind people are those who truly take pleasure in their time on earth."

There's a small noise behind me, and Sister looks over and says, "Now, here's someone you'll remember." I turn to see Mary-Anne Wilson and her cereal-spattered tunic standing awkwardly at the lounge-room door. How weird . . . has Mary-Anne become a nun? At twelve!

"Hi, Mary-Anne."

"Hi, Allegra," she says, walking past to sit down. I get a whiff that tells me she's still eating Perkins paste.

"Telephone for you, Eileen," says Sister Claire, popping her head into the room. Sister Josepha—who must have an alias—gets up from between her two former students on the couch and disappears to take the call.

There is now a nun-sized hole of silence between Mary-Anne and me. Not sure how else to fill it, I say: "Did you come to bring Sister Josepha a present too?"

"No," she says, pushing her glasses back up her nose and looking slightly puzzled. "My family is staying here for a while. Well, my mum and my sister and me. Dad's still at home—he doesn't know we're here. He's gone a bit cracked."

"Really? You're staying? What's it like *sleeping* here . . . in a convent?" I ask.

"It's all right. The nuns are pretty nice . . . they let mothers sleep over with their kids sometimes. I've learned how to play Chinese checkers."

"Oh," I say. "Well, that's fun."

Even though I did end up letting Mary-Anne be my

partner in art last year, I still feel kind of bad about telling her earlier that she was pathetic at gluing matchsticks straight. I want to escape her sad face, but I hear my *good self* saying instead, "Do you want a quick game?"

Mary-Anne has the board set up in a jiffy, and she chats almost happily about her new high school, where she's definitely made one, and *possibly* even two, friends. Sister Josepha comes to the door, smiles a little and slips out again.

Mary-Anne's eyes focus hard through her smudged glasses as she moves each of her marbles. Whenever it's my turn, her tone changes slightly as she tells me about her mum with a migraine who hasn't got out of bed since they came to the convent, and her older sister, Jennifer, who refuses to eat anything but grapefruit and celery. Apparently Jennifer's hair is falling out. Mary-Anne would like to go home but she's not sure that she can look after her mum and her sister all by herself *again*—even if the nuns kept up with dropping off meals.

I can see a winning path across the board but decide to ignore it and let Mary-Anne win.

"Do you want to play best of three?" she asks.

"Nah, better not. My grandmother told me not to impose."

● ● ●

I get home to find Matilde winding up the hose after her sunset watering. Everything is thriving in the vegetable garden and she looks slightly calmer than usual. I think of her work at the Singer and all the things she told me it pays for: the mortgage for our home, the electricity we use, the food we eat, my piano lessons and swim-squad training and the university education she wants me to have. Does working and paying those bills mean that Matilde has achieved financial freedom? Maybe Matilde is also a spirited woman, just in a different way from Joy.

So I decide to give it a shot before bed. After hovering for a while at the door of the front room, I slide in and ask Matilde outright if she's a women's libber.

"Such a question, Allegra! What business would I have with being a women's libber?" she snaps, looking up from a pile of paperwork. "I am too busy making ends meet, looking after this house and caring for you to have the time to even think about anything else. That 'libber' nonsense is for the women who do nothing but take up time and space with their empty round-and-round talk. Don't be bringing those ideas into this house. You need to get through life simply by getting on and doing!"

I hope Annabel Renshaw and her classifying eyebrow don't ask me again.

I really don't know what I am, exactly.

■ ■ ■

Ever since I arrived at high school more than six months ago I've made myself invisible to Lucinda Lister. Passing her on the gym stairs I've looked away, lining up at the canteen I've looked overhead and queuing to take a book out from the library I've quickly looked down, flipping through the pages. I've made no eye contact with her at all, and she's managed to look straight through me every time we've come close to one another. Each afternoon—when she's sitting on the bumpy back row of the bus, arms and legs entangled around her boyfriend, who goes to the school opposite— every other first former has sneaked a gawk, but I've acted as though Lucinda and her antics are completely invisible to me. Only now she really is invisible. She hasn't been on the bus, entangled or otherwise, or walked home from the stop closest to our street for almost three weeks. And there's been no hint of Deep Purple being played in, or smoke rings coming out from, the Lucky Listers' garage.

"Hey, Legs, have you heard about Lucinda Lister?" Annabel Renshaw says in a low voice while packing away her history workbook before we walk to phys ed.

"No . . . what about her?"

"She's preggers! Katrina Jenkins told me. The whole of ninth grade knows."

Preggers . . . Lucinda preggers . . . I wonder if the Lucky Listers' Fruit Tingles mother knows about that. I only know *preggers* means having a baby because Patricia told me in one of our letters that lots of the girls at her school up in Armidale drop out because they get preggers and have to stay at home and look after their babies. I can't imagine Lucinda Lister looking after a baby in that smoky garage.

Perhaps Matilde knows about Lucinda being preggers and thinks it's contagious, because after school, while serving up warm doughnuts for my afternoon tea, she says with a disapproving look, "I do not want you to go anywhere near that Lister girl's house, and you are to keep well away from their garage."

"Why, Matilde?" I ask, checking her knowledge and testing her reaction.

"It is for your own good that I tell you to keep away from that girl, and that is all you need to know. Now, eat your doughnut, Allegra, so you can go and make a start on your piano practice."

...

I finished *To Kill a Mockingbird*, our English novel, in just over two nights and three days. I wish I could start it all over again, not knowing the ending, and be carried along with Scout, Jem and Dill and the happenings in Maycomb, Alabama.

The only other person who's finished it too is Annabel Renshaw, and she's fallen completely for Scout and Jem's father, Atticus Finch. She tells me proudly that Atticus reminds her of her own father, especially when he talks about equality and justice. I can't tell her that Atticus reminds me of my father too, because Annabel's seen Rick driving his van and knows he's a carpenter, not a lawyer wearing a suit and fighting for a black man to get a fair hearing. But somehow when I read the last line of the book, "He would be there all night, and he would be there when Jem waked up in the morning," it's Rick's face that I picture in the lamplight next to Jem's bed.

Mr. Dewhurst, the cool teacher who wears long sideburns and purple velvet trousers, tells us to pair up so we can prepare a class presentation. We have to choose our favorite Atticus quote and tie it to a theme in the novel. "Do you want to work on it at my place tomorrow?" asks Annabel, presuming that we will be partners. "You can come home with me after school. . . . I'll ask Mum if you can stay for dinner if you like." I'm happy with her presumption, and luckily when I check with Matilde, she's fine with me going to the Renshaws' place—and even staying for dinner. I think it's mostly because of Annabel's viola and flute, and it certainly doesn't hurt that Matilde knows Annabel is with me in advanced English.

Annabel's house is pretty much a mansion; two stories of solid sandstone and wrought iron overlooking the harbor, with a paved path winding through formal gardens before it arrives at a double front door. "Mum won't be home from uni yet; it's her late day," Annabel explains, taking a key from under a brass umbrella stand. "She's gone back to study sociology. Dad jokes with his friends that he's 'bedding an undergraduate.'" Whatever that means.

I follow Annabel into a large timber kitchen where she grabs a packet of Tim Tams from a walk-in pantry and a bottle of Orchy orange juice from a side-by-side fridge. We set ourselves up at a long dining table in a very posh room at the end of the hall.

There's no mucking about with Annabel; she gets down to work straightaway. "So . . . I think my favorite quote is right here—see, this one, Legs. I've underlined it in pencil," she says, taking small nibbles around the edges of a Tim Tam while I read it out loud: "Our courts have their faults, as does any human institution, but in this country our courts are the great levelers, and in our courts all men are created equal."

"I read it to Dad when he got home last night, and he likes it too, very much. It's why I want to be a lawyer."

"Yeah, that is a good quote," I say. "But I actually underlined another one. It's here, close to the end, after Scout tells Atticus about Boo Radley. She says, 'Atticus, he was real nice . . . ,' and Atticus replies, 'Most people are, Scout, when you finally see them.'" Annabel is nibbling and nodding pretty politely, but I don't think she's really that taken with my choice of quote.

"Well, good afternoon, girls! It's looking all very industrious in here." It's Annabel's mother in embroidered denim flares with matching vest, holding a three-ring binder and a takeaway chook. "And this must be Legs, or do you prefer to be called *Allegra*?" she says with a pretty-mum smile. I tell her that Annabel is really the only one who calls me *Legs* but that's okay, I don't mind if she does too.

"Well, I'm going to call you Allegra . . . it's such a strong and lively name," she says, leaning over for a Tim Tam. "And don't worry about this stuffy old Mrs. Renshaw business; you can call me Jen. How's the assignment going?"

"Good, thanks, Mum," says Annabel. "We just have to agree on an Atticus quote."

"I'll leave you to it, then; I've got to finish my philosophy essay that's due tomorrow. Now, don't fill up on biscuits and spoil your dinner. We're having chicken."

Jen disappears and doesn't surface again until Mr. Renshaw's Jaguar pulls up in the garage with a deep thrum.

Annabel's mother is quite altered now, and stationed in the kitchen . . . more Mrs. Warwick Renshaw than jeans-wearing Jen. The embroidered denim flares and vest have been replaced by a Liberty-print floral dress nipped in at the waist. She has coral-colored lippy on, and her long hair is now tied back in a clip. She looks like a completely different person.

"Something smells good," announces Mr. Renshaw, walking into the kitchen with a briefcase under his arm and a kiss on the forehead for his wife. The empty oven is turned on high, and heating up, it sends out the smell of what must have been other nights' dinners. Jen looks over from the pop-up tidy and gives me a half grin. While Mr. Renshaw is changing upstairs, Annabel and I set the table in the eating nook and Mrs. Renshaw plates up the takeaway chook, which has been nowhere near the oven. She tips shop-bought coleslaw and potato salad onto large heirloom platters. They seem way too special for the meal. She zaps some frozen peas in a microwave oven; I've never seen one before. "Such a time-saver," she tells me. "Warwick bought it for my birthday a few weeks ago. It was the first one available at David Jones, and I did a whole beef silverside dinner in it the first night we got it, white sauce and all."

We sit down and discuss the two quotes over dinner with

Annabel's father and *both* of her mothers in a strange double act that seems lost on everyone but me. Mr. Renshaw unreservedly agrees with Annabel and favors the quote about the courts and all men being created equal.

"Interesting that it's all *men* created equal," says Jen, picking up her husband's napkin that he dropped without noticing. "I think I like Allegra's preferred quote about seeing people for what they are." Mr. Renshaw doesn't seem to see or hear Jen, but asks his wife, "Is there any mayonnaise to go with this chicken? It's a tad dry." Mrs. Renshaw hops up from her meal and gets a jar of mayonnaise out of the fridge. She puts a few blobs into a little crystal dish and places it in front of her husband with a smile . . . or was it a smirk?

Mr. Renshaw continues talking about the quote and tells Annabel to get a pen and paper so she can take down some notes.

"It might be better, Warwick, if the girls think it through for themselves," says Jen.

"Oh, yes, of course, don't fuss, dear," he replies. "I'm just steering them in the right direction. Now, what's for pudding?"

Mrs. Renshaw opens a tin of peaches and serves them up at the kitchen island bench with heavy-handed scoops of Blue Ribbon ice cream while Mr. Renshaw, pouring himself another red wine, takes us through some further thoughts about law, courts and justice. A bit further along he shares that he hasn't actually read *To Kill a Mockingbird:* "Too many judgments to get through to bother with fiction."

"I've read it," says Jen, putting a bowl of peaches and ice cream in front of her husband, who looks like he could do with a few laps around the park in his sandshoes instead of a large serving of *pudding*. "I thought Calpurnia was a fabulous character."

"These peaches would do nicely with a splash of my brandy," says Mr. Renshaw, with which Mrs. Renshaw, who has only just sat down, gets up again and fetches the brandy from the next room.

The kitchen door opens and there's Annabel's brother, Barnaby, carrying his muddy rugby boots and looking red-faced and quite spotty.

"Here he is," says Mr. Renshaw, projecting as though he's announcing the arrival of someone important. "You must be ravenous, Barnes. Your mother has made chicken. How was rugby training?"

"Good, thanks, Dad—actually pretty exhausting." I've never seen Barnaby before. He's a boy version of Annabel, only a couple of years older with a slightly off-center nose. He kisses his mother—twice—first on the forehead and then again on her cheek when she stands up and gives him her place in the nook. He looks over at me sitting next to his sister, waiting for an introduction.

"Oh and Barnes, this is Annabel's friend from school . . . *Leggo*," says Mr. Renshaw, polishing off the last of his *pudding*, a smear of ice cream on his chin.

"Dad, it's *Legs*," corrects Annabel, slightly embarrassed.

"Actually, her real name is Allegra," says Jen, lighting up a cigarette by the sink.

I feel myself blushing and tell them that either *Allegra* or *Legs* is fine.

"Good then," says Mr. Renshaw, refreshing his glass. "What say, Barnes, while the girls hop in and do the kitchen, you grab your plate and join me in the cedar room? *Four Corners* is starting in just over five minutes."

"Sure, Dad, see you in there," says Barnaby, his mother passing him a plate covered in foil.

"Are we going to watch *Four Corners* with your dad?" I ask Annabel while carefully wiping up a silver-edged platter.

"No. I usually just help Mum clean up after dinner— she's got a heavy load with Gender Studies this semester."

Soon after the washup Rick arrives to take me home. He looks out of place in his flip-flops at the double front door.

"So how was that?" he asks as I climb into the van.

"Yeah, good," I tell him. "But I'm still kind of hungry. I don't think their mum knows how to cook, and she seems a bit all over the show, like she hasn't worked out what sort of woman she is. Actually, Rick, it was like Annabel has two mothers."

CHAPTER EIGHTEEN

STEPPING OFF THE BUS AND WALKING DOWN OUR STREET, I'M looking forward to the school holiday break when suddenly my focus is tugged between two big surprises waiting for me outside Number 23.

The first, and by far the best surprise, is Patricia Faith O'Brien sitting on our fence, holding a small bunch of gardenias and a big bag of Twisties. She looks planet-sized pleased as I skip over and give her a noogie, rubbing my knuckles across the top of her head. But Patricia is every bit as confused as I am about the second, not-so-good surprise: three angry women are standing on the footpath, calling out Matilde's name as though she's done something wrong.

"What's going on?" asks Patricia, swinging her arm around my waist.

"I don't know. They weren't there this morning," I say, taking a Twistie from the opened packet and leading her to the front porch.

Matilde is waiting on the other side of the door. She opens it quickly, ushers us in and deadlocks it closed behind us. She looks switched-on *bátor* but is actually so distracted that she doesn't realize there are two of us walking down the corridor behind her.

"Who are those women outside, Matilde?" I ask. "And why are they calling out your name like that?"

"Never mind about them—they are not important," she says dismissively, walking to the kitchen where she lifts the tea towel uncovering a rack of ladyfinger biscuits, still warm. She only acknowledges Patricia after she accepts the bunch of gardenias and starts arranging them in a vase, when she says: "So you are visiting us again, Patricia. You are in luck; my cabbages are flourishing."

A loud bang on the front door makes the three of us jump.

"Wait here," says Matilde. "I'm expecting a Bolton's delivery."

The man with the gray Plasticine face bursts in and drags four massive bags of fabric into the front room. He looks hurried and hot and way angrier than usual. When he makes his way back toward the front door, I can see that he has egg yolk dripping down the sleeve of his brown shirt.

"Now get cracking," he barks at Matilde. "And don't cave in to that lot out there if you know what's good for you." I really hate the way this man speaks to my grandmother.

"Wait! Before you go . . ." Matilde's voice stops him in the corridor. "I still haven't been paid for my last job."

He swings around as though my grandmother has stolen his wallet. His Plasticine nostrils are flaring, and his brow is molding into an even angrier shape. "You'll be paid when the boss decides your work is worth paying for and not one minute before!"

"There is nothing wrong with my work," says Matilde, her switched-on *bátor* rising up from a deep place now, reinforced and convincing. "It was done on time and the quality is good. You know that and your boss knows that."

"*My* boss is *your* boss, so don't you forget *that*. There are many hungry outworkers far better than you who'd be happy for this work from Bolton's." He slams the front door behind him. And for a few minutes the women out front stop calling Matilde's name and yell bad things at him instead.

I'm boiling the kettle, hoping that Matilde will sit with us at the table and have at least one of her ladyfinger biscuits before Patricia polishes them all off, but instead she runs her hands up the back of her head and says, "I need to make a start on these pieces immediately." She looks exhausted before she's begun. "There is bean soup and cheese noodles prepared in the fridge, Allegra. You can heat that up at six o'clock." She starts walking toward the front room. "And Patricia, there is plenty if you would like to stay for dinner. But you must call your mother and ask for her permission."

A small smile starts in Patricia's eyes and spreads across her face. I'm not sure if it's the thought of more of Matilde's tucker or the fact that my grandmother actually asked my best-ever friend to stay without me having to beg or do anything that made her the slightest bit proud.

Matilde slips back into the kitchen to tell us one more thing before she saddles up to her Singer: "Allegra, you are to stay out the back. Do not go to the front door, or look through the windows, and you are definitely not to go out onto the street. Is that clear?"

"Yes, Matilde." I'd agree to anything now that Patricia is here—and staying for dinner—with me at Number 23.

Matilde does get cracking, but the sound of her Singer is almost drowned out by the continuing noise from out the front of the house. She turns up Liszt's *Transcendental Études* on her gramophone, but the angry women outside turn up their sound too, and it's certainly coming from more than just three of them now.

"I reckon there's at least ten out there yelling your nana's name," says Patricia, using the black pick-up stick skillfully to lift two red sticks off the floor of my room.

"It's so weird," I say. "She mostly just keeps to herself. . . . I've never known anyone to be angry with Matilde before." I move three sticks, trying to pull out the blue one, and then I have to admit softly, "Except maybe the people in my family."

"Wait here, I'm going to take a look out the front." Patricia's got the game pretty well stitched up and is way more interested in what's happening out on the street than beating me again in pick-up sticks. "Matilde told *you* not to go to the front, Ally, but she didn't say anything about me."

"Okay," I say, feeling squeezed between the instructions

of my grandmother and the erupting idea of my best-ever friend. "But be careful. Go through the kitchen door and then you can sneak along Joy's fence line . . . you know, on the other side to where Matilde is working. I'll wait here and make noises like we're still playing pick-up sticks."

Patricia moves pretty quickly and is back in my room before eighty-apple-pie.

"There's nine of them out there . . . I counted . . . and now they're holding up signs," she says, slightly puffed.

"What do the signs say?" I'm really hoping Patricia's reading has improved.

"I looked real quick, so I only saw two of them straight on. One I couldn't make out, but the other one says *Scab*."

"*Scab?* . . . Why would they say *scab?* That's just really *weird*." I'm wondering if those women think my grand-mother Matilde is a Riffraff.

Rick doesn't say anything about the angry women when he arrives home, but I know that he's seen them because soon after, he comes to the kitchen door and suggests that before dinner we go for a paddle. I think he wants to get us away from Number 23 and let the waves wash over us and do their work.

"Go grab your togs, girls. And Al, leave a note for Matilde on the hall table to say I'm taking you out for a while," he says. "Actually, write down straight up, Al . . . *My father is taking me to the beach!*"

I don't want to make Matilde livid with all that's going on, so I write instead: *We're going for a drive with Rick.*

I explain to Patricia what a paddle involves and tell her

that it will be really cool because we can take it in turns with Rick on the board and then he can also teach her how to ride the waves.

But she doesn't seem all that excited. "I'll just watch you from the beach, Ally. I don't have a swimsuit."

"I've got an old one you can wear. I've grown out of it, but it'll still fit you."

"Nah, it'll be more fun just to watch."

I'm sure Patricia will change her mind when she sees how cool it is to ride the waves, so I bring the extra suit anyway. We join Rick at his van out the back. I slide in along the bench seat beside Rick, and Patricia tucks in snugly next to me. Rick sits forward, revs the engine and takes off down the side drive, turning sharply into the street. A startled woman jumps out of the way, her fist waving and her sign bending toward us. The sign reads in big black letters: **STRIKEBREAKER.**

"What's a strikebreaker, Rick?" I ask, looking back to make sure I've read the words right.

"And what's a scab?" adds Patricia, also looking over her shoulder.

"Those women are just a bit hot under the collar and taking it out on Matilde. They'll be gone soon enough." Rick is flipping over the Beach Boys cassette with one hand and steering with the other.

"Will Matilde be safe there all on her own?" I say, suddenly thinking we should go back. "I don't think we should be leaving her."

"They're not going to hurt her, Al Pal."

"But what's happening, Rick? Why are they so angry? I don't understand . . . can you please tell us what's going on?"

"Really it's nothing to worry about," he says, tapping his fingers on the steering wheel in time to the music.

I turn down "Good Vibrations." "You're fobbing me off, Rick. What's happening?"

Rick stops tapping and glances at me sideways. "Okay, Al . . . look . . . those women are on strike. Do you know what that is?"

"Kind of," I say at the same time as Patricia says, "No."

"Well, they want better pay, so they've all stopped work at the factory. They're trying to negotiate with Bolton's to give them more money. But if Matilde and the other outworkers keep up their sewing at home, that means Bolton's can still get the work done and their orders filled and then they don't need the women at the factory after all. The strike is broken."

"Is it bad to be a strikebreaker?"

"That depends on your perspective, Al."

"But Matilde is just doing what she's always done—her piecework from home—and if she doesn't work, then she doesn't get paid, not a red cent."

"Yeah, that's exactly right."

"And if she doesn't get paid, she can't pay for everything we need."

"Well, she doesn't pay for *everything* we need, Al. I work too."

"I know . . . but you've got that sickness."

"What sickness?"

"The *Játszik* sickness . . ."

"The *what* sickness?"

Rick and Patricia both turn toward me so that I feel flanked, and now I'm wishing I hadn't taken the conversation from strikebreaking to the *Játszik* sickness. I lean forward and turn up "Good Vibrations." "Don't worry about it."

"What are you talking about, Al? Come on, don't *you* fob *me* off now." Rick turns the music down again.

He's not going to let me off the hook, I can tell, so I explain reluctantly, "I heard Matilde telling that Polish lady, the one who came around for tea, that you had a sickness and she called it the *Játszik* sickness. She said it's why you can't contribute much money."

"Jeeeez," Rick mutters under his breath, and turns up "Good Vibrations" louder than before. He doesn't tap his fingers on the steering wheel this time; he just stares straight ahead.

"She wasn't really mad about it, Rick, she was just explaining why she needs the money from the piecework. But ... well ... maybe ... maybe I didn't hear her properly." I don't think Rick is hearing me now.

We don't speak again until we pull up in the car park at the beach. Rick gets his board out of the back and hovers there for a while before he sticks his head in the side window of the van.

"I'm going to catch a few waves. You two can wait here or down on the sand." Rick's obviously changed his mind about taking us for a paddle and wants the waves to wash his stuff away all on his own.

"And Al ... by the way ... sometimes your grandmother

can be a bitter old woman. I don't have that sickness, not like her husband had. I just like to place a bet every now and again. It gives me something to be hopeful about."

I'm relieved about that, in a worried-guilty sort of way.

"Looks like we didn't need our swimmers after all," I say to Patricia.

"That's okay, Ally. I can't actually swim," she says, watching Rick walking toward the water. "Well, at least your dad hasn't got that sickness."

"Yeah, but now he's mad at Matilde all because of me," I say, and I start to feel a sickness of my own rise up in that part of my heart that gets congested when my dad and grandmothers press hard and cold against each other.

■■■

Patricia and I arrive home from the beach bone dry. Coming up the back porch, I hear Matilde on the phone at the end of the hall. She doesn't normally speak much on the phone, especially in the middle of a rush job.

"Of course I understand. I need the work just like you do, Nora, but this could be our only opportunity to change things for good, to make things better for all of us, the piece-workers. We are the ones treated worst of all." She sees us come in, turns to the wall and lowers her voice. Only it's a Matilde-style lowered voice and still just loud enough for me to hear every word.

"With this strike at the factory, Bolton's needs us now more than ever, and so we have this small window of power.

We should seize this opportunity to be paid fairly and to be paid on time. It could be our only chance."

Matilde goes quiet. She is listening. She is nodding. She is pleased: "Good. This is good, Nora. Can you speak with your sister also? I will call Katia and Irena."

She hangs up and walks back to the front room, looking like something important has been settled. I follow her in, hoping it's a good moment to ask if Patricia can stay for a sleepover. "Yes, yes, she can stay," says Matilde, sitting back down at her machine. "Your friend Patricia is a good no-nonsense girl. She is welcome here."

■ ■ ■

Patricia is fascinated that Lucinda Lister is preggers. I told her when we were chatting in bed last night. And now after breakfast she wants to talk about it again, this time fishing for more details: "Do you know who the father is?"

"No, I don't know," I say, and the truth is I hadn't even thought to wonder about that.

"We should visit her, Ally—we could take her some Twisties. I'd like to meet her."

"Matilde would be livid if I went anywhere near the place. She told me to keep well away from there, and from Lucinda."

"It's not like the mumps, Ally. You can't catch preggers."

"I know that . . . but I don't want to make Matilde mad, especially in the middle of this rush job with all the other stuff that's going on."

"Yeah, I suppose," says Patricia, but then she comes up with an idea. "Tell you what, why don't you write Lucinda a note and I can drop it off at her place. That way *you* won't be going there—you'll be staying away like Matilde told you to, but you can still send her your sympathies. Don't you feel sorry for her?"

Lucinda isn't the sort of girl anyone normally feels sorry for. She's always been the girl across the road that has everything: a blond ponytail, a pool, a dragster, cool parents, a mixed party with eighteen friends, and Alpine Lights. But now that I think about it, there's no one hanging around in the garage anymore, her pool has gone murky, and it seems like her dad and his station wagon aren't coming back. I'm not sure where a baby fits in . . . whether that counts as more of *everything* or if it is actually something to feel sorry about.

Patricia seems pretty sure it's something to feel sorry about, and she's usually spot-on, so I write Lucinda a note on my old Holly Hobbie stationery:

> *Sorry you're preggers. I hope these Twisties make you feel better.*
> > *From,*
> > *Ally*

Patricia slips out the back door and down Joy's side path to deliver it across the road to the Lucky house. I play both hands of Go Fish by myself on my bedroom floor, using two different voices out loud so Matilde is none the wiser.

For three days now Matilde has pedaled hard, despite the angry women holding up their signs—and calling out her name—and the growing crowd of neighbors staring at what's become quite a sight outside Number 23. The man with the gray Plasticine face has arrived at the same time each night, branded with dripping egg yolk and bringing more bags of fabric and a fresh round of barked instructions for Matilde.

And now some of the women are shouting *Áruló . . . Áruló . . . Áruló.*

I'm thinking that word must be Hungarian, so I sneak a look in the dictionary Matilde keeps on the bookshelf. And there it is: *áruló* in Hungarian means *traitor* in English. My birthmark warms up and starts to pulsate.

I take a tray of tea and honey toast in to Matilde. I make the tea extra warm, sweet and milky and spread the honey extra thick. Once I've set the tray down on the table next to the Singer, my arms surprise me by moving forward and wrapping themselves around Matilde's bony shoulders. My face nuzzles into the back of her head. She smells brave. She smells able. She smells really tired. Matilde actually stops sewing. She exhales and reaches her left hand up to my forearm, which I turn upward . . . slowly . . . deliberately . . . so that my special mark lines up with the numbers written on her wrist.

And suddenly there is Kimberly Linton's father, standing large and looking menacing in the doorway of Matilde's front room.

"Sorry to disturb such a tender scene, but I have come to

let you know that it's *you* who is dragging the chain, and now that I'm here, I can see all too clearly why."

Mr. Linton moves forward and stands over Matilde at her machine. It's easy to trace the origin of every festering feature of Kimberly Linton. He has that same cruel expression Kimberly gets when she's about to lash out.

So this time I decide to strike first.

"My grandmother is not dragging any chain," I say, picturing Mr. Linton as a scrunched-up essay in my pocket. "She's hardly had any breaks in more than three days."

"Is that right, little miss," he says without looking at me. Then, stepping in closer to Matilde, he sprays: "Well, how is it, then, that your work is so slow and the quality is so poor? And as if that's not bad enough, I hear you're stirring up trouble with my other outworkers. If you want to be paid anything—*anything at all*—for this job or any other, you'd better pick up the pace and keep your mouth firmly shut!" Mr. Linton's spittle is going straight into Matilde's face.

A memory vapor of Kimberly's burning words is whirling around the room:

I have an alive mother to buy for, not a dead mother, not a dead mother, not a dead mother like you.

And now it's mixing with the threatening words of her father: *Pick up the pace . . . the quality is poor . . . keep your mouth firmly shut.*

My solar plexus is pushing up something that surfaces with a burst of *bátor:* "You leave my grandmother alone! You're a bully just like your horrible mean daughter!" I fly at him and pull at his arm with all my might.

193

Matilde flinches like something is coming her way, but Mr. Linton turns and pokes his thumb—hard—into the middle of my spine. His breath smells of meat and vinegar, and he pushes me down toward the door with his other hand at the base of my neck: "Now settle down, little miss—you have quite a temper there."

He must have hit a nerve. I can't help but let out an echoing shriek as I land—*thump*—on my knees in the corridor. And now he's above me, looking down, but I don't care if he hurts me. I will not let this bully from Bolton's Fashion House see me cry.

Matilde jumps up and is breathing hard by my side. "You . . . *you disgusting pig*. Do not *ever* touch my granddaughter. Do you hear me? Ever! How did you even get into my home? My front door is locked," she demands loudly from the floor next to me.

"What . . . you want me to come to the front door with those mad women bellowing out there? Knock on your front door like a visitor!" Mr. Linton is snarling. "You work for me, remember, and I'll use any entrance I like." He looks like he thinks he owns everyone and everything in the world.

Matilde, satisfied that I'm not injured, stands up and takes him in—head on—but suddenly she seems paralyzed.

Joy is here.

For the first time ever, Joy is here inside Number 23—and she's holding a shovel.

And now she is speaking: "I don't think the police will care who works for whom, Mr. Linton, when I tell them you have committed the crime of trespass by coming through my property, and worse than that, you have just assaulted my granddaughter." Joy beckons me toward her.

"Christ, what is this, surrounded by bloody grandmothers!"

"Yes. *Yes* you are," says Matilde, regaining movement. "Now, leave immediately, through the front door."

"You'd better hotfoot it and finish that order," he snorts. "I employ you. I pay you good money. I'm the one who allows you to work from home. You need me."

"And we both know that with this strike at the factory, *you* need *me*." Matilde is looking a whole lot of B words: Bold, Balanced, *Bátor* and Backed up.

"I will finish the work that you can't get done by the women on strike if—*and only if*—you pay me for the last job." Matilde is most definitely a spirited woman; how did I ever think that was even a question? "And I want full payment for this next one, immediately when I hand it over. With an extra dollar per garment from now on. In fact, I want you to agree to that for all of the outworkers."

Mr. Linton looks what Rick would call snookered.

"But before you go, Mr. Linton," says Joy, quickly handing Matilde a pen and paper from next to the phone on the hall table, "Mrs. Kaldor will write that agreement down, and you will sign it." I've never seen this before: Joy and Matilde working together.

"I'm not signing any such thing."

Whisky Wendy has arrived, looking every bit like another grandmother. "I've called the police and they're on their way," she says.

"Your choice, Mr. Linton, father of *dear little Kimberly* and *pillar of the church*," says Joy. "You can leave through the front door into the path of those egg-throwing women, or through my place into the hands of the police. Signing the agreement sounds like the easiest way out to me." Annabel Renshaw would definitely classify Joy as a women's libber.

Patricia, who'd gone up to get Rick, bursts in with a flushed face just ahead of my dad, who looks ready for action. He stops himself short when he takes in the scene. He beckons me toward him, and I move from beside Joy to behind my dad. He says nothing, but his rib cage is fully expanded and he seems taller than ever before.

I can't believe my eyes.

The Bully from Bolton's is shaking his head, but he's signing the agreement and he's doing it on the ironing table with all of us watching. Matilde looks sideways at Rick and Joy and gives them both a pea-sized half nod. Then Joy and her shovel lead Mr. Linton out the back through the brown gate and down the side of Number 25 with Rick coming up behind like a cattle dog. Patricia and I move to the front window and watch as Mr. Linton tries to turn left out of Matilde's house, but Rick stands in his path and turns him around so that he has no choice but to walk through the middle of the angry ladies with their signs, and their name-calling, and an enthusiastic round of pitched eggs.

CHAPTER NINETEEN

THE SINGER HAS STOPPED ALTOGETHER AND SO HAS MATILDE. She has finished the rush job, but now that it's over she seems completely exhausted. The man with the gray Plasticine face comes first thing for her perfect pieces, but Matilde can't even go the door. She asks me to check that he has brought an envelope containing two hundred and twenty-two dollars, which I bring to her bedroom and count out on her nightstand. Then she asks that I help take the garments out to his car "while I put my head down on the bed, just for five minutes."

After lunch I check on Matilde, and she's still lying down. Just before dinner I check her again. She is murmuring in a disturbed sleep. I leave her a tray of tea and honey toast, whispering softly that it's on her bedside table, but when I go in after dinner, the tea and toast are untouched and cold, and Matilde's face is blotchy and hot.

And now Matilde's words are making no sense at all.

"Do not let them see that you are weak, Elsa, *never.* Never let them see the slightest sign of weakness in you. They must think that you are strong. The strong ones are spared."

I bend over Matilde, telling her it's not Elsa, it's actually me, her granddaughter, Allegra. She takes my hand and says with warm breathy words, "Here, have this corner of my bread. Take it. Quickly, do what I say. Eat it to keep up your strength."

Matilde is holding out her empty left palm, which hangs limply from her numbered wrist. I obey her instructions and move my hand, taking the not-there bread, and afterward I loosen the buttons at the top of her blouse. Her words change to Hungarian so now I don't understand anything she is saying.

But then Matilde uses one word that has recently opened a door inside of me.

Belinda.

"*Belinda,*" she says again. And then switching back to English, "I survived hell to give you life, and still you were taken from me."

I hold Matilde's hand in mine and lay my head gently down onto her chest.

"But I am here with you, Matilde. I am here," I say. "Belinda's daughter. Her *alive* daughter."

■ ■ ■

Rick is seeing Dr. Scully off at the door.

I hear the doctor tell Rick that Matilde needs to have complete bed rest for at least a week: "She's suffering from fever and quite possibly exhaustion. Just light meals for now, and call me again if you have any concerns."

A few hours later Joy appears on the back porch. That's twice in two days that my grandmother has stepped through the brown gate and into Number 23.

"Now, I'm no Margaret Fulton," she says, looking as proud as punch and swinging her tie-dyed silk scarf over her shoulder. "But I tried my hand at making a lasagne. *With pineapple pieces!*"

Not even Patricia can stomach Joy's lasagne, and I don't think Matilde would go anywhere near it, even in full health. So the light meals are mine to prepare. I bring down Matilde's cookbooks, and Patricia and I decide to have a go at making a pot of spring-vegetable soup. We pick carrots, beans and spinach from Matilde's garden, chop them and simmer them in some chicken-bone broth that Matilde keeps in her stockpot in the fridge. We add parsley and shallots, salt and pepper, more salt and a sprig of chopped mint—that's Patricia's idea, she says its freshness might cool Matilde down. The soup turns out a bit salty and looks kind of greasy but after I wipe Matilde's face gently with a face washer, the way she does mine whenever I'm sick, and pop a few pillows under her head, she eventually swallows five small mouthfuls—then one more—which I feed to her slowly from her favorite dented silver spoon.

Patricia and I agree: that should keep the wolf on the other side of the door.

Rick tells us the next day that the house needs to be kept extra quiet so Matilde can rest, and it's time to take Patricia back to Glebe. He agrees that I can come for the drive in his van to drop her over there to her mum.

"Hey, Ally—here—sneak your pj's into my bag," Patricia whispers as she packs up her things, which are scattered around my room. "When we get to Wendy's place, let's ask your dad if you can have a sleepover with me. My mum won't mind, and Matilde will be resting so she won't say no."

I hand my pajamas to Patricia, but I'm not really sure that Rick can make a decision like that.

We arrive at Whisky Wendy's, and Patricia jumps out of Rick's van. I follow her in "just to say goodbye," I tell Rick, who stays firmly put. He has no interest in going inside Wendy's place; I think he was put off from the last time we were there. Patricia plays hopscotch around the holes in the floor and bounces into the back room, the one I walked through the day we brought Joy home, the one with the cane furniture, fishbowl and poster about women's lib. There's a circle of women sitting under a cloud of cigarette smoke, some busy with notepads and pens, and others with little kids on their knees or playing at their feet. There seems to be some sort of a meeting going on.

Patricia O'Brien's mother is Hula-Hoop happy to see my best-ever friend after four whole nights of her being away. She ruffles her hair. Then Patricia, with a pleading burst, asks: "Can Ally stay here, Mum, just for one night? Her nana Matilde is sick as a dog."

"Oh really, sick as a dog? That's no good," says her mum. "Well, yeah, it should be all right for her to stay here for a bit. That okay with you, Wendy?"

"Actually, we could do with some help from you two girls looking after these little ones at the moment," Whisky Wendy replies, wiping up a spill on the floor.

"Can you come out and speak to Ally's dad, Mum? He's waiting outside in his van." Patricia's already scooped up a tiny boy with one rosy cheek high onto her back.

Luckily, Patricia O'Brien's mum is really pretty, with moss-green eyes framed by glossy black hair. Rick seems a bit taken with her. He looks like he'd go along with just about anything she suggested.

"I suppose one night is okay, Al Pal. You two have been pretty useful helping out at Number 23 while Matilde's been sick, so yeah, I guess you can stay."

"Glad to hear they've been pulling their weight," says Patricia's mum, leaning slightly forward into Rick's wound-down window.

And just like that the sleepover is bedded down.

Rick starts pulling out and I realize that I have something important to tell him. I tap hard on the side of the van and he stops with a jolt.

"Can you make sure you give Matilde the rest of that soup we made? It's in the large stockpot at the back of the fridge. Maybe with some small fingers of toast if she's up to it. Don't heat the soup up too hot. And you might have to feed it to her, Rick, one small spoon at a time. You will look after her, won't you?"

"I'll give it my best shot, Al."

"Promise?"

"Promise. You have fun with your friend. Matilde will be all right."

...

"The best you can get at the Salvation Army shelter is one night, two tops. But that's it. You can't stay during the day. They kick you out." The lady speaking in Wendy's back room has a baby across her lap, its head nuzzled under her blouse, and one slightly bigger pulling at her skirt. "That's why most women stay at home, whatever the circumstances. They don't leave, *they can't*, they just put up with it. . . . It's too disruptive to take off with little kids, especially when you've nowhere to go during the day."

"And when the Salvos kick you out in the morning, there's a limit to how long you can spend in a library with three under three," says another lady, who is pushing a stroller back and forth with one hand.

"Or a shopping center, without a cent in your purse," pipes up another.

All the other ladies are blowing smoke from different-shaped lips, nodding and agreeing with whatever is said. Patricia is busy building a fort out of blocks with four toddlers on the floor and doesn't look like she's paying much attention to the conversation going on around the table. I'm on the floor too, sorting the blocks into sizes and colors and passing them to Patricia one by one. But I'm taking in every word.

"We need somewhere we can stay with our kids, during the day as well as overnight," says a lady with a slightly old face but a young-sounding voice.

"And help getting a job would be good," says another woman who Matilde would think needs a brush through her hair. "If I had a job, I could get my own flat. I'd only need something small. And my twins start school next year, so I could work during school hours. That would be enough. Yeah . . . I reckon we could survive on that . . . at least we'd be safe at night."

"And some legal representation to get custody of the kids and what's rightfully ours," says a woman as she stubs out one cigarette and lights up another.

"What is rightfully ours?" says a lady with red welts around her neck.

Wendy plonks down a plate of grilled cheese on toast: "It depends on your circumstances, but if you own a house together you should get at least half of its value—that's if you get a good lawyer and go through with a divorce proving he was at fault."

"*Gawwd*, who can afford a good lawyer!" replies the red-welted woman.

"Too right," agrees another woman with a croaky voice,

reaching for a second piece of toast. "But we certainly need some sort of legal help to make the break away for good, so we can build a decent life for our kids."

"Yep, and in the meantime a safe place to stay, just for women and children, no men. A place that's *run by women*," says a lady blowing smoke from her nose.

"You're spot-on there!"

"Run by women who actually understand what's going on, out there in the real world."

"And more than an overnight shelter. A *refuge*—somewhere safe where we can stay on for a while."

I'm remembering Joy telling me that Liberty Club was trying to set up a safe house, something that she also called a refuge. She spoke about it the night we took the net down to the creek. I look around at the little kids on the floor, playing and giggling. Wriggling like tadpoles.

"And then we can support one another," their mothers agree.

"Exactly. Somewhere we can actually live, just till we sort ourselves out."

■ ■ ■

I help Patricia bathe a pile of kids. We wrap them in towels and roll them into the lounge room, some chuckling, some squealing and all of them wanting us to roll them again. Wendy gives us a plastic bag full of pajamas, and Patricia makes a game of finding the tops that best go with the bottoms that are close to the right size for each child.

When we've dressed them all, Patricia announces, "So everyone, listen! Go get under Ally's wings on the mattress. Quick, run, onto the floor in the front bedroom. It's time for the Blanket Show."

Patricia stretches an orange-and-purple crocheted blanket across the open wardrobe doors, and with soft toys and a doll she performs a puppet-show story about a princess who is being chased by a monster. She does the actions and the different voices, and the kids all love it as much as they love Patricia.

"Run your fastest, run your fastest," screams a little girl no more than four. "Or the monster will get you and hurt your mummy." She is wriggling in closer to me.

"But then . . . along came . . . *Brave Aunty Bear*!" says Patricia from behind the blanket. "She's old, but she's strong and she's powerful, and she tells the monster, 'Bugger off, you horrible monster. Leave the princess alone. Go back to Monster Land and never come near here again.'" Patricia does a very convincing Brave Aunty Bear voice.

"Yay," calls out the little girl, "and leave all the kids alone too!"

"Yeah," says Patricia's Brave Aunty Bear voice. "'Leave all the baby princesses alone and the baby princes too. Go back to Monster Land and have a big sleep and think about how you can be a good monster.' And so he stayed away forever and ever, and they all lived with full bellies happily ever after." Patricia comes forward with the toys in her arms, and together they take a bow in front of the blanket stage.

The kids are cheering and I'm thinking that Patricia

would make a really good teacher. Though her spelling could be a bit of a problem: I might have to help her with that.

···

We're sleeping head to toe again, this time at Wendy's, with Patricia planning where we'll go in our van once we've painted a red-and-yellow sunset down the sides and a purple peace sign on the back.

With my close ear I'm listening to her rattle off a list of all the places around Australia that she knows, and it seems like a lot, but with my distant ear I'm listening to the women who are still up talking with each other in the back room.

Finally Patricia drops off to sleep so I can hear the conversation with two ears instead of one, and I can make out most of what they are saying.

"It took me months to work up the courage to leave the first time, but those church places just want to patch you up and send you back. One of the God-botherers at the last place I went to had the hide to say to me, even before I was stitched up, 'Just go on home, don't ruffle his feathers and think of the children.'

"Well, I *am* bloody well thinking of the children, and that's why I'm never going back. *Never again*. He'll probably kill me next time. Then who'll look after my kids?"

I think the lady speaking is the one who liked the cheese on toast.

"It actually happens," says another one. "It happened to

my friend's cousin. She got her head slammed into the fridge door, over and over, until her husband left her with blood pooling from her mouth to die alone on the floor while the baby was asleep in the cot. Apparently what triggered it was her telling him she was pregnant again. With *his* kid!"

This is so awful. . . . I don't want to hear any more, but I can't stop listening.

Now the lady speaking is raising her voice. "It was the only time the cops ever came. *Afterward!* Too bloody late then."

"Those cops are *useless*," they're all chiming in.

"Righto, enough! It's urgent now. We can't wait any longer for a place to just become available. You know what? There's an empty house down the road here, all boarded up, a bit past where Lesley was squatting with her friends from uni."

"What street is it in?"

"West Street, I think."

"Yeah, yeah, I know the one," pipes up the lady whose friend's cousin had her head slammed into the fridge door. "The BLF green-banned it a while ago, which means the developers haven't got their greedy hands on it yet. Actually, I think there might be two empty places there, side by side."

"What's the BLF?" asks the red-welted woman. She doesn't seem to know as much as the others.

"It's the builders laborers' union—you know, the blokes who usually fight for the workers to get them better wages and safety. But now they're on to stopping developers from

207

putting their wrecking balls through houses and parks, to build filthy high-rises everywhere and expressways. They're using workers' solidarity to put green bans on some sites," explains Whisky Wendy.

"If we break into one of those green-banned houses, we could set ourselves up there and claim squatter's rights."

Whatever that is, it gets the women excited, and they start speaking louder and quicker and over the top of each other, and I lose track of which one might be saying what.

"You know, when you squat, there are ways you can tap into the water and the sewerage—that's if they haven't poured cement down the pipes. My little brother's a qualified sparky; he'd probably know how to hook up the electricity."

"It could be a great spot to set up a refuge."

"It could be the *perfect* spot to set up a refuge!"

"Good location."

"Just sitting there empty."

"And free."

"God, that sounds good."

"Okay then, let's do it. What do we need?"

"Well . . . tools to break in, for a start. A shovel under the window will do the trick. And once we're in, we'll need to change the locks."

"Is someone writing this down? A couple of shovels, new locks and then a way to secure the place."

"Wendy's cricket bat works well."

That gets all the women laughing loudly.

"Maybe more than one cricket bat, then," someone suggests.

"It'll need a good clean-up, no doubt . . . so mops and buckets, Ajax, stuff like that."

"And mattresses, sheets and towels. A kitchen table and chairs."

"Clothes for the kids."

"And clothes for the women."

"A fridge, we'll need a fridge."

"What about food?"

"And what about a phone? We'll definitely need to get the phone connected."

"If we're going to do this, we have to act quick smart, and once we've set up, we should get the media involved— you know, get their support. We need to let this city know what's going on and why we're going to these lengths to set up a refuge."

"Absolutely. We need to tell women's stories, get the public and the politicians on board, no more passing it off as just 'domestics.' Let them know that women and kids are suffering—*something horrible*—in silence, some of them dying at the hands of these bastards."

"Has anyone got contacts in the media? What about you, Wendy? You'd have some, wouldn't you—from, you know— your efforts with Parramatta Girls Home?"

"Yes, well, I've certainly got a few. Peter at *This Day Tonight*, he's a decent bloke . . . a good journo. He might be interested."

"And what about you, Beryl? The *Women's Weekly*? The *National Times*?"

"Yeah, sure, both are worth a go."

"And the radio—wouldn't it be good to get onto that John Laws show?"

"Righto. What say we assemble in the park in West Street at three p.m. tomorrow with what we need and go in! Does everyone agree?"

By the sounds of things, they do.

"So, Cathy, you're on locks, electricity and plumbing. Beryl and Wendy, the media. Margaret, you can be in charge of the break-in and security: shovels, cricket bats and brooms. Everyone else, try to get your hands on cleaning stuff and get in touch with women you know who can help us, or the ones who could use refuge accommodation, and tell them what's happening. But be careful: we need to get the address out to the women who need it, but not to their bastard men.

"So . . . this is it! Enough is enough: we're taking control. By this time tomorrow, looks like we'll have ourselves a *refuge*!"

A cheer goes up and so does the stereo. Things go from sounding like a meeting to sounding like a party and it goes on well into the night.

That part of my heart that remembers building the pretend fort with blocks on the floor with the toddlers today senses that their mothers might be about to build a real one—with shovels, bats, mops and brooms—tomorrow.

CHAPTER TWENTY

Rick is waiting in his van outside Wendy's place, listening to the radio. His elbow is resting on the open window, and he's staring straight ahead. He has come to take me home.

Patricia walks me out slowly. Looking down at the path with her arm around my waist, she's mucking about like she's going to trip me over with every step.

I guess this is it.

We give each other a quick hug and promise to write often. We agree that we'll start saving—every red cent, from this moment on—for the van with a sunset, peace sign and curtains.

"I could get a job at the greengrocer," I tell her proudly, thinking that's a good start. "Joe actually offered me one, you know, not that long ago." I'm working hard to sound upbeat, as well as inventive, coming up with ways to earn money that might impress Patricia.

"At Joe the Robber's! Gaaawd . . . your nana would hate that! And that creep probably wouldn't even pay you. Maybe you could just set up a shop outside Number 23 and sell Matilde's spare fruit and veg—it's heaps better than Joe's—and that way you could drive the robber out of business. Hey, you could sell some of her cooked tucker too. Yeah, you could do that, Ally. Tell you what: I'll make you an apron in dressmaking, with 'Tildie's Tucker' appliquéd on the front." Patricia's eyes are twinkling, slightly watering, probably at the thought of the good tucker and all the money we'll make.

That part of my heart that misses someone while you're still holding them clamps hard around Patricia's shoulders. I say a quick "see ya," give her a noogie and climb up into the van.

But just before we push off, Patricia O'Brien's mother runs out. Her denim wraparound skirt is flapping open above the knees, and she asks if she could speak with Rick for "just a quick minute."

"By the looks of that sign on your van, you're a carpenter," she says with a voice that sounds like the spoken equivalent of a wink. "Any chance you could help us with something real important later today?"

"What needs doing?" Rick asks, not looking at her knees.

Patricia O'Brien's mother explains to Rick that Wendy lets battered women stay in her house, women with no support and nowhere to go. Women at the end of their tether, with little kids, who are scared for their lives. And young girls too, runaways, some of them pregnant, some of them thrown out by their mothers or bashed by their fathers. Some of them are "home girls"—*you know, wards of the state*—who slip into Wendy's via the lane behind her house and leave messages for each other on the pin board on her back wall.

Patricia O'Brien's mother tells Rick what they are planning to do later today: "We're setting up a refuge for women and kids . . . you know, like a safe shelter where they can stay . . . in one of those green-banned houses just down the road. We just need someone strong, who has tools, who knows how to use them to change the locks."

She explains that what they're going to do is not illegal because the houses are just sitting there empty—nobody's using them, and squatters actually have rights—it's a fact—rights recognized by the law.

I'm not sure if it's hearing about mothers and children being scared for their lives or young girls being bashed and thrown out of their homes, or if it's more the high notes of Charlie perfume wafting through the window, but Rick has scribbled down the address on the back of his hand, and we're heading for the hardware store with a promise to meet them just down from the empty house in a bit over an hour.

"I'm not going to have time to get you home and then get back before three o'clock, Al Pal, so you'll just have to come along and keep your head down and stay *schtum*. Matilde doesn't need to know about this. . . . Agreed?"

"Agreed," I say, suddenly feeling more like I imagine you do at twenty-six than twelve, and thinking that maybe I might be about to see Rick in action doing something a bit Riffraff. The thrill of that prospect lightens the heaviness inside of having to say goodbye to Patricia for now.

...

When Rick and I arrive in West Street, a small group of women is standing outside a peeling white house with a sloping tin roof. It looks nothing like Number 23 or Number 25 or a convent, and it's attached to a mirror-image house, every bit as dilapidated, on its right. The front windows of both houses are boarded up, and I can't picture anyone cooking chicken paprikash, making Morello-cherry strudel or even frying up soggy fish fingers with frozen mixed veg inside those dirty flaking walls. Or, for that matter, reciting times tables, practicing piano or learning to play Chinese checkers.

Rick blows out hard, from the back of his throat. He doesn't seem sure where to park the van.

And then we see Patricia O'Brien's mother hailing us down with big swinging waves and—*whooshka*—she's inside the van sitting right next to me.

"Have you got everything?" she says to Rick, panting slightly.

"Yep, I think so. I bought new locks, and all my tools are in the back."

"Beaut. We're just about set, then."

"Is Patricia coming?" I ask hopefully.

"Patricia . . . oh no, she won't be coming—she's back

at Wendy's looking after the little kids." Her green eyes are darting and she's sounding distracted. "Look, pull up here, there's a spot opposite the house. I'll get the women to gather down the street a bit. Once we break in and establish ourselves, we're going to call up the papers, and maybe the telly too." Her voice is quickening, starting to sound kind of excited.

I can tell that Rick is definitely not excited. He has that same face he had in the church when Joy didn't show up on my Confirmation day. He leans toward me and says in a low voice, "We'll be making ourselves scarce before any television people appear, Al, I'll tell you that for free."

That's disappointing because I wouldn't mind seeing the television people arrive with their lights, cameras and action. But actually, I'm pretty surprised that Rick has even come this far and is sticking with the plan, especially now that Patricia O'Brien's mother has swapped the wraparound skirt for overalls.

And then I get another surprise.

It's Joy.

Today she *has* shown up. She's standing in her halter-neck sundress next to Wendy across the road. Wendy is holding a cricket bat and Joy has a picnic basket in one hand and a mop in the other. I didn't even know that Joy owned a mop. Maybe her job will be to clean up this dirty house— that's a strange job to give Joy; she's not big on cleaning up.

The group of women is growing, in size and noise and energy. Some have arrived with buckets, some with feather dusters and brooms, and others are holding up shovels and signs.

Patricia O'Brien's mother jumps out of the van and tells Rick to stay put until she gives him the signal. She moves swiftly from woman to woman, and it looks like she's giving each one a quick message.

They all move in a pack a little way down the street.

I glance at my watch, the one Matilde gave me for my tenth birthday. It tells me it's just before three.

Then Patricia's mother stands out front, and with a big voice she leads the women assembled together in a rhyme:

> *Two, four, six, eight,*
> *What do we repudiate?*
> *Violent lives we can't escape!*

Another woman holding up a shovel moves the rhyme to a chant:

> *Women have been relegated*
> *Deflated—isolated—berated*
> *Obliterated*
> *Time now for us to be elevated*
> *Compensated—educated—celebrated*
> *LIBERATED*

All the women are joining in and their chant becomes a rallying call.

Women's liberation's going to smash the cage
Come join us now and rage, rage, rage
Rage, Rage, Rage

Even Joy, it seems, is starting to *rage, rage, rage.*
They're all getting louder.

Rage, Rage, Rage

They start marching toward the house.

Rage, Rage, Rage

I'm feeling quite hot in this van.

RAGE, RAGE, RAGE

"When I go in to change the locks, you stay put, Al. Don't get out whatever you do. I won't be long." Rick seems pretty clear about that. And that's okay with me; I've got a good view sitting here across the road from it all.

I'm starting to get thirsty.

We didn't have much breakfast at Wendy's this morning; actually, come to think about it, we didn't have any breakfast . . . or lunch. I could do with a glass of cold water.

Patricia O'Brien's mother, having led the women to the gate of the house, is still chanting. Then, looking our way, she nods at Rick in the driver's seat of the van. He seems a bit reluctant to get out. I think he'd rather stay and listen to Race Number Two at Randwick. But Rick opens the door, whips around the side and gets his toolbox out of the back.

Watching Rick cross the road, I move the dial of the radio away from the horse races. It moves past a "hard-earned thirst needing a big cold beer" and past Johnny Cash singing "Sunday Morning Coming Down." Things are sounding fuzzy until the dial lands clearly on music I recognize: Mr. Franz Liszt. And he's partway through "Liebestraum No. 3."

It's getting hotter in here, and I'm starting to feel a little bit dizzy.

More women are arriving, mostly in overalls, some holding balloons.

And now one has arrived holding a lute.

She is not like the others.

She's gliding, not raging.

She doesn't have a shadow.

But she does have a beard.

None of the women in overalls talk to the one with the lute.

She is moving about on her own, seemingly unnoticed, between them.

Until now: She touches the side of Joy's arm. Joy turns and mouths with wide-eyed surprise: "Oh, St. Liberata!"

The rest of the women's bodies are moving like they're still marching, and their mouths are open like they're still chanting. I'm within the music of Franz Liszt, which is softening my lens and filtering my focus.

But even though Mr. Liszt's music is playing inside the van, he isn't the conductor here in West Street today. It's St. Liberata who, with a maestro's nod, mouths, *It's time*, and raises her fingers to the strings of her lute. She's suddenly apparent to all the women there, and her inspiration brings up their shovels and mops, brooms and balloons.

In one fluid movement the women leap forward, their shovels deftly levering off the boards over the windows and getting in under their frames, opening the house to the air and the light. The door is kicked in by a number of legs, and the women send out an orchestral roar that echoes through the empty rooms and back onto the street.

Rick gets busy with his tools, driving his drill into the opened door. He wipes his brow with his sleeve and continues punching out an old lock before replacing it with a brassy new one. He turns and meets Joy's eyes as she walks with purpose up the small path. They both stop moving for a moment before she briefly wraps both her arms around his strong back and disappears inside, pulling a small glass bottle from the top of her sundress.

Leaning with my head out the window, I'm catching the freshening breeze. Rick is walking toward me on his way back to the van. He's safe; no telly people have arrived so far, so it looks like he won't be filmed for the six o'clock news. But that part of my heart that files away footage knows that this clip today—and its accompaniment—should be stored under B for Breakthrough.

CHAPTER TWENTY-ONE

When I get home to Number 23, I keep my word to Rick and stay *schtum* about his role with the refuge. I can see he's kept his word to me, too, because Matilde is sitting in a straight wooden chair on the back porch in the half sun. She's looking much better but complaining about being waterlogged by salty spring-vegetable soup.

"Every time I opened my eyes, there he was again, waving that spoon in front of my mouth. And just look at that clothesline. What a way to hang out the laundry. Men! The socks are not in their correct pairs, and the shirts are all clumped."

Rick winks at me and walks up to his flat.

"Where is Patricia?" asks Matilde.

"Oh, we dropped her home," I reply. "She said to say thank you, Matilde—she really liked staying here."

Matilde doesn't ask about my sleepover at Glebe, and I

don't mention it either. I think with her being as sick as a dog, she mustn't have even noticed I was away overnight.

•••

I'm making a collage of spring leaves for art class and call into Dave's Mixed Business and Milk Bar after school for more Perkins paste to stick it all down. On my way into Dave's shop, I almost bump into Lucinda Lister on her way out.

"Oh . . . hi, Ally," she says in a voice that sounds thinner than usual. And then, looking grateful in an embarrassed sort of way, she adds, "Hey, thanks for those Twisties."

"That's okay," I say, sort of embarrassed too. "It was Patricia's idea—she thought you might like them."

"Well, I did. She's a cool chick, that Patricia."

"Yeah, she is . . . a cool chick. . . . She's my best friend but she lives in Armidale now, so I don't get to see her that much anymore."

"Guess you must miss her, then."

"I do, actually. I miss her a lot."

"Do you write letters to each other?"

"Yeah. Every other week."

"That's cool." Lucinda is looking at me longer than usual, like she might have changed her mind about wanting to be invisible.

"Are you walking home?" she asks. "I can wait for you, out here, and then . . . we can walk together."

I'm not so sure about this: walking with Lucinda Lister for all the world to see, now that she's preggers. Matilde

221

would be livid if she caught the slightest whiff of me doing that. But there's something about Lucinda today, a look around her outline of lowered expectations and crushed opportunity that makes me feel sorry for her. Plus I'm a bit intrigued by her situation. So I whip in, buy the Perkins paste and join her back outside the shop.

Lucinda unwraps a Cherry Ripe and we set off for home. "I liked your note too, Ally—no one else wrote me a note," she says, taking bites between slow steps. "Except for my deadshit dad, but that wasn't exactly what you'd call a nice one."

"What did your dad's note say?"

"Oh . . . you know, that I'm an embarrassment to him, that he won't be helping raise a baby. And that I should just get rid of it."

"How do you do *that* . . . just get rid of a baby?"

Lucinda stops chewing her Cherry Ripe and comes to a halt. She gives me a sharp look. "Ally, you are obviously smart, but *deadset* you can also be pretty bloody dumb. There *is* a thing you can have called an abortion, you know!"

"Oh, yeah," I say, but I didn't know. "Are you going to have that . . . that thing?"

"Nah, Mum says over her dead body. I think mostly because she's so spitting mad that Dad left, and now she reckons that it's all *his* fault that I'm pregnant, so she won't be going along with anything he wants to happen."

"Is this your dad's baby?" I ask.

Lucinda throws her head forward and spits out

chocolatey-cherry goop onto the footpath. "Jeez, Ally! No! *Yuck* . . . what do you think I am? It's my boyfriend's baby!"

"Sorry . . . it's just when you said your mum thought it was all your dad's fault, I thought that . . . *anyway* . . . sorry. What does your boyfriend think you should do?"

"I don't know. Mum won't let him anywhere near me. He's tried calling me at home a few times, but Mum's put the phone in her room. I've heard her say, *'This has nothing to do with you—keep away—you've done enough damage,'* and then she just hangs up."

Lucinda no longer looks like the girl who has everything. That part of my heart that beats to another person's pulse starts pumping out more Patricia than me and comes up with a sudden idea.

"Hey, why don't you write your boyfriend a note, and I can give it to him on the school bus? You could make a plan to meet him somewhere and, you know, talk about things. You could sort it all out."

Lucinda looks at me, impressed—actually very impressed— like I've just earned a permanent spot in her garage and maybe, if I wanted it, a drag on one of her Alpine Lights.

"Come to think about it, I take back what I said about you being deadset dumb, Ally. For a First-Form Dropkick, that's actually a pretty smart idea." She punches my arm, which hurts only slightly, and quizzes me about what her boyfriend looks like—just to make sure I get the note to the right guy. Once I pass that test, she tells me his name is Rob . . . *Robert Fuller.* She chucks the Cherry Ripe wrapper into a bush and shoots off ahead, saying she needs to get the note written and dropped off to my place before her mum gets home from work, because before all this happened, her mum used to let her roam free, but now she has her on a tight leash . . . *like a dog.*

"Don't bring it to me at Number 23," I call out after her. "Take it to Joy's place, my grandmother next door, you know, the one who lives in Number 25. I'll get it from her letterbox as soon as I can."

"Okay, Ally . . . First-Form Genius! You'll be our Leo—our go-between."

I'm not sure what that is exactly, but Lucinda makes it sound like it's something important. So I head home feeling thicker than an outline and more solid than a shadow, which is almost enough to eclipse the worry of Matilde finding out that I've been walking the streets for all the world to see with *that Lister girl.*

■ ■ ■

Robert Fuller doesn't look like anyone's father.

He's short, with a sprinkling of pimples across his forehead and tufts of fluff on his chin, and he doesn't seem in the least bit responsible. He's playing corners in the back row of the school bus—laughing—grunting—snorting—as he pushes a slightly beefier boy off the seat and into the aisle.

Somehow I'm going to have to get this note to Rob quick smart, but it's looking like I won't have a chance before we reach my stop, which is coming up soon. He's surrounded by his friends, and they'd all be very suss if a First-Form Dropkick goes anywhere near a fourth former on the back row.

I stay on the bus. Past my stop, and the next one and then a few more. Finally the kids thin out and Rob is one of only two boys left on the back seat. They've both settled down to looking at footy cards. The bus jolts to a halt; Rob collects his cards, jumps up, flicks his friend on the neck with an elastic garter and gets off on his own. I gather my bag and get off too. And now I have to follow him. This is weird, very weird, but it *was* my idea and I can't let Lucinda down.

Walking along the gutter with his bag slung over his shoulder, Rob has a different way about him now. I'm walking at the same speed a few paces behind. I wait a bit longer and then, after a deep gulp, I call out.

"Robert . . . *hey, Rob* . . . wait. . . . I have something to give you."

He stops, turns around and studies me. Puzzled, he says, "Yeah, what? What have *you* got to give *me*?"

"It's a note . . . from Lucinda . . . your girlfriend."

"*A what* . . . ? Who says she's my girlfriend?" He has a dismissive tone, but I see a definite flash of curiosity in his eyes.

"Well, anyway, here it is." I'm trying hard not to sound like a First-Form Dropkick. "I'm Ally—I live across the road from Lucinda," I say, passing him the note. "If you want to write back to her, I'll be on the school bus tomorrow morning."

I start the trek home, trying to think of an excuse for Matilde about why I'm so late.

...

It's the first Wednesday of the month, so Matilde's sister is here with us at Number 23, and like on all first Wednesdays she's staying for dinner. She likes me to call her Aunt Helena and to greet her with a kiss on both cheeks. She always brings chocolates for me and mending for Matilde. Everything about Aunt Helena is long: her arms, neck and fingers, her nose and her scarves, but mostly her stories she likes to tell me about the luxury cruises she takes to exotic locations with her dear friend Marta, her adventurous travel companion, because her husband, Bence, is *much too busy* to leave the business.

Things are always strained when Helena is here. I don't even know why Matilde invites her or why Helena would bother coming, given the way things are between them. Matilde seems to put so much effort into her cooking and cleaning before Helena arrives that she hasn't any energy left to be the slightest bit nice, or to respond with anything more than a tick of her tongue to the suggestions that her sister makes. And Helena makes a lot of suggestions.

"I am telling you, Matilde, your hydrangeas would be a much brighter blue if you just took my advice and scattered your coffee grounds around them. . . ." Matilde keeps mashing the potatoes—hard, from the shoulder—her eyes looking down and the sinewy muscles in her forearms flexing.

Helena studies the floorboards and announces as she sits down: "I don't know why you don't put a little felt on the bottom of the chair legs to stop these dreadful scratches on your floor. . . ." Matilde pulls her chair in—slowly, closer to the table, with a long screech—and picks up her knife and fork without so much as a word.

"This sausage is better than the last time you made it, but it could still do with something—yes—I would definitely add a little caraway, and perhaps a good shake of nutmeg. . . ." Helena lifts her chin slightly and narrows her eyes to a creative squint, the way she does when she talks about colors, travel, music or flavors. But Matilde ignores it all and starts clearing the table before her sister's even finished her meal—scraping the other untouched sausage into a container for the fridge and clanging the dishes loudly at the sink.

I'm glad to escape the one-sided conversation that seems to change the oxygen-to-nitrogen ratio in the dining-room air, with the excuse of taking Rick's plate of dinner up to him in his flat.

"It's an especially good dinner because of Helena's first-Wednesday visit, but it's pretty tense down there tonight," I tell Rick, plonking into the Jason recliner next to his TV. "I don't get it. If I had a sister, I'd just be nice to her and make sure we had fun together."

"Reckon you would too," says Rick, getting a beer from his fridge. "But some sorts of people . . . no matter what . . . they can't manage to have fun together."

"What sorts of people?"

"Sometimes the ones who have shared a hard past, Al. It kind of thickens the membranes that separate them."

"What do you mean?" I ask.

"Well"—Rick takes a swig—"you know that Matilde and Helena survived the war together, right? But what you mightn't know is that they were the only ones in their whole family who did. . . . I have to remind myself about that sometimes." Rick has a look like he's suffered too.

"When the war finished and they finally made it all the way home, they found out they'd lost everyone: their mother and father; their little sister, Elsa; their aunts, uncles, cousins, the lot. Those two women can busy themselves with their separate lives and distractions, but whenever they get together that's the sad truth of things . . . looking them square in the face." Rick's going for another beer.

"But wouldn't that just make you feel closer to each other, Rick—you know, because you went through all that, the same stuff, and you survived it together *and you're the only two left*. Shouldn't you understand each other's sadness?"

"It doesn't always work that way, Al," Rick says quietly, tapping the side of his beer can. "Sometimes you just can't bear each other's sadness on top of your own."

■ ■ ■

It's been three days now since I got the note to Robert Fuller, but when I've seen him on the bus each day since, he's looked more interested in playing corners and garter flicking than getting a reply to me to pass on to Lucinda.

That is, until this afternoon. Rob struts down the aisle from the back row, and while I'm talking to Annabel Renshaw, he casually drops his shoulder into me and lets an envelope slip from his hand onto the floor at my feet. Lucinda will be relieved . . . it has her name written on it in small scrawly letters.

Annabel Renshaw's thick eyebrows shoot high as I scoop up the envelope and stuff it into my bag. I continue on like that didn't happen, telling her about the runaway girls who leave messages on Whisky Wendy's back wall. Thankfully Annabel's sufficiently captivated by that story to be distracted away from asking what I just put into my bag. She says a quick "See ya—got to go to orchestra practice" and gets off at the next stop.

And later, at mine, there's Lucinda waiting with a Cherry Ripe and a Coke outside Dave's shop. She's been there every afternoon, looking hopeful, then disappointed when I've stepped up empty-handed. But now she's beaming and mouths, "At last," as I hold up the envelope.

"Finally," she exhales.

"Yeah, finally," I reply, sharing her relief and a moment of preggers solidarity.

I wait in silence while Lucinda rips open the envelope.

"Rob's going to ditch school Friday and wants me to meet him . . . at lunchtime . . . when Mum's at work. He reckons it could be a bit tricky, but he's got a solution in mind. Ally, don't tell anyone, will you? You got to promise."

"Mum's the word," I assure Lucinda.

And so I learn exactly what it means to be a go-between, carrying notes for the next week between the girl who had everything and the boy who doesn't look at all like a dad, sneaking the odd peek at what each of them writes. They are counting on me—they need me, in fact—and while it's what Rick would call meddling and it's certainly against Matilde's rules, I feel my shadow solidify by being in on the plan.

CHAPTER TWENTY-TWO

LUCINDA LISTER IS MISSING.

The neighborhood kids are hanging out with her brother, Mark, now quiet in the garage, and their mothers are dropping off casseroles in CorningWare dishes and baked slices in Tupperware containers with quick awkward hugs for Mrs. Lister on her front porch.

And now Mrs. Lister has crossed the road; she is standing at our door. I can hear her telling Matilde that she wants to speak with me.

"Did she mention anything to you, *anything at all*, about plans to run away from home?" The flicks and wings in Mrs. Lister's hair have dropped, matching her expression, which is lank and lifeless. She's out of the crocheted pantsuit and into a gabardine skirt and flat navy espadrilles. I don't know where to look. She's staring straight into my face, hard and unflinching, a lioness hungry for morsels of information about her cub.

"Allegra was forbidden to have any contact with your daughter," announces Matilde, as though that's a perfectly reasonable thing to say. "I don't think my granddaughter can help you." She is obviously offending Mrs. Lister but thankfully saving me from having to lie or, worse still, confess that I was a go-between. "Perhaps if Lucinda is missing, you should contact the police," continues Matilde, matter-of-fact.

"That was my next step," responds Mrs. Lister sharply. "But I wanted to check with Lucinda's friends and the neighbors first. Most of them have been very helpful, but clearly that's not the case here." She marches off, heading back down the path, but stops at the gate, fuming. She turns around and lobs squarely at Matilde: "I don't think with your family history, Mrs. Kaldor, that you, *of all people*, have any right to sit up there on that high horse."

If I had the saliva to speak right now, I'd ask Matilde what family history Mrs. Lister is talking about. Instead that part of my heart that writes a vocab list for my brain is sending up a whole lot of M words: Meddling, Meeting, Mum's the word, Missing and . . . My fault.

Less than an hour later, a police car pulls up outside the Lucky house. The garage clears of teenagers, the porch clears of mothers, and my heart is trying to pull back from its nervous canter to a keeping-it-under-control trot. I can't say anything to Matilde. She would be *beyond* livid if she knew I'd had any contact with *that Lister girl*—and worse still, that

I might have actually played a part in her going missing. Instead I wait for Rick's van to arrive after work and follow him up to his flat.

"Why the gloomy face, Al Pal?" says Rick, looking like he's had a good day.

"I need to tell you something."

"Really? This sounds serious."

"It is pretty serious—I think."

"Well, come on in, Al, step into my office, pull up a chair."

Sitting at Rick's Formica table, I shake my head no to the can of Passiona he offers and the handful of beer nuts he holds out with a ready-to-listen grin. Instead I go on to explain that over the past week Lucinda had been dropping off envelopes for me in Joy's letterbox and that I'd been passing them on to her boyfriend, Rob Fuller, the guy on the school bus who's—"you know—the father of her baby." I tell Rick that they needed my help to get the notes to each other because Lucinda's mother had her on a tight leash, like a dog, and she wouldn't let them have any contact, not even over the phone, ever since Lucinda got preggers.

"I was their go-between, if you know what that is, because they couldn't see each other face to face. I was the one in the middle passing their notes back and forth, just helping them a bit, so they could sort everything out. And I know I shouldn't have been a meddler, Rick, but I read the last note, the one from Rob right before Lucinda went missing."

"Hold on . . . when did Lucinda go missing?" Rick looks up midnut, surprised. Worried surprised, not good surprised.

"Her mother found out she'd gone yesterday morning, but I know that she left the night before because they were meeting down at the beach . . . down there at midnight."

"*Crikey*, Al. She went to the beach on her own *at midnight?* How old is this girl?"

"Fourteen. Going on fifteen," I assure him, but as I look at Rick's expression, that doesn't seem so old anymore, even to me.

"Anyway . . . Rob's dad is standing for council elections and he said that if his parents found out about Lucinda having a baby, they'd *kill* Rob, because any sort of scandal would kill his father's chances of ever becoming mayor. Rob got the money together so they could travel to Canberra and Lucinda could have this thing called an abortion. Do you know what that is, Rick . . . the *abortion* thing?"

"Yes, Al," says Rick, looking down at his thongs. Then, giving up on the nuts altogether, he says, "I do know what that is. *So* . . . how long ago was all this?"

"They were going to leave early yesterday morning, but then Lucinda found out that her mum was taking the day off work, and she wanted somewhere to stay the night before they left, after they met at the beach, so she could still get away early. I told Lucinda about Whisky Wendy's, and that she helped girls in trouble, but I told her not to tell Wendy that she'd found out about her place from me. They were meant to be back on Wednesday night, and now it's Thursday night and Mrs. Lister is going mental."

"You have to tell Mrs. Lister, Al . . . you have to tell her everything you know. It's a bloody shame you got involved with this . . . *jeeez, Al.*" Rick is rubbing his fists along his thighs toward his knees. "I should never have taken you to Wendy's."

"It's not your fault, Rick."

"Well, maybe not, but that's not how *someone's* going to see it."

"Who? Matilde?"

"Don't worry about that now. C'mon, we need to get you across the road to speak with Mrs. Lister."

■ ■ ■

All hell has broken loose.

Mrs. Lister listened quietly at first, taking everything in and offering me a second Monte Carlo biscuit as Rick and I sat side by side on the white cane settee in their swirly-yellow-wallpapered sunroom and I coughed up all I knew about Lucinda and Rob's plans to have the abortion thing. But then, when Rick said, "That about sums it up; we'd better push off," Mrs. Lister chucked a complete mental, and now she's following us back across the road to Number 23—Cyclone Tracy at our heels—this time demanding to see Matilde.

"Forbidden to have any contact with my daughter! Really . . . *Really!*" Mrs. Lister is wild-eyed and yelling at Matilde, who has come to the door with her apron half off and her mouth fully agape, trying to make sense of the stormy outburst.

"So how do you now explain that your *perfect little*

granddaughter organized for Lucinda to have an abortion? Yes, that's right—you heard me correctly—an abortion! *The hide of her! The hide of you!*"

"Now, c'mon, Tracy, that's stretching the truth a bit. . . ." Rick is working hard to secure things to the ground. "Al didn't organize an abortion; she was just passing notes between Lucinda and her boyfriend."

"It was more than that, Rick—you heard it yourself. She organized for Lucinda to stay at some *den of iniquity* . . . overnight! *Whisky Wendy's, for the love of God!* Hiding my daughter from me, so she could be spirited away, and now she's gone to Canberra with that imbecile . . . for an abortion!" Mrs. Lister looks like she's about to suck up all the tessellated tiles on our front porch, blow off the roof and scatter our garden furniture three streets away. It's hard to picture Matilde's expression in the wake of all this: I can't bring myself to look anywhere near my grandmother's direction. But no doubt she's shocked. She's *disgusted*—knowing this time for certain that her perfect granddaughter is a Riffraff.

"If she ends up dead like Belinda . . . *Christ Almighty*"— Mrs. Lister moves to a Category Five—"your family will have *not one but two deaths on their heads!*"

The barometric pressure in my heart plunges. For one elongated moment things go strangely calm and my ears feel full of cotton wool. I'm no longer hearing the fury around me; I'm pulled into the eye of the storm. There's no sound, no gusts, no squalls. But then—*bang*—I'm surrounded by the eyewall and circled by a ring of severe weather. The cyclone reintensifies, unleashing a lashing for all in its path.

"Go inside, Al. Now . . . *GO!*" Rick's voice breaks through, giving an in-case-of-emergency instruction.

I run to my room, slam the door shut and slide in under my bed.

I want to take cover. I want to take cover here in this dark space forever.

What have I done? Something bad? Is it something very bad? Have I maybe killed Lucinda Lister? Why was Mrs. Lister saying . . . "dead like Belinda"? What did my family do? How did my mother die? According to Mrs. Lister, that's on my family's head. . . . Is it on my head too?

I nudge up against something hard. It's the box of Mother's Day stall gifts from the past seven years, sitting under my bed and pretty much forgotten from one year to the next. I'm wishing more than ever that they'd had a destination other than here in the dark collecting dust in a box. I wish they'd been given to *an alive mother*, unwrapped with a pretty-mum smile and gratefully received with a warm hug. Not kept for a dead mother, a dead mother like mine.

The silver figurine of the mother angel holding a baby is at the top of the box. *A Mother's Love Is Forever.* I'm holding it tight and hoping that's true, but I'm thinking that if the death of my mother is on my head, then I'm no angel, that's for sure, and maybe there's no forever either, and I am definitely, completely and utterly unlovable.

"Allegra!" Matilde is back in the house, calling down the corridor and into the kitchen. "Allegra, where are you?"

"Al." Rick is somewhere out the back. "C'mon, Al, we need to talk."

They can keep calling all they like. I don't want to talk. I don't want to listen. I'm staying here forever. I'm better off in the dark.

I move farther under the bed and feel my quilt hanging down on the wall side touching the floor; I loop it up and tuck it under the mattress all the way along and make a tight chenille hammock. I can hear Matilde and Rick both calling out the back now, their voices moving separately from near the chook shed, behind the compost bin and down the side path. I climb into my bed, roll across to the far side and down into my new hiding pouch. It's dark and suspended between the mattress and the wall. Matilde is still calling out my name, and now she has opened the door of my room and is looking under my bed. I'm invisible. Clutching the mother angel inside the chenille hammock, I can easily imagine what it's like inside a warm dark womb, yet to be born, a heartbeat other than my own giving me life, keeping me safe until I'm thrust into the world. I'm going to stay here. I'm going to sit out this cyclone, to the point where they'll be so planet-sized pleased to find me alive that they can't possibly stay shocked or disgusted. They'll just go back to loving me in their own weird and separate ways.

The mother angel is warming up; she's the same temperature as my hand. The mother angel has a pulse. It's faint but it's unquestionably there, and I can feel it pressing against my thumb. Some of its beats are short dots, some are long dashes, and now a pattern is emerging. Three short dots, three long dashes, three short dots again. It repeats over and over, again and again.

Matilde's voice is coming from the strangest direction now. . . . Her voice is coming from the other side of the fence, in at Number 25. For the first time in my whole life Matilde has actually gone through the brown gate and is talking very loudly to Joy:

At Joy.

"Well, if she's not here, where could she be? It's nine-thirty at night, and she is nowhere in the house or anywhere out the back; she has disappeared. And Joy . . . I blame you! Yes, I do, you! It is you and your crazy friends who have filled her head with all this women's-liberation nonsense and deceit and running away from home. . . . *You* have put Allegra in danger."

"I don't know what on earth you are talking about, Matilde. I would never put Ally in danger." Joy is clearly caught by surprise at this accusation but is firm with Matilde.

"Yes, Joy. Yes, once again you have done it—you have pushed a young girl to have an abortion. It must have been you who gave Allegra the idea to send Lucinda to that ridiculous Wendy woman."

"You are speaking complete rot, Matilde. I've done none of those things."

Matilde starts bellowing with a belting, blaming beat, "It wasn't enough for you to take Belinda, to take her from me, my only child . . . and her baby too."

The mother angel's pulse is getting stronger. The dots are definite, the dashes unmistakable.

"You are wrong, Matilde, and you are cruel. Harsh and cruel!" Joy's emotions are thickening the air in my hiding pouch. "You fabricated that explanation in your bitter head so you never had to face the facts. *You* pushed Belinda, you pushed her with *your* version of her future—her life was never her own. You made her feel that she had to make up for all the things you thought the world had deprived you of. You *made* her study medicine. She didn't want that; she just wanted to be with Ally." It would take hundreds of colored glass bottles to catch Joy's unleashed emotions now.

"You pushed and pushed Belinda until she felt she had no choice, and when she was pregnant again she just couldn't face the thought of your disappointment, your judging and your disdain. It was you, not me, who forced her to make the decision that led to her death."

"No! It was you!" Matilde is screaming. "You stole my only daughter and her unborn child. You killed them both. You deprived Allegra of her mother and a baby sibling."

My heart is punctured . . . BLAMED FOR BELINDA.

I picture the dirty labeled bottles hidden away under the bench in Joy's glasshouse. Is my dead mother on Joy's head? Matilde thinks so . . . and that's why she hates Joy. But I don't want to think that. I don't want to hate Joy. But I could have had an alive mother with a pretty-mum smile *and* an alive sibling, not be this kid on my own revolving around this angry adult world. Joy has bottled all that blame, but now she is blaming Matilde. Who is it? Who should be . . . *blamed for Belinda*? I love Joy and she loves me. I love Matilde and she loves me. I am their flesh and their hearts and their histories. They are my left side and my right side. I am their future.

I can't stand this. I can't stand this anymore. I can't stand this sadness throbbing inside my body, hurting my head and pounding my soul.

The mother angel is pulsing hard.

Three dots, three dashes, three dots.

She is sending me a message. What does the mother angel want me to do?

Three dots, three dashes, three dots.

"Stop! Stop, both of you!" It's Rick. My dad is in there with my grandmothers at Number 25. "First you don't bloody speak for years, and finally when you do . . . this crap! No wonder Al's shot through. You might like to remember where I fit in. It's my daughter who's missing, and I'm going to get on and find her."

For a moment that silences both of my grandmothers.

"Look," says Rick, sounding like he's taken in a deep breath. "She might be at Wendy's. She knows that Wendy helps girls in strife—maybe she's gone there."

"How on earth would Allegra know how to get there?" Matilde demands.

"She's been there with me—a couple of times," Rick confesses without remorse.

"What! She has been there to that crazy woman! You are both . . . both . . . *unbelievable*! Take me to this place, Rick, immediately. I need to get my daughter's only child." Matilde is demanding this of my dad. Joy is sobbing that she's going with them, to bring her granddaughter safely home. And before there could be time to catch any tears in little glass bottles, I hear the van doors slam and the sound of its motor whiz down the drive. I am alone in the dark with the mother angel and her offbeat pulse.

Three dots, three dashes, three dots.

She is pulsing harder now.

S . . . O . . . S

Save Our Souls

Three dots, three dashes, three dots.

She is feeling hotter now.

Three dots, three dashes, three dots.

What am I to do now?

Three dots, three dashes, three dots.

S . . . O . . . S

Smash Our Sadness

The mother angel wants me to smash our sadness. I have to smash those dirty labeled bottles. I have to smash Joy's emotions and Matilde's bottled-up anger. I have to smash it all. . . . I have to smash BLAMED FOR BELINDA.

■ ■ ■

Simone de Beauvoir pops up from her pond as the mother angel and I burst through the brown gate. She follows us into Joy's glasshouse. I work hard at the cupboard under the sink until it springs open, revealing the thirty-two bottles labeled BLAMED FOR BELINDA. And now the mother angel is swinging at the bottles, swinging hard, smashing them one at a time in all directions, spraying colored glass and tears and emotions into the air. They are all over the walls, dripping down the windows and shattered across the floor.

DEVASTATION, the mother angel decides, has to be smashed too. There it is high up on the shelf, a whole row without a story, obscured by SELF-ACTUALIZATION.

And down it comes . . . *smash* . . . *smash* . . . *smash* . . . into a hundred tiny pieces.

DEVASTATION is released—*everywhere*—and now it is no-where.

The mother angel's pulse is quickening, but it no longer has a pattern. Dots and dashes, *daaash, dot,* dot, dashes and dots. It's pounding, missing beats, racing ahead as though it has an end in sight.

My muscles are weak, my flesh is hot and my bones feel old, achy and tired. My eyes aren't working the way they usually do. And now I am falling . . . *falling* . . . onto my knees . . . *falling* . . . onto my elbows . . . *falling* . . . onto the floor. The mother angel and I are lying on the linoleum surrounded by shattered glass and released emotions and bottled blame with Simone de Beauvoir coming in and out of focus nuzzled into the crook of my elbow.

"Hold on, Allegra, hold on," whispers Simone. "You can transcend this disequilibrium."

My heart flutters. It misses a beat. It races toward another . . . *and it stops.*

CHAPTER TWENTY-THREE

Something is pushing from behind my eyes, and after a couple of shoves they open against a heavy load. My mind tries to find the right channel. It lands on a fuzzy white room.

I'm floating on a bed in that white-room ocean. The outline of Matilde is at my side and a statue of Rick is on an outcrop by the window. There's a pulsing, a whooshing and a mid-range beeping. I want to call Matilde and Rick in, let them know I'm still on the surface, but the weight of outside wins out and pulls my eyelids down.

I have become a hot climate: a furnace hovering just above the earth, heating cold deserts and warming all oceans. My blood is a river of embers, my throat a burning pipe and my fiery fingers aflame.

Joy is a torch: a humming, singing, scorching torch, caressing and weeping white-light love.

Coming up again. It's dark now. I am alone. The room is

slightly aglow. A silver figurine is shimmering from the other side of the window. It's the mother angel. Her lips are moving; they are forming a heart shape. They are whispering now with the words coming toward me in engraved running writing.

A
Mother's   *A*
Love   *Mother's*   *A*
    Love   *Mother's*
        Love
        Is Forever

I want to follow the mother angel into the night.

But Patricia has arrived at the door, standing firm opposite the silvery window. She is a plaster mold but feels real in the room in flesh and blood and future. She is holding a book with blank pages and waves at the angel outside. The angel's smile sends back a million glass pieces from shattered bottles that light up the room. She speaks now in capital letters:

OUR SADNESS IS SMASHED

The sun is pushing out the last of the dark, the mother angel has gone and I'm here in the damp and cool. And with me, asleep in chairs either side of the bed, are Joy and Matilde. Rick is curled in a ball, anchoring my feet to the bed. We are all together in the one room.

"I'm thirsty," I say to no one in particular.

I don't have to choose between them: Joy and Matilde

have taken each of my hands. Rick is on his feet and reaching for a glass.

They are not livid or disgusted or looking at me as though I'm a Riffraff. But they have glistening eyes that seem to have gone back to loving me, in their separate ways, and in this small space they have no way of avoiding each other.

■ ■ ■

"Arrhythmia," says a man dressed like a doctor with a serious frown. "Her heart rhythm remains irregular; profoundly so, I'm afraid. Did she have a fever in the past week, or was she taking any medication?"

"No," reply Matilde, Joy and Rick all at once.

"Or was it ever suggested, when she was born, that she had any type of congenital heart defect?"

"Certainly not," clips Matilde as though that would be some fault on her part.

"She was born a picture of perfect health," Joy chimes in proudly.

"And she's been strong as an ox ever since," adds Rick.

"Well, it's a puzzle, especially in light of all that. And the fact she's been so unwell here for days." He takes the stethoscope from around his neck. "Mmmm . . . a bit of a mystery, really. Sometimes in young people it can be caused by an imbalance brought on by stress, but that's rare.

"Allegra, I'm just going to listen to your heart again. Is that all right with you?"

It takes some effort but I nod, and the doctor warms the

metal end of his stethoscope in his cupped hand and places it against my chest. I can see in his eyes as he listens that I'm still not right.

"There are medications we can try, but of course they come with side effects," he says, and I can tell by the looks on their faces, just the thought of that is giving Matilde, Joy and Rick side effects too.

"I'll write something up to start this afternoon and we'll see if that makes a difference. It might take a bit of trial and error. Meanwhile she'll need to stay in, with plenty of rest, at least for another week or so." The doctor takes the clipboard off the end of my bed and disappears into the corridor. I can't keep my eyes open any longer and sink back into a deep sleep.

■ ♦ ■

"Twisties for breakfast—that'll sort you right out." Patricia is here, really truly here. Not a cold plaster mold but my best-ever friend, with a pleased-to-be-here grin and hair smelling reassuringly of green-apple shampoo. She's telling me that she's managed to sneak in—and what's more, find me—before visiting hours have even begun.

"What time is it?" I ask, my eyes feeling crusty and voice husky.

"Almost six-thirty," she says. "In the morning, in case you're a bit muddled up. I came straight from Central Station; Mum put me in a cab as soon as the overnight train pulled in. Cost me a fiver; good thing I've been babysitting a bit lately. Mum and I were coming down from Armidale next week, but she said we could bring the trip forward by a few days after Wendy rang up and said you were real crook."

I take a Twistie from Patricia's outstretched hand but just hold it for now, saving it for later.

"So how are you feeling, Ally? Have to say you look all right!"

"Okay . . . I'm okay . . . better than before."

"Wendy told Mum your heart's buggered up. What happened?"

"Oh, it just kind of sped up and got out of beat. And it couldn't get back . . . into its beat. The doctor says it's something called arrhythmia. He's put me on some medicine. But it takes a while to start working."

"What made your heart get out of beat? You didn't bump into that chunderous Kimberly Linton, did you?" Patricia pulls a face, and the sight of her twinkling brown eyes rolling in toward each other in such a funny way warms up my chest and recharges my stomach. I eat my Twistie.

"Nah, it wasn't Kimberly. . . . I haven't seen her for ages, thank God. I was in Joy's glasshouse, with that mother angel I bought at the Mother's Day stall. Remember the silver statue, holding the baby girl?" And feeling the tent snugness of just Patricia and me alone in the white room, I take a chance and tell her something I would never dream of telling anyone else.

"It was pretty weird, Patricia—she wanted me to smash those BLAMED FOR BELINDA bottles, you know, the ones we found at the back of the cupboard the day we got the mulberry leaves for Simone. The mother angel wanted them smashed, she wanted me to get rid of them all."

"Jeez, Ally . . . a statue of an angel wanted you to smash bottles! That is weird. That is *very bloody weird.* Don't tell the doctors; they'll check you out of here and send you to the loony bin. But you know . . . *I kind of get it.*" Patricia hands me another Twistie. "Did you smash them all?"

"I think so. . . . I think she did it, mostly."

"Well, it was *always* weird, Ally. I don't mean you, I mean all those bottles full of Joy's tears, kept in that cupboard. You know what? They're better off smashed." Patricia dips into her calico bag and gets out a packet of playing cards. "Reckon you're not up to Spit, but do you want a game of Go Fish?"

"Okay, if you want," I say, pushing myself up with my elbows. Patricia sits cross-legged at the end of my bed and deals us seven cards each. "Does Joy know her bottles were smashed?"

"I don't know. She left with Rick and Matilde to go off to Wendy's looking for me. It was pretty late; I don't remember what happened after the bottles were smashed. I just woke up here."

"Do you have any threes?" asks Patricia, looking up briefly from her cards, then back down. "Why were they looking for you at Wendy's? And why were those three even together? I thought they didn't speak to each other."

"Go fish," I say, and I tell Patricia about Lucinda Lister going missing and her mother going mental and blaming

Matilde *and maybe me* for Lucinda *and, get this* . . . the death of Belinda. And Matilde going mental and blaming Joy for me going missing and the death of Belinda and—*guess what?*—my brother or sister too.

"Do you have any queens?" asks Patricia.

"Go fish," I say, and I tell her about Joy blaming Matilde for the death of Belinda *and maybe Lucinda too* and Rick blaming them both for me going missing *while all along* I was hiding in a pouch I'd made with my quilt along the wall side of my bed. I tell her that I could hear all the blame and sadness and pain that they'd bottled up for years, that was out now, out and being hurled around like a weapon.

"Do you have any aces?" I ask Patricia, and then I tell her that the mother angel heated right up in my hand and sent me a message with her hot beating pulse; it was completely clear, just like Morse code. She wanted me to take her to the BLAMED FOR BELINDA bottles and smash all our sadness and set free the emotions that had been bottled and labeled and stored away in the glasshouse but were still there in the air at Number 23—and Number 25—and even in Rick's flat, Every. Single. Day. And it was there too in their nonspeaking language, pulling me and pushing me, until it burst out into the world with a whole lot of yelling.

"Jeez, Ally . . . that's enough to bugger up anyone's heart." Patricia passes me two aces. She brings over my water glass and holds the straw while I take a long sip. I lay my cards down and rest back against the pillow, feeling exhausted.

"Reckon you don't so much need medicine, Ally," says Patricia gently, gathering up my cards. "You just need your mob to settle their score and stop revving you up with all their own stuff."

•••

I doze on and off for the rest of the day. Each time I wake Patricia is still there. Sometimes she's playing cards by herself on the floor—Concentration—sometimes she's curled up in the chair by the window, working on something that looks like patchwork, and sometimes she's sitting at the end of my bed smelling the same and looking reliable.

I dream of the mother angel.

She's holding a cherub—it's me—with a birthmark on my pudgy left wrist. She tells me the birthmark is on precisely that spot because it's where she has kissed me one thousand times. It's her mark of love, not a stain of someone else's pain.

Now the mother angel is swimming in a rock pool and I'm on her shining-shell back. Her arms are moving through the clear water. Against the sandy bottom I see she has flipper-fins rather than hands. She tells me not to be afraid of the waves or the current or the deep waters below. She urges me to take in all the fresh air I need before I dive down, and to make sure to exhale the old air powerfully when I surface again because by then it's no longer nourishing my cells.

And the mother angel sings my soul a song.

Inspire, expire, inspire, expire
Balance yourself, Ally

251

Drawing from within
Expel this expired disequilibrium.

St. Liberata is playing her lute while the mother angel, wearing white robes, is brushing my hair with long tender strokes. She hands me the brush, and herself as a statue, and kisses my birthmark again, more than twelve times.

Her lips press against my pulse and beat out a message. But it's different this time, not Chaotic or Confused: it's Calming, Confirming and Clear.

S . . . O . . . S
you have
Saved Our Souls
by
Smashing Our Sadness
now
Sing . . . Our . . . Song
Ally
Sing . . . Our . . . Song
Tell them, Ally, tell them that your soul has a song to sing.

• • •

Joy, Rick and Matilde come into the room with different versions of what might bring a heart back into beat. Rick is holding a jar full of air from Bondi Beach and a parcel of hot chips. As he hands me a second chip—salty and warm, dipped in tomato sauce—Joy insists on a few sips of lemon myrtle tea from her old silver thermos and places a large red and green bloodstone crystal onto my chest. Matilde has prepared her liver dumpling soup, which quite frankly has never been a favorite of mine. She's bringing a third spoonful up toward my mouth when Sister Josepha arrives and saves me from having to swallow any more of the livery mush. She has brought a scapular of St. John of God, the patron saint of cardiac problems, *apparently*. She leans me forward and positions it around my neck, with one piece of cloth sitting above my heart and the other hanging down my back.

Despite their fussing over me, everyone seems pleased to see Patricia sitting cross-legged in the corner of the room. And they're all there together when the doctor arrives. He scans the scene, and my chart, and sets up his stethoscope to once again listen to my heart. He looks up and announces, sounding quite disappointed, "I'm afraid the medication isn't doing what I'd hoped. We'll have to try something else, perhaps even surgery. I'll confer with my colleagues. We'll speak again tomorrow." Joy gives a small gasp and Sister Josepha bows her head and gently closes her eyes.

"That won't work either," blurts Patricia, moving forward from behind the adults.

"I beg your pardon?" says the doctor.

"You can try anything you like, but none of it's going to work."

In the split second it takes for the doctor to settle his stethoscope back into his pocket, his bearing changes from capable-professional-in-charge to bowled-over-bloody-astonishment. He's staring at Patricia, who is less than two-thirds his size, and she returns his gaze with a bold certainty before she continues, "Her heart's all out of whack because of her mob, this lot in here, and all their stuff they load up onto her."

While the adults look around at each other, Patricia comes in close and mouths at me: *If you can ride a wave, you can climb a tree, and if you can climb that mulberry tree, you can do this. Go on, Ally . . . tell them.*

My pulse slows down and I'm sucked into the vacuum that Patricia has created. It's a void, a free space, a chance for my heart to find its own rhythm. And there it settles to a steady beat.

And I tell them.

"It's not enough that you all love me. Not anymore. *Please . . .* you have to stop hating each other."

· · ·

She introduces herself as Stephanie and tells me she's *What's Called a Social Worker.*

"Do you mind if we have a little chat, Allegra?" she asks.

"No . . . that's all right," I say, partly because she seems kind of nice but mostly because I'm stuck in this bed and Stephanie with her big forehead, hoop earrings and multi-colored panel skirt is standing between it and the door.

She pulls a chair in close and with a friendly smile, but awful breath, asks me if I like school, play any sport, and whether I've seen *Picnic at Hanging Rock* at the pictures? I answer *Yes, No* and *No.*

She's seen *Picnic at Hanging Rock*—just last week—and she tells me, her large hazel eyes framed by clumping mascara, "It was beautiful, with lovely scenery and haunting music, but I found it really quite *spooky*." Then she asks, as though we're friends in the playground, "What's your favorite movie you've ever seen at the pictures?"

"I don't have one," I say. "I don't really go to the pictures." She seems a bit disappointed by that answer and says, "What about telly then? What's your favorite show?" I explain that we don't have a television set at Number 23 so I can't help her there either, and I'm starting to wonder what a social worker is, exactly. But before she can fire another question at me, I tell her that I have been to the Opera House, to see a ballet called *Onegin* for my twelfth birthday, with my grandmother Matilde.

"Lucky you," she says, sounding a bit too enthusiastic. "That must have been wonderful. I've never seen anything at the Opera House. Is Matilde the grandma you live with?"

"Yeah, well I live in her house, I sleep there, but I go into Joy's next door a lot too; she's my other grandmother. And Rick, that's my dad, he's out the back in his flat above the garage—of Matilde's house, not Joy's house, even though he lived there when he was little because he's actually Joy's son, not Matilde's son—but now he lives on Matilde's side of the fence."

"So how do you find that, Allegra?" asks Stephanie, who I'm guessing had a tuna sandwich for lunch. "Do you all get along?"

"Yeah . . . I get along with them all," I say.

"Oh, that's good. But do *they* get along with each other?" Maybe it was tuna with onion.

"They don't really need to get along with each other," I tell her, turning my head down and a little away from her line of bad breath so that now I'm facing the open window.

"Why not?" she asks.

"Because . . . well, they don't usually need to speak to each other. And if they do, they just give me the message and I take it between them."

"What sort of messages do you take between them, Allegra?" This Stephanie is pretty nosy.

"Just stuff, things they need to know . . . mostly about what each of them is doing with me, if they're taking me places, you know, on their own."

"So you're something of a go-between then, Allegra?"

How does Stephanie *What's Called a Social Worker* know about me being a go-between? Does she know about Lucinda Lister?

"How does that make you feel, Allegra?" she asks.

She should have said she's Stephanie *What's Called a Busybody.*

"Allegra?"

"I'm tired now," I tell her, and roll over onto my side, away from her stinky-breath questions.

CHAPTER TWENTY-FOUR

THE NURSES ARE DOING THEIR ROUNDS: A WHITE WHIRL OF chatting efficiency; medicating, observing and recording before dimming the lights, when Rick appears with messy wet hair "for just a quick visit."

He sits down in a chair at the side of my bed.

"Wanted to pop in on my way home from a surf and say good night, Al Pal."

But it seems like he's here for more than that. After a while he goes on to say, "And also, I wanted to tell you that Lucinda Lister is back home. I thought you'd like to know."

"Did she have the abortion thing?" I ask, looking down.

"I don't know about that. But she's home safely, so that's the main thing. I saw her leaving for school this morning in her uniform."

Rick seems relieved, and he knew that I'd be relieved too. And he's right. I am relieved to know that Lucinda is home, back with her mental mum and gone-away dad, and that our family doesn't have *two deaths on its head*.

And as though he's reading the other thoughts looping through my mind, Rick adds, "And those things Tracy Lister said . . . when she went right off. She had no right to blame you for the situation her daughter wound up in. That was never your fault, Al."

My dad takes my hand and holds it in his, just like it might be something breakable. He holds it for more than two-hundred-apple-pie. His hand is brown and broad and sits salty around mine, giving us both something to look at before he finally says, "Al, I want to talk to you . . . in an adult way."

I nod, still looking at Rick's hand.

"I know they sent the social worker in here to see you yesterday. She and the doctor spoke with me afterward about their take on things, on what might have landed you in such a bad way." Rick lets out a long breath, as though it's one he's held on to for a long while. "So it's probably about time I told you my take on things too.

"After your mum died, there was a whole lot of blaming that went on between Joy and Matilde—and between the two of them and me. We had different stories in our heads about what led to Belinda's death, whose fault it was. No matter what, we just couldn't take on each other's point of view, let alone each other's pain. So we were stuck. Stuck in our different corners, coping with being broken in our own different ways.

"But one thing we did have in common was you, Al." He squeezes my hand gently. "And while it was tough living bang-up against each other's anger and grief, we all dug in and we stayed where we were, to look after you. Because you were so little, Al . . . and you didn't have a mum." Rick looks so sad. "We weren't really doing it *together,* but none of us could have cared for you on our own, giving you everything you deserved . . . everything your mum and I had hoped to give you. Everything your grandmothers believed, in their *wisdom,* that you needed.

"We were all mad as hell at each other, Al, but we were mad about you, and we only ever wanted what was best for you."

The four chambers of my heart are pounding.

Rick and Belinda

Joy and Matilde

Lub dub—lub dub—lub dub—lub dub

My left side

My right side

Lub dub—lub dub

My upper atriums

My lower ventricles

Lub dub—lub dub

"There was this terrible tension between us, but we thought we were doing a good job keeping it from you. I guess we thought if we just didn't speak to each other, then you wouldn't pick up on it. But you were smarter than that. You *are* smarter than that. And I realize now that the way we did it hasn't been good. *It's been bloody unhealthy.* And it hasn't been fair to you, Al, not one bit fair."

It's sadder than sad seeing my strong dad with tears in his eyes. I want to comfort him, but I'm stuck too.

"The way you've had to circle around us and scoot between us, trying to keep things ticking along. Loving us equally and not taking sides. Carrying messages over the fence, from one house to the other, and up to my flat—back and forth—softening them up, making them less brittle. None of that was fair. We made you orbit around our separate adult worlds rather than us orbiting yours, as we should have done, in unison."

I want Rick to comfort me too.

Lub dub—lub dub

"And now it's making you sick, Al." Rick takes both our hands, mine inside his, up to his face. He wipes his wet cheekbones. *"We've bloody well made you sick."*

Lub dub—lub dub

"All of this should have been settled years ago, and I'm sorry, *so sorry,* that it wasn't. But I've got a plan, Al Pal. I'm going to fix this. I'm going to fix this, and I'm going to get you well."

Lub dub—lub dub

I picture those four chambers working separately, pumping hard for survival. Receiving blood—sending blood—receiving oxygen—sending oxygen. Each blood cell has been reddened, nourished and used, over the years of my life.

Lub dub—lub dub—lub dub—lub dub

And now that I'm starting to understand this poly-elliptical force squeezing my chest—with what my dad has shared through his tears in the hospital tonight—I know that my heart needs to pump with a rhythm of its own.

Lub dub—lub dub—lub dub—lub dub

And work hard to get rid of the waste.

CHAPTER TWENTY-FIVE

THREE DAYS ON AND EVERYTHING SMELLS LIKE LIFE RESUSCI-
tated outside of that hospital: the sprinkler-wet grass at
the side of the road, the sun-faded salty hot seats inside
Rick's van, even the petrol being pumped into our tank at
the Amoco station by a big-bellied man. We're on our way
up the coast, just my dad and me, his board and a tent in
the back and a lineup of surf tapes to play as we go.

I was in hospital for twenty-three days: one million, nine
hundred and eighty-seven thousand, two hundred apple
pie. And now that I'm out, with my heart settled down,
Rick's looking slightly older to me: older around the eyes,
the shoulders and jaw. It's older in a good way, in an *I'm taking charge* way . . . in a *Maybe he should be called Father every
now and again* way.

When the doctor came by my bed to say that the medication finally seemed to have stabilized things so there was

no need for surgery, and that he was happy for me to be discharged to go home, Joy was completely tickled pink. Matilde simply straightened her skirt and assumed the pose of a nurse ready to continue the routine and care at Number 23. But then Rick announced—just like he was the decision maker and Joy and Matilde *had no say in it at all*—that I wouldn't be going home yet because he was taking me up the coast for a bit of a break; a medicinal dose of sun, sand and sea.

After a few moments of table-tennis glances between the adults, they stepped into the corridor for a word, out of earshot—*my earshot*—and that part of my heart that shoots invisible arrows at targets on the backs of their heads fired a few as they walked out the door, hoping to stun Matilde into being less sharp, Joy less emotional, and Rick into sticking to his *Father* plan.

"What did you tell them, Rick—you know, what did you tell Joy and Matilde—when you spoke with them in the corridor outside my room in the hospital?" I ask now, rolling up the stiff window as Rick gets his driving eye in on the highway.

"It wasn't a long conversation, Al. I just told them *straight out* that I won't be bringing you home until they've made their peace with each other. Simple as that."

"Do you think they can actually do that, Rick?" I say, looking across at him. I'm pretty sure that they can't, and I'm feeling uneasy at the thought of never seeing my grandmothers again. Rick shifts in the seat and changes his grip on the steering wheel as though he's not so sure now either.

"I think it'd take a complete miracle for Joy and Matilde

to be at peace with each other," I say, but Rick says nothing, just keeps driving until he pushes in the *Morning of the Earth* soundtrack and hits play. A few songs along he turns up the volume of "Open Up Your Heart" to full bore.

There's no formula for happiness that's guaranteed
     to work
It all depends on how you treat your friends and
     how much you've been hurt
But it's a start, when you open up your heart
And try not to hide, what you feel inside
Just open up your heart

There's no dreamer who's ever dreamed, and seen it
     all come true
Takes a lot of time and breaks a lot of hearts, to see
     an idea through
And love's just a simple word, its truth is easily lost
And sorry's said so easily, nobody counts the cost

But it's a start, when you open up your heart
Give your love to others, they become your brothers
You open up your heart, come on, make a start
Try not to hide, what you feel inside
Just open up your heart

"Hang on, Al Pal, I'm pulling a U-ey!" Rick spins the van around at the traffic lights so that rather than heading north we're suddenly driving south.

"Where are we going now?" I ask.

"Just want to let Sister Josepha know we're going away for a while," says Rick.

"Sister Josepha? But she's not even my teacher anymore—she hasn't been all year."

"I know, Al," says Rick. "But if we're going to need a miracle for Joy and Matilde to make their peace, then Sister Josepha's probably our best shot."

Rick tells me to wait in the van while he ducks into the convent. "I won't be a tick," he says. He's there for about as long as a Monday-morning assembly and afterward walks out with Sister Josepha by his side, looking all signed up to pull off a miracle.

She's probably promised to petition the patron saint of grandmothers at each other's throats.

Sister comes to my window and says in a thanks-be-to-God voice, "I'm so pleased to see you up and well again, Allegra dear. Yes indeed, I can see all the color has come back into your cheeks." She pats my arm and then walks around to Rick's side as he climbs into the van. She closes the door for him and gives a small wave. As he starts up the engine, she follows through with a nunly nod—I fancy it's a nod of respect, and maybe one of recognition—she's looking at Rick like he might be related to that Jesus sitting on top of the convent telly: the one who could well be a surfie.

Heading north up the highway again, Rick seems pretty stuck on "Open Up Your Heart." He's set it on repeat, so it's coming at us through the dashboard, over and over. We listen in silence, and by the end of the fourth time the words are wearing a groove inside my head, and I'm getting a bit stuck on it too. It starts to strum the strings that bind my rib cage to my core and vibrates all the hairs on the back of my neck.

There's no formula for happiness that's guaranteed
to work
It all depends on how you treat your friends and
how much you've been hurt
But it's a start, when you open up your heart
And try not to hide, what you feel inside
Just open up your heart

Those strings loosen and lengthen and reach toward my dad across the bench seat of the van. Then *he* just opens right up and says, "Words make you think, Al . . . but music makes you feel." With his eyes straight ahead and his foot pressing harder to the floor, after a while he adds, "And when words fail, I reckon music speaks."

"Yeah . . . I know what you mean," I reply. "And it kind of gets the stuff above and below your mind to speak up more clearly too." Then something floats in from one of those places—a whispered suggestion taking hold as a question, "Do you think that self-knowledge is on the side of happiness, Rick?"

He takes his eyes off the road for half-an-apple-pie, and looks over at me, his expression puzzled but kind of impressed, as though he might have to work on his answer for a while yet.

We drive through the late afternoon and on past the

curtain of nightfall, an appetite starting to bite at us both. "I could eat the horse and chase the jockey," says Rick. I laugh at his joke and tell him I reckon I could do that too.

Just after the Bulahdelah Bends we stop at a petrol station for *a burger with the lot*, and Rick tells me, as though I'm a driver too, "Always pull over where the truckies are lined up, Al. They know where to stop for a decent feed, and they'll give you a hand if you need any help." He has beetroot juice dripping down his chin as he leans over the white paper wrapping on the hood of the van, polishing off the last bites of his burger. A truckie walks past and it's as if he's read Rick's script because he gives us a friendly "G'day . . . bloody good burgers, hey!" He looks like he's going inside to order three.

Back on the road I'm trying hard to stay awake and be a fit pal to ride shotgun with Rick, but I feel myself sinking, jerking gently, in and out of sleep. I stretch out across the seat with my head nudging Rick's thigh; gear changes, road noises and *Morning of the Earth* music soothe me and start to elongate time. Rick turns the music down slightly and I'm not sure how much longer we drive, but I wake up with the engine off and the seat entirely to myself.

"We'll catch a few z's here, Al," whispers Rick, covering me with a couple of towels. He climbs into the back and I sleep solidly in that van, way better than I did any night in the hospital.

I wake in the early light to Rick revving up the engine and we're heading off, up north again. "At this rate we'll be able to make it to the beach break just in time for Dawn

Patrol. You're going to love Crezzo, Al. It's pure magic out there."

The road becomes bushy at the sides and bumpy in the middle, and even though the beginnings of a salty sea breeze make Rick keen to speed up, he has to slow down to navigate around potholes and the odd fallen branch.

Then a sign announces CRESCENT HEAD, and after passing through a small town that has yet to begin its day, we pull up in a car park overlooking a sweeping curve of long sandy beach. It was well worth the drive. Perfect waves are rolling in rhythmically in neat lines, golden and glassy, each one with a frothy white trim. They are cooperating, not competing, and look ripe to be ridden. My dad is right: it really is pure magic out there.

I climb out of the van and am taking it all in with my eyes, nose and skin when Rick calls out, "Come here a sec, Al—I've got something for you. Over here, in the back of the van." Walking around, I join my dad as he gets out his board . . . and then another one, smaller in size. "I wanted to get you something special for your birthday next month, Al Pal, you know, because you're going to be a teenager and all," he says, kind of shy. "But I'm not good at choosing jewelry or girl stuff like that, so I was at a bit of a loss, then . . . well, I thought . . . your own board might be the ticket."

It's a McGrigor—*apparently*—and it sure is the ticket, a really good ticket. Way better than jewelry, and even better than those tickets to the ballet Matilde organized, though I certainly won't be telling her that.

We inspect the board together, and Rick points out its features: six foot ten, single fin, and believe it or not, although secondhand, only two small dings! I love the idea of my very own board, and I let my dad know, without any doubt, with a whopping tight hug. Then it hits me like a dumper wave: this ticket means riding the waves out there, in the surf, without Rick . . . *on my own.*

We each polish off a can of baked beans and share a Coke before pulling on our togs to start the climb down the large rocky cobblestones toward the water. Rick carries his board as well as mine and tells me to watch where I put my feet. We cut a left and walk across a footbridge to the sand. I'm pretty puffed. It's taken a lot out of me just to get here. My legs are shaky, and my chest feels kind of hollowed out and empty inside.

"You okay, Al?" says Rick.

"Yeah, I just feel a bit weak." I don't tell him, *And a lot nervous too.*

"That's not surprising; you were laid up in that hospital for more than three weeks. It's going to take us some time to get you strong again." He looks over at me and adds, "There's no rush. The waves have been working here forever; they're not going to stop anytime soon. Let's sit down here for a bit so you can get your breath."

And so we sit, for more than a bit, above the line that divides the wet and dry sand, and together we watch the waves. They're rolling in consistently and their rhythm is relaxing. From here they look gentle, but I know that within, they are strong. And I'm thinking that they are kind of like Rick: you can rely on them doing what they do, again and again.

I'm almost hypnotized staring at the sea. Everything seems static yet calmly changing. I dig my toes into the sand and massage the balls of my feet against the ancient grains. The sun is getting higher and warmer and I'm warming up with it.

"Starting to pick up, Al?"

"Yeah, beginning to."

"Can you smell that air coming in off the salt water?" says Rick, inhaling slowly. I follow his lead and breathe in the air. "You know what I reckon, Al? . . . The cure for everything is salt water. Yep, think about it: sweat, tears and the sea. They're all made up of salt water. The first two can pump out your pain and the last one—the sea—well, it washes it away."

My dad Rick seems to be turning into a *Father* and a philosopher.

"You know what, Al Pal, we don't need to jump in and ride these waves just yet. There's no hurry. If you look over to your right, that's the estuary where the river meets the ocean, and in behind there is Killick Creek. C'mon, follow me. We'll make our way over there and you can lie on the board till you get used to it . . . there's no swell to deal with there in the creek."

A few minutes later I'm lying facedown on my McGrigor in the calm channel of the clear creek. Rick is ahead of me, paddling slowly on his own board, and he tells me to hold on to his leg rope. He tows me along gently just out from the sandy shore, and in tandem we follow its line. I move slightly forward on my board so that my eyes are just above the water's surface, my chin dipping in and out and creating ripples from the board's tip. Tiny fish are darting back and forth below, just missing each other in a search for whatever tiny fish search for in their tiny-fish world. All sandy colored, they blend in perfectly with the shallow corrugated floor of the creek, and when I move my arm through the water to the bottom, scooping up and letting go of handfuls of sand, they are camouflaged completely. I wonder if those fish have feelings. Friends? A heart? I wonder if they know they are fish.

Rick points to little crabs just ahead, running sideways for refuge by the water's edge. They have different-colored shell houses that they bury along with themselves in response to our floating past. "Hermit crabs," says Rick, moving my attention away from the fish. Even little crabs need their safe houses.

My back is warm in the sun, my arms and shins are cool in the water, and right now I couldn't be more comfortable. I'm freshening and feeling a growing list of B words . . . Buoyant, Bolstered and Blissful.

"Let's have a quick dip in the surf before we set up camp," Rick suggests.

We leave our boards on the sand and wade out to dive under waist-high waves before Rick scoops my arms around his neck so I'm hanging on to his shoulders. He swims me out beyond the foaming break to the green-glazed surface with deep water below, and we float on our backs, spread out like starfish. The water inside me expands and I can't make out where the edges of my body end and where the sea begins. I feel like I go on forever.

"We'll catch a wave in," says Rick, noticing that my fingers have gone kind of pruney.

"How can we do that?" I ask. "We don't have our boards."

"We'll bodysurf in . . . I'll show you how. C'mon, up on my back." Rick swims us both to just behind the breaking waves and talks me through his bodysurfing technique.

"It's all about timing, Al. You've got to have patience to wait for the right wave. And position—you've got to be in the right spot when that right wave comes along. Righto, let's move to where we can stand up, and I'll give you a demo."

We swim in until our feet hit the bottom, and Rick says, "So once I pick my wave, I'm going to dive forward and make myself as rigid and streamlined as possible. I'll put all my weight on the hand of my outstretched arm and kick hard. I want to feel like I'm within the wave."

Rick lets a few waves go through, says they're a bit messy, but then he lines up a perky one with a promising blue face.

"Here comes a good 'un, Al . . . hang on tight . . . watch me now, right arm out front . . . here we goooo!"

We take off. It looks like half the wave is above us and half is below, and my father, Rick—the philosopher— becomes a flying fish with me on his back, and we are heading for shore.

CHAPTER TWENTY-SIX

RICK SETS UP OUR TENT ON THE HEADLAND BETWEEN TWO gum trees for shade and ties some rope from one trunk to the other to use as a line to hang out our wet things. He unpacks a blow-up mattress for me but says he's happy with his sleeping bag just down on the grass.

By now I'm really tired and go for a rest inside the tent. I wake sometime later to find Rick having a yarn and a beer with three men who had also set up camp. Two brothers, *apparently*, Glen and Matt and their dad, Darce. They're all busy waxing their boards.

"Here she is," says Rick, as though he might just have been talking about me. "This is my girl, Ally."

"G'day there, young lady," says Darce. "I hear from your dad that you've got your own board. A McGrigor to boot." He has a wide grin and lifts a big crocodile-skin hand to his mouth to take a swig of his beer. "Good on ya, Ally, we don't see many girls out there in the surf."

"Another coldie, Rick?" asks Matt.

"Nah, better not—thanks, mate," says Rick. "Al and I need to get on and get some supplies in town before the shops shut."

"Tell you what, if you pick up some spuds, we've got buckets of fish here for tucker," says Darce. "The flathead've been biting a bloody beauty and we're gonna cook 'em up on the fire tonight. We certainly can't eat 'em all, even with Fat Matt here to help, so you and little Alligator there are welcome to join us."

Glen, all brown and blonded up, flashes a white smile and a chipped front tooth while Fat Matt looks more puffed-up proud than embarrassed.

Rick and I take them up on their offer and get back from the shops with a big bag of spuds. We're greeted with a roaring fire ringed by beach chairs in the middle of the camp. Darce is gutting the fish, Matt and Glen are scaling them and I'm given the job of wrapping the potatoes in foil and pitching them carefully into the hot coals at the spots that Darce thinks will cook the perfect spud. Once the fire has settled, Darce carefully places parcels of foiled fish on the died-down flames and pokes them a few times. Then we wait for what will take, according to Glen, "no more than two beers" before it's done. "Possibly three," ups Darce. Rick only has one beer and I have a Coke—that's two in a day, Matilde would be livid—but I don't think her livid reaches out here under the stars in Crezzo.

The fish tastes smoky, slightly tinny, but delicious, and I lick the last of it off the foil as my spud cools down. The spud is burnt in parts on the skin but fluffy on the inside and golden all over thanks to the big dob of butter that Darce slaps on when I open mine up.

"Blokes' tucker, so we don't have a salad to serve ya, Alligator," says Darce. "But don't be too disappointed—we do have dessert."

He cuts five bananas longways through the skin and into the flesh with his penknife, stuffs bits of Old Gold chocolate into the slits, wraps the bananas with foil and places them on the hot embers that now look like way-off city lights. The bananas don't take long, and we each peel one and tuck in without speaking. As I finish the last of mine, I think for the second time that it really is a good thing that Matilde's livid doesn't reach out here, because she certainly wouldn't like to hear me tell Darce and his boys: "That's the best thing I've ever tasted in my whole entire life."

■ ■ ■

A golden sun is rising and Rick, Darce and the boys are paddling out together for Dawn Patrol. I'm taking it easy this morning, just watching from the beach.

After a while Fat Matt comes in, towels himself off and plonks himself down on the sand next to me.

"It's getting kind of messy out there," he says, sounding puffed. "Okay if I sit here for a bit?"

"Yeah, sure," I say, keeping my eyes on Rick out the back.

"I hear we've got something in common, Alligator," Matt says, on the friendly side of matter-of-fact. "Not the best thing, but something at least."

I look across at him, wondering what I might have in common with Fat Matt.

"Yeah . . . we've both lost our mums," he says, looking younger now that he's away from his big brother. "And your dad tells me we were exactly the same age. You were only three, just like me."

I nod, thinking, *Rick never actually told me I was only three.*

"But he said you're lucky enough to have two grans. That's cool."

"Did he say that? The lucky bit?" I'm kind of surprised that Rick would say that. *Think that.*

"Yeah, I'm pretty sure he said the lucky bit. My grans had both gone by the time my mum died. Would have been good to have had them around after we lost her."

A few waves later I ask Matt, "How did she die . . . your mum?"

"Cancer. Sixteen years ago now. And yours?"

"Actually, I'm not really sure. . . . I've never been told that part of the story."

"Probably time you asked, then," says Matt. "I'm sure your dad would tell you. He's a good bloke, your dad, and he seems like a pretty straightforward sort of fella."

"Yeah, he is. . . ."

"Probably do him good to talk about things while he's up here surfing in Crezzo. Hey, we'll give him a few extra beers tonight," says Matt, like I'll be in on the plan. "That can get a bloke talking. It'd be good for my dad too, to have a yarn. Get some stuff off his chest. We've got a tough job to do in the morning."

■ ■ ■

Later that evening we're all sitting around the campfire, and Rick's about five beers deep. He offered to cook dinner, and while the others just took it in their stride, it almost stopped me in mine: I've never known Rick to cook dinner before. I've never known Rick to cook anything at all.

I watched closely. Rick said no to a sixth beer, but he had two as he turned the steak and eggs, another with his food on his lap and two more sitting around the campfire yarning afterward. I lost count with Darce, but from what I could tell nothing came off his chest, except maybe a few rounds of a smoker's cough. Rick's chest seems to stay completely intact.

And now we're back in the tent, settled on top of our sleeping bags.

"Good night, Al," Rick says from down on the ground.

"Good night," I say, although I'm not really ready for sleep.

"Rick . . . ," I whisper. "You know how in the hospital you told me you had a story in your head . . . about what led to my mum's death? Well, I don't care if it's different from Matilde and Joy's. . . . Can you tell it to me now, your story about Belinda?"

I'm not sure if it's the beer, the dark tent or simply

because I'm almost a teenager now, but Rick does more talking in the next thirty minutes than he's done with me in the last thirteen years.

He says, "Okay then, Al, I'll give you my version of events. I reckon others might dispute it, but it's as close to the truth as I know it."

And his version of events from all those years ago goes like this:

"When I was eighteen, still living with Joy, I was deadset keen on the girl next door, Matilde's daughter, your mum . . . Belinda. She was beautiful, in every way—inside and out—with this fiery mind and crazy imagination."

It's a weird sort of warm thinking of Belinda on my side of the fence.

"She was creative too, Al, ace at drawing and painting and sculpting. She was always angling to use Joy's pottery wheel. It was kept in the glasshouse—before it was overrun by all those bloody bottles.

"Belinda spent hours at that wheel and would turn a flawless pot, then give it a little squeeze or a twist, so she made it what she called 'perfectly flawed.' She was delighted with imperfections . . . guess that's why she liked me." Rick pauses for a while before going on.

"She really wanted to go to art school once she finished the Leaving exams, but Matilde, well, she had other ideas. Your grandmother was hell-bent on Belinda going to uni and becoming a doctor, because that's what she was set to become herself, in Budapest, before the war got in the way."

So that's where the doctor thing comes from.

"Well, I almost put an end to that, because halfway through Belinda's last year at school we found out that you were on the way, Al. And this might be hard for you to hear . . . and I don't want you to take it the wrong way . . . but Matilde was fuming, she could barely speak to Belinda, and she couldn't even look at me. She wanted me as far off the scene as possible, to stay on my side of the fence."

Rick rolls over and I can see his outline facing me.

"But once you arrived, Al, you were this little package of love and potential, and Matilde's heart softened right up. In her eyes you were pretty much perfect. And Belinda, well, she fell in love the second you were born, when she reached for you with both hands and brought you in to her chest. You stayed there for months. Your mum couldn't stop gazing at your face, said it was like the sunrise: glorious and a little bit different every day."

I wish I could remember my mum's gazing face.

I wish I could hear her voice and listen to her words.

"Joy was mad about you too, of course. She and Matilde had been good friends over the years that they'd been neighbors, helping each other out because both of their husbands had failed them in one way or another. And now they had you, a granddaughter in common, to bind them to each other forever . . . only it didn't quite work out that way."

I just can't imagine my grandmothers as friends.

"Belinda did go to university to study med," says Rick. "I think she did that mostly because she couldn't disappoint

Matilde again. She threw herself into it and got some pretty good results too."

My mum was smart, smart just like me.

"But honestly, I think she would have preferred just to stay at home with you for a while, going at your pace and doing her art thing."

I bet Belinda had a pretty-mum smile.

"We moved into the flat above Matilde's garage—your mum, you and me—and Matilde kept a desk in Number 23 for Belinda so she could study. Matilde and Joy cared for you during the day while Belinda was at uni and I was at work. I focused on that, bringing the money in. I'm not proud that after your mum died some of it went out again placing bets, which didn't impress Matilde because her husband ruined himself through gambling, but I'm getting on top of that now."

So that's why Matilde thinks she has to pay for everything.

"Joy and Belinda were pretty close. Belinda was the daughter Joy had always wanted, with the bonus of bringing a baby girl into her world. They pottered and planned and spoke about things Belinda would never talk about with her own mother."

There are certainly things I'd never talk about with Matilde.

"And despite it all, Belinda and Matilde were close too, in that way that mothers and daughters can be, especially when a baby links them together."

Rick rolls onto his back. "Then something bad happened, Al. When you were about three. Belinda didn't tell me, but she found out she was pregnant again. I wish like hell that she'd told me, because we would have got through it together—I'm sure we could have survived it."

And I wouldn't just be this one girl on my own. I'd have a brother or sister too.

"But she just couldn't face Matilde, not again, because by then Matilde was telling anyone who'd listen that her daughter Belinda was more than halfway through her medical degree. So Belinda confided in Joy instead. She told Joy that she felt herself sinking, that she just couldn't be a mother of *two* children, as well as finish her degree, and work as a doctor, she didn't feel ready, and she didn't think Matilde would cope with another disappointment and blow to her plans.

"And Joy didn't tell me at the time, but she was worried that Belinda was headed for a breakdown, and she was worried about what that would mean for you, and for me. So she helped find a place, a clinic in Bondi with proper doctors where she could be 'fixed,' and she gave her the money for the operation.

"It was the abortion thing, Al, like Lucinda, but I was completely left out of the plan." Rick's voice is shaky now, and I'm feeling a bit shaky too. "Joy took Belinda to the clinic after I left for work one day and picked her up once it was over. I came home in the afternoon and found Belinda resting 'with a headache.' By the next morning she was doubled up in pain on the bathroom floor.

"Then she started screaming; she told me, *'Just get Joy.'* I ran into Number 25 and once Joy got there, she told me the truth about what had gone on and we took Belinda back to the clinic. But they didn't want to know about it, not now that there were 'complications.' I wanted to go to the hospital there and then, Al, but Belinda was hysterical, said they'd call the police, and she was terrified that Matilde would find out as well, so she insisted that we just go back home.

"She had a really rough night, and the next day she was pale and shaking and all burning up. I put my foot down then. Just carried her to the van and got her to hospital . . . but it was too late."

Behold My Mother.

"They said she had an infection, a thing called septic shock. . . .

"She died a couple of hours later."

My mother angel.

"So, Al, that's why you don't have a mum. And it's why everyone left behind has been hurting and blaming. It's why Matilde, in that clamped-up taut way of hers, hates Joy—she blames Joy for taking Belinda to the clinic where she had the procedure that led to her death. And Joy, well, she's mad at Matilde for the pressure she put on Belinda that meant she felt she had no other option, and she's sick-sad that Matilde blames her.

"But I can see it behind Joy's eyes—in that forced-happy face—that she does blame herself to an extent for what happened. And while I've tried not to blame her too—and the way she cut me out, gave me no say in what happened—that's been hard over the years. And if the truth be known, on some level, Al, Joy blames me for Belinda dying after being pregnant again. And I . . . I blame myself too."

Rick stops. His words hang with a sad weight in the tent.

My mother angel wanted all that sadness smashed.

I roll off my air mattress and lie on the ground next to my dad.

The cool earth vibrates beneath me.

I'm neutralized.

Soothed and strangely energized.

I can't see or hear my mother, but I feel her.

I put my arm over Rick's chest; to comfort him, and that comforts me.

My mother angel wants my soul to sing our song.

"I don't blame you, Rick," I say for her, and I say for me. "And I don't blame Joy, and I don't blame Matilde. And I can tell you, Belinda doesn't blame any of you either."

Our breathing falls into sync.

"If you forgive yourselves," I whisper with our next falling breath, "then maybe you can forgive each other."

We inhale the salty air.

"There's a huge lot of good in you, Al," Rick says. "Just like your mum. And you should know . . . despite it all, I do see the good in your grandmothers too. You've got the best parts of each one of them."

I really love hearing my dad saying that.

"I want to be like you too, Rick," I tell him.

"My Al Pal," he says, putting me under his wing.

The chambers of my heart open up to each other.

My *good self* is reaching toward ready.

Ready to be charged by the best parts of all four.

Able now to become me.

■ ■ ■

There is a shadow outside our tent. It's sticklike and moving, prodding me out of a rock-solid sleep. Rick is lying still on the ground next to me, snoring gently, unaware that the walls of our tent are breathing in and breathing out. But I'm aware, and know without doubt that they are definitely moving in response to the motion of the stick shadow on the other side of the canvas.

It comes in closer and now I see it's more of a baton than a stick, and it's bringing up the beginnings of the twilight before sunrise. It's tuning up the day: the waves and the breeze. I hear low oboe murmurs from the other side of the campfire, where Darce, Matt and Glen have been sleeping in their tents.

The murmurs become more—they join the morning song—each one with a frequency, a voice and a rhythm and it's then that I recognize the first bars of Franz Liszt's "On Lake Wallenstadt." Nature's orchestra is playing out as a melody in my mind. I open the slit of our tent just wide enough to see the boys and their dad silently moving with their boards on their heads. They must be doing a *Pre-Dawn* Patrol.

I watch from the headland as the three of them climb down the still-dark rocks. In a straight line they launch themselves onto their boards and paddle across a border of small breaking waves.

They are the first out and into the clear water, even before anyone else has appeared on the beach. But they are not interested in positioning themselves to ride the pristine morning waves. Instead, once out the back they sit up, straddling their boards with their feet in the water. In the lifting light I see them orient themselves toward the horizon and then link their strong arms.

After some time, Darce pulls a small flask from his board shorts and holds it up to the sky. Together their gaze follows a cloud of ash that Darce releases into the air before it drops gently onto the sea. They bow their heads and sit silently surrounded by a circle of ash, now floating on the water. It seems to mean something to all of them . . . be something of all of them . . . and nothing to do with me. I go back to our tent and lie down on my sleeping bag next to my dad.

I don't know why Franz Liszt woke me to witness this private mystery, and I'm not fully sure of what I've just seen, but that part of my heart that beats by baton, and ritual, tells me that it was connected to something quite sacred, and a tune everlasting.

■ ■ ■

"Hey, Alligator, you gonna stand up on that McGrigor today?" Darce calls out to me from his car window as I get my togs off the line. "Reckon today might be as good a day as any," he adds, egging me on. He's obviously noticed that for the past six mornings I've paddled out behind Rick on my board but only caught the whitewash lying down rather than the green curves standing up.

Rick says that I'm doing "just fine," building up my strength with my paddling while learning a healthy respect for the ocean. But now, prompted by Darce, I'm feeling that today might be the day to change my position and spring up onto my feet.

"Got something here to fuel you up, young lady," says Darce. "I've been to the bakery and back while you were still in your *boudoir* getting your beauty sleep."

He pulls a loaf of white bread from a brown paper bag, tears it in two and passes me half. I copy what Darce does, dipping my hand into the warm softness within the brown crust, and then I down it with the carton of chocolate milk he lobs at me through his car window.

"If you want to surf like a bloke, Alligator, you don't need to be built like a bloke, but I reckon it's gonna help if you eat like a bloke," he says, scooping out another handful of warm bread with his big crocodile paw. I sure don't want to look like Darce, but I don't mind eating his version of blokes' food.

I follow Rick down onto the rocks this time, carrying my board on top of my head. *Today's the day, today's the day, today's the day,* my heart tells my feet as I hop from one rock to the next. "I'm going to go for it today, Rick . . . I'm going to stand up," I say, committing myself aloud so I won't wimp out. "Reckon you will, Al," he replies, pleased, like it's something he's been waiting to hear. "It's a good day for it too: there are nice breaks happening right along the beach and we can find a few waves all to ourselves."

He looks across my shoulder toward the ocean. "Surfing is a mix of battling against nature and going with it, Al," he explains. "You fight against the waves to get out, fight against gravity to stand up, then you harness the energy of the wave to ride it safely in to shore. And when you're trying to get to where you need to be, out the back before you surf in, just like in life, you don't need to take every wave head-on. Pick the ones you can push through and the ones that are best to duck under . . . like I taught you on the board paddling out the other day."

We walk along the sand till we get to the spot Rick thinks is just perfect. "See that rip, there to the right of the sandbar? We're going to use it to get ourselves out. Rips can be swimmers' enemies, Al Pal, but surfers' friends."

We paddle out. I'm tucked tightly in behind Rick until we're carried in the sandbar gutter by the pull of the rip. Once we finish our free ride, we paddle on farther, making our way out the back through the rolling crests. I push the rails of my board with my hands, and knee it down in the middle, to duck-dive under the oncoming waves. Rick nods at me like he knows I've been listening and beckons me over to him ahead in the clear water. This is a place where Rick likes to talk.

"Okay, Al, we're at the mercy of the ocean now; we can't control it so we've got to work with it and take what it gives us. It forces us to use all our senses and adapt quickly. Don't be scared, Al. Just be ready. Do you remember the day you popped up on the front of my board at Bondi?"

I tell him, "Yep, I'll never forget."

"You're going to do the same again, Al, only this time on your own, on your own McGrigor. And I'll be right behind you. But first you've got to pick the right wave, one with a solid blue face, and you've got to decide where you're going. Not knowing where you're going is dangerous for a surfer and anyone else nearby. You're going to use the energy of *your* wave, commit to it and give it back a good burst of your own energy too. Once you feel that wave grab you from behind, then spring up, get onto it, get into it—and whatever you do, Al, don't forget to lap up the joy."

I wait for my wave. I'll know it when it comes. I will see its face and it will recognize mine too.

And here it is
This is the one
I'm paddling hard and fast
If I can ride a wave, I can climb a tree
If I can stand up on my board on my own . . .
I can be free
I spring up
And then I'm standing—woohoo—I'm standing
My knees are bent
I'm staying low
Locked into the wave
I'm gliding-dancing-flying
Toward the shore
Suspended and held
By nature's hand

I go from not being able to do it, to not being able to stop. I catch wave after wave, losing count and all track of time. Rick can't wipe the smile off his face, and Darce and his boys watch from the rocks, cheering me on until they paddle out too and the five of us spend the rest of the day surfing together with them calling, "It's yours, Alligator!" at every good wave.

■ ■ ■

We're all pushing off in the morning, so Darce has planned a farewell feast.

"Chicken Honolulu, and I'm going to need you all involved in its preparation," he announces, picking up twigs for the fire. He gives us each a chicken breast in a plastic bag and tells us to pop it onto the middle of our camp chair and sit down on it *very slowly* and stay there for two beers, "Or in our young Alligator's case, two Cokes."

Once that's done and the chicken is flattened out, Darce places our squashed breasts on cheese slices that he's centered on large pieces of foil and then tops them with pineapple rings from a Golden Circle can. He wraps them up into foil parcels and, like he's done with every other meal he's cooked, pokes them into the embers of the hot fire.

"You're gonna love this one, Alligator," he says, beaming with confidence. I don't have the heart to tell him that I don't like cooked pineapple and probably won't like sat-on chicken either, especially if I end up with Fat Matt's breast that burst out the sides of his plastic bag and had to be peeled off the canvas chair. Blokes' food was good for a while, but suddenly I'm missing Matilde's beef goulash, spaetzle dumplings and fisherman's soup.

Darce slaps his cooked creations into hamburger buns and tells me, "Get your chops around that grub," which I do, mostly for his sake, while he watches on with a cook's anticipation, lighting up a smoke. Despite the cooked pineapple it tastes good, surprisingly good, and when Darce asks, "So what do ya reckon, Al?" I say, after a second bite, "Bloody delicious!" He unleashes such a big belly laugh that it becomes a croak, then a cough, then a whole-body wheeze. "There you go . . . you learned how to make chicken Honolulu . . . and you got out there and learned how to ride that McGrigor like the bloody Duke . . . all without traveling to Hawaii. What do you reckon, boys? Here's to our surfing Alligator," he says between deep wheezes.

Darce raises his beer, then quite a few more, until his eyes get red around the rims and watery in the middle. He tells Rick that meeting us on this trip was "bloody fantastic" and that this girl here—Alligator—"is every bit as good as a boy and in some ways a good deal better." He says that he'll never forget watching me learn to surf and that to do that straight out of bloody hospital was a gutsy bloody thing to witness. He raises another beer to Rick and says that he's "a great bastard, real persistent," and one of the best bloody dads he's ever seen in all his travels up and down the bloody coast. "Pardon my bloody French, Alligator . . . and here's to you again, young lady."

Glen suggests it might be time to turn in, but Darce says he's just got one more thing to say—to get off his chest—and that is, having kids is the best bloody thing that could ever happen to a bloke, and that even though he would have loved a daughter, he's been blessed to have three sons, and that it breaks his heart to see some bloody bastards not look after their kids because you never know what's round the bloody corner and when you might lose one and be left with nothing but ashes.

He says that losing their mum was "a big bloody blow," but that they did all right. "Didn't we, fellas? Four men, just on our own with me giving it a crack to be Mum and Dad. And I tell you what . . . you've made your old man bloody proud every bloody day, and at least my princess was spared from the worst blow of all . . . losing our Trev. . . ."

We all sit silently looking at the fire until Glen fills us in: "Our brother Trev died in a car accident eleven weeks ago."

"I'm very sorry to hear that, mate," says Rick.

We keep watching the fire.

"And now, now there's just . . . just the three of us," says Fat Matt, wiping a large tear away with his free hand.

Darce goes quiet and his bottom lip starts to tremble. He loses interest in his beer. Glen and Matt stand up and put a hand under each of his elbows, pull him out of his camp chair and say good night. They take Darce, each with an arm around his back, weeping quietly, off toward the direction of their tent.

That part of my heart that feels engorged with someone else's sorrow lifts me out of my camp chair and onto my feet.

I catch up with Darce, so I can tell him, in case I never get to see him again, "You're a good dad, Darce, and a good mum too. And a bloody great bloke."

I wrap my arms around his middle and rest my face against his smoky chest. His weeping becomes a whole-body wheeze, then a cough, then a croak, then a big belly laugh; and even though I shouldn't be doing all this swearing, I am kind of pleased that I have, because I think that tonight under the stars at Crezzo it might have just helped slightly reverse a situation.

■ ■

"Where are my mum's ashes?" I ask Rick as we get ready for our last night in the tent.

"She was buried, so there are no ashes, Al. She was buried in Waverley Cemetery. We could visit her grave when we get home, if you want to do that."

"Nah, not really," I say, climbing into my sleeping bag. "I just wish I could remember her face. Sometimes I think I do, but then when I zoom in it's just a mirage or something."

We're lying in the dark and after a while Rick says, "I've got something that might help you remember, Al. I brought it with me and was waiting for the right time." He gets up and starts rustling through his bag. "I'm sorry you can't see your mum, Al, I really am, and I'm sorry that the two of you can't ever have a good yarn, but I've got something here, so you can kind of smell her." Rick brings a plastic bottle to just under my nose and says, "Take a whiff, Al. Inhale your mum."

The smell is familiar and comforting and at once old and new. It ties loose strings from my long-ago memory to my more recent life. Happy strings which, tied together, make sense. The smell is green-apple shampoo. It's the smell of my best-ever friend, Patricia Faith O'Brien, and now my dad is telling me that it's my mum's smell too.

I inhale again and whisper to Rick, "I miss Patricia."

CHAPTER TWENTY-SEVEN

IT'S A LONG DRIVE HOME ON THE EXACT SAME ROAD THAT WE took to get up to Crezzo. I'm looking out the window and thinking about soon turning thirteen—*a teenager.* Some pockets inside me feel thirteen, but others feel more like thirty-two. It won't be the exact same me returning to Number 23, that's for sure. I'm suntanned for a start, and Rick reckons I might be a bit taller and that I'm definitely a good deal stronger. "You've got surfer's arms, Al, and I reckon you're starting to get surfer's abs." He gives me a soft prod in my side across the bench seat and looks kind of pleased with every bit of me.

And a surfer's presence in my head and direction in my feet, I say to myself, wondering if those things can ever be seen.

We stop at the petrol station at the Bulahdelah Bends for a "burger with the lot." On my way back to the van I walk past a truckie eating a burger on the benches by the bin and

I say, "G'day . . . bloody good burgers, hey!" He gives me a thumbs-up and a look like he'd be ready to help if I needed it. I'd better get all this swearing out of my system before I next see Matilde; she would never *pardon my French*. I start eating my burger alone over the hood because Rick says he needs to make a quick call from the phone booth inside the gas station, and once he's done that, and he's polished off his burger in seven big bites, we hit the road again, and I hit play on *Morning of the Earth*.

It's late afternoon when we finally slide down the drive-way of Number 23. Suddenly I realize how much I've missed home, and I can't wait to see Matilde and Joy. I leave Rick to unpack the van, and I run up the steps to the back porch and in through the kitchen door. I want to tell Matilde all about our trip . . . the places we've been, the cooking we've done, Darce, Matt and Glen . . . and my own McGrigor: well, maybe I won't tell her *everything;* I'll leave out the bits that would make her deadset livid.

But Number 23 is empty. Strangely, Matilde is not at home. I've never known Matilde not to be home in the late afternoon before. I go from room to room. The fridge is looking all but empty, the Singer is cold, and unfolded washing sits on top of the cane basket in the laundry. Then I see something that's so unusual, I double back to take a second look: Matilde's bed is unmade.

I go to the side fence, through the brown gate and weave past Joy's wind chimes into her kitchen. If my grandmothers still spoke to each other, then perhaps Matilde might have let Joy know where she was going; to the post office, or up to the shops. She might have asked if Joy would like something from Dave's or a lemon from Joe's. But I can't remember that ever happening, and here at Number 25 there is no sign of Joy either. Her teapot is cold, her sweeties jar is empty and her bed is also unmade—though I have to admit that's not so unusual.

There's one last place to look for Joy: the glasshouse. I'm kind of uncomfortable going to Joy's glasshouse, having left it a mess of smashed bottles last time I was there. I approach the door gingerly, and Simone de Beauvoir pops her head around the trunk of the magnolia tree. She looks happy to see me but just as uncertain as I am about the glasshouse door being opened again. She saunters over to be by my side and nuzzles into my left ankle.

I pick up Simone and together we open the door. There is no sign of Joy in the glasshouse and no sign of any of her emotions either. Instead, on the far side, under the glass window is a potter's wheel, and drying on the bench is a series of pots, in all shapes and sizes, with little twists and indentations.

There are glazed pots and vases too, in purples and greens, oranges, turquoise and reds, out as if on display. And glazed alphabet letters . . . I count them out: two As, two Es, two Ds, two Ns, an I, S, L, G and a B. On the windowsill nearby is a menagerie of small clay animals: rabbits, bears, ducks and whales—even a penny tortoise. Simone looks up at me, perhaps hungry and hoping for boiled lettuce, but it could be that she has a question: *Are you going to get to work and smash all of these too?*

"Allegra!" It's Matilde. She's calling me from over the fence. "Allegra," she calls again, with a levity and lilt that sound almost like love. I have for a long time suspected that Matilde cooks with love, mends with love and hovers with love, but she's never sounded like love . . . not before now.

"I'll see you again soon," I assure Simone, putting her down by the water-lily pond.

I pop back through the gate and into Matilde's open arms. Today she even smells like love.

"I missed you, Matilde," I say, with my two arms around her back now long enough to touch on the other side: I have her completely encircled. Releasing slightly after a hug that she's actually returning, I realize that our eyes are now almost at the same level. So Rick is right, I have definitely grown, but it could also be that Matilde has shrunk.

"And I missed you, Allegra, I missed you very much." She seems to be pushing through feeling awkward to get to a warm place. "I didn't expect you back before dark." Matilde is wearing her gardening clothes and has a bucket at her feet filled with small spades, hand trowels and her Dutch hoe.

"Were you in the garden?" I say, a bit puzzled. "I didn't see you there before . . . before I went over to Joy's."

"Let me look at you again, Allegra. Yes, *yes*, I think that you have definitely grown to be taller," she replies, not responding to my question. "You must be hungry—it's past six o'clock. I haven't anything cooked, but still we will eat."

Even though Matilde's fridge is short on supplies, her pantry is—as it has been my whole life—full. Shelf after shelf is stockpiled with pickles and preserves, chutneys, relishes and jams, sauces and all varieties of bottled fruit. Throughout my childhood I've often wondered if Matilde was preparing for famine, a food strike or perhaps another world war. But right now all her harvesting, preserving and bottling means that on short notice she is prepared for dinner. By the time I've showered and changed, she is putting a colorful meal out on the table. It looks nothing like spuds wrapped in foil or chicken Honolulu, but I know it will be familiar, nutritious and completely delicious.

She sets down a large serving of sweet and sour summer pickle made up of cabbage, onions, purple peppers and carrots that she's scooped from a jar labeled CSALAMADE into her best porcelain bowl, the one with butterflies around the middle. Into smaller bowls with the same pattern she dishes up pickled gherkins, shredded beetroots and hard-boiled eggs. I don't think Darce and the boys would consider this good "blokes' food," but after weeks in hospital, and then up the coast, I'm looking forward to *getting my chops around Matilde's grub.*

"Here, Allegra, take this plate up to your father before we sit down," says Matilde, hanging her apron on the hook near the stove.

I catch a wave and hear myself say with a burst of *bátor,* "Maybe he'd like to eat with us down here."

Matilde lowers her eyelids for three-apple-pie and inhales. She lifts her head and slowly exhales. Then—*right there*—at that moment there is a shift. Matilde's head, heart and soul pull a U-ey and she says, "Well, because you are safely back home, yes, for tonight, you can invite him down here for dinner." She doesn't use Rick's name, but an invitation is an invitation.

I'm absolutely bowled-over *bloody* astonished. But of course I don't tell Matilde that—especially the "bloody" bit—and instead tell myself, *Just act cool, Ally, like it's perfectly normal that Rick should join us for dinner—at the same table—sitting down together—like a family.*

"Thanks, Matilde," I say, jumping up and running out the back door and up to Rick's flat before she has a smidge of a chance to change her mind.

"Are you sure she invited me, Al?" says Rick, standing at his door in a towel.

I'm about to sweeten it up, give it some oomph and say something like, *Absolutely, she suggested it right out of the blue, with a beaming smile, saying she'd be deadset delighted if you joined us for dinner,* but I stop myself and instead shoot for the truth and tell him exactly how it came about. "Well, I suggested it, but Matilde agreed, and an invitation is an invitation." I prod him in the ribs and add, "Please come, Rick. . . . Don't fob me off now."

That does the trick, and for the first time in my whole entire life, my dad, Rick, has a seat at our table.

CHAPTER TWENTY-EIGHT

I SLEEP IN LATE . . . THAT'S WHAT TEENAGERS DO, *APPARENTLY,* and I'm eight days off being thirteen. I'm surprised that at ten past eleven Matilde hasn't blasted me out of bed, calling me a lazing-bones-sleeping-head. I soon learn why; she isn't here. Matilde, it seems, has gone out, again. She has left breakfast prepared for me, though: liverwurst, tomato and cheeses, splayed out on a plate in the fridge.

"So you're awake," says Rick at the kitchen door. *"Finally,"* he adds with mock irritation. "Can you be ready in five, Al? You need to be somewhere."

"Where?" I say, spreading more liverwurst on a piece of rye bread. "Do I need my togs?"

"Not this time, Al Pal, not today."

I meet Rick by the van and we're off again to I don't know where. After a while it becomes obvious that we're heading in the direction of Glebe. "Are we going to Whisky Wendy's place?" I ask.

"Close, but no cigar," says Rick, whatever that means.

We pull up in a street not far from Wendy's. It's the one I went to with Rick a few months ago when St. Liberata signaled *It's time* to the women, who then burst into the run-down boarded-up house before Rick jumped out of the van and changed the locks. This house and the one next to it look slightly cleaner now, and both have WOMEN'S REFUGE painted down low in big orange letters across their front wall.

"Here we are," says Rick. "Remember this place?"

"Are we going in there?" I say, feeling puzzled.

"Not me, I won't be going in, Al—just you," says Rick, keeping an eye on the twin houses across the road. "Go on, out you get, and in you go."

I don't understand why we've come to this place again, and why I should be going in when last time Rick made me stay out, and why Rick now seems to be a whole lot of C words: Cagey, Concealing, Coaxing and quite frankly a Colossally Coy Carpenter.

I'm just one C word: Confused.

Rick toots the horn and the most amazing thing happens. Out from the twin house on the left skips—*actually runs*—my best-ever friend, Patricia Faith O'Brien! We reach each other in the middle of the road, and we hoot and hug and happily fall all over each other laughing. I'm engulfed by a whirl of reunion and a wonderful whiff of green-apple

shampoo. It's even better than camping at Crezzo and standing up on my own McGrigor.

"What in all the world are you doing here?" I ask Patricia.

"I live here now—we moved back down from Armidale.
Wendy sorted Mum out with a job helping with the women
in the refuge, and I'm going to help too, with the little kids,
when I'm not at school. And guess what? Next year . . . Mum's
looking at going to uni to study social work, part-time. Beats
pumping gas in a servo," she says, all very quickly and full of
excitement.

"Hey, look at you, Ally, you're so tanned and strong!"

"This is the biggest best-ever surprise," I say, giving her
a noogie.

"Well, keep your undies on, 'cause you're about to get a
bigger one," says Patricia, swinging her arm around my waist
and leading me into the house.

The place is packed with women, young, not so young
and old, and kids . . . *kids everywhere:* toddlers and babies,
primary-school kids, and some kids who look bigger than
me. Little ones in high chairs, preschoolers running and
screaming happily up and down the corridor, quieter ones
coloring in together on a low table, others jumping off bunks
onto a pile of pillows and boisterous ones wrestling, rolling and chortling down on the floor. Tired-looking mums
are feeding them, scolding them, chasing them, separating
them, putting on Band-Aids, setting some up with a Chinese checkers board, comforting and cuddling and telling
them loudly to "take that racket outside."

In a corner of the small lounge room Patricia O'Brien's

mum is at a desk, on the phone. She has a pen in her hand and half a frown on her face. Even so, she's saying with an upbeat voice, "No, that's fine, we'll fit you in. Four kids . . . How old's the baby?" She writes something in a notebook and looks at a roster on the wall. She sees me, smiles and gives a warm wave. She still has her overalls on.

"C'mon, let's keep going," says Patricia.

I follow her toward the back door and hear a voice in the kitchen that sounds a lot like . . . *and actually is* . . . Sister Josepha. Yes, it's her—in half a habit—looking hotter than Hades as she stirs a big aluminum pot balancing on a tiny stove. It smells like minced meat.

"Allegra, dear!" Sister stops stirring. "How lovely to see you. And looking such a picture of health, what's more. Yes indeed. Is your father with you?"

"No, he just dropped me off. I don't think he wanted to come in," I say, actually quite stoked to see Sister but still kind of confused: Has Sister Josepha joined the Sisterhood? She has two child helpers; a middle-sized boy grating carrots and a slightly older girl chopping celery. "We're making a big brew of spaghetti bolognaise *together*, aren't we, children? We have thirty-eight to feed tonight, at last count." She turns off the gas flame and puts the lid on the pot. "But that can wait for now. Come with me, Allegra. There is something quite glorious I'd like you to see."

While the two houses look separate from the front, they are open to one another out the back with a large common yard that flows from each kitchen door. The yard is a hive of activity with people weeding, planting and watering, and my first glance tells me that by collective effort it's a space under transformation. It's being turned from a yard into something more like a garden.

Just as I'm processing that, my second glance grabs me, just like my first wave did with its solid blue face, which I recognized as mine and which took me to the safety of the shore. There are two faces here that I recognize now. They are the faces of both of my grandmothers, Joy and Matilde.

Matilde is in her gardening clothes, the same ones she was wearing yesterday. She is directing a thin woman using a Dutch hoe as to where a little trench in the soil should go, while she follows steadily behind her, planting seedlings in finger-sized holes. She looks up and doesn't really seem surprised that I'm here. She gives me a pea-sized-pleased smile. I'm smiling back. The slight vibrations around the edges of her mouth spread and push up the fleshy parts of her cheeks, and her smile grows, creating lines like rays stretching from her blue eyes out to the wisps of gray hair touching her temples. She pauses, wipes her brow and points across the yard with her spade, to Joy.

"You will like very much what your grandmother has created over there. Go, go and see it for yourself, Allegra."

Joy is working at the end of a winding stone path. I approach from her right side. It seems that she is finishing off some sort of small maze. She swings around with a genuine happy face, nothing switched-on about it: relaxed, ready and real.

"Ally, my darling heart! *Oh, Ally, I missed you*, every day I missed you." She takes me to her chest, and I have to bend down a bit in the knees to settle into my berth in her harbor.

"What's going on, Joy?" I whisper. "What are you doing here, *with Matilde?*"

"We're making a garden, Ally, isn't it wonderful! The men from Rotary came and secured the back fence and made a swing and a slide for the children. So we thought—well, it was Sister Josepha's idea really, but Matilde and I agreed—that we could create a garden together so that there was food to feed the women and children and things of beauty to lift their spirits. Matilde is working on the herb and vegetable beds, and I'm planting the blossoms, the ferns and flowers. And it won't surprise you to know that I'm in charge of embellishments as well," she says, looking thrilled. "Would you like to lend a hand, darling?"

I help Joy place the same glazed pots and vases that I saw yesterday in her glasshouse along the path to the maze. "Your mother, Belinda, made these," she says without any fuss, and without pulling a glass bottle out from her bra. Then together we find spots among the flowers, pavers and stones for the little clay animals, putting a green penny tortoise in the middle of a miniature pond.

"Why don't you call Matilde over, darling? There's a job to do now that's best done by the three of us, together. Actually, pet"—Joy changes her mind—"you wait here; I'll let Matilde know." She trots off.

My eyes follow as Joy approaches Matilde, says a few words, and Matilde responds with what could be best described as *grace*. She comes over and stands at the edge of the maze.

Joy opens a cardboard box and produces the glazed clay alphabet letters, which she shares out between us. We look at each other's and realize what they spell . . . and we know the order that we need. I can smell Patricia behind me and feel Sister at my side as I lay down my B. Matilde's next with an E, then Joy with an L, me again with an I and Matilde with N, and so we go on until we have set to rest, in glorious colors, with the odd little dent . . . BELINDA'S GARDEN.

We stand silently, not knowing quite what to do next. Patricia dips her hand into the box. "And what about this?" she says, pulling out the silver mother angel. "Where are you going to put her, Ally? She needs a safe spot, somewhere up high where the little kids can't get to her. Looks like you're sorted out now so she won't need to be coming down again anytime soon!"

At that we look around at each other and can't help but laugh.

Matilde's eyes release fine silver threads, flowing in streams that run down her flushed cheeks. I understand her. I go to her. I take her hand and I kiss her wrist.

And that part of Matilde's heart that has long needed darning is pulled together with one continuous stitch that weaves the silver threads into rows, reversing the direction at the end of each one, then fills in the framework. So that now it is reinforced, strong, and good to go on.

EPILOGUE

ONCE JOY STOPPED BOTTLING HER EMOTIONS, A VALVE RE-
leased within Matilde and her tears started to flow freely.
Tears for interrupted life as she mended; tears of receding
anger as she gardened; and healing tears of loss, grief and
sadness as she pickled, preserved and baked in her kitchen.

They flowed too when she occasionally gave me, during the years that followed—over sewing, seedlings and
servings—her story and *her version of events,* including her
time in Auschwitz, escape from Hungary and the betrayal
she endured when her husband left her in debt with a small
child and fled back to Budapest.

Then on the day that the women decided to name not
just the garden but the whole refuge after my mother, so
it became known as Belinda's Place, Matilde shed tears of
honor, remembrance and renewed purpose that reset her
course for the next twenty-five years. She joined Joy and

"her crazy friends" volunteering, mostly in the garden, often with the children and sometimes helping out with the cooking and the cleaning. She would let Rick know directly—speaking with him respectfully—when a tap at the refuge needed fixing, furniture needed collecting or a lightbulb needed to be changed.

Matilde had many tears of joy too. They flowed when I received my final-year school results, finished my PhD in psychology, and when Patricia graduated with her diploma in early-childhood education, wearing the red silk pantsuit she'd made with Matilde.

Tears of pure delight welled up in Matilde when I gave her a ballet subscription with center-stage seats and we didn't have to *climb all those impossible stairs.*

And they enlivened her eyes the first time I brought Tom home to our regular Friday family dinner, with Rick on the barbecue and Joy slipping through the brown gate with a new signature dessert: "tinned two-fruits trifle with custard, caramel and marshmallow pieces!" Matilde saw instantly Tom's *good self,* Joy his spark and Rick that he was a bloody great bloke. For me it was Tom's kindness that raised my respect and locked in my love.

But Matilde's tears never flowed more than when I told her, throwing the dough one hundred times against the side of the bowl to Liszt's "Hungarian Rhapsody No. 2," that sometime early the next spring she would become a great-grandmother. She later held my newborn, kissed her wrist and wished out loud "nothing more than she be her own person."

■ ■ ■

And today the tears are mine.

We are preparing the food for Matilde's funeral.

I have thrown the dough again for this, my most important strudel. Molly has spread her great-grandmother's pink-stained bedsheet across the kitchen table, and Joy has brought down the last bottle of Matilde's Morello cherries.

"So typical of Matilde," says Joy, moved, amused and touching on admiring. "In a way she has prepared the food for her own funeral."

"I'll put on 'Un Sospiro,'" says Molly.

I place my palm down on the back of Joy's soft hand: long-lived and elegant. Molly joins us, placing her small pink palm—plump with potential—down on the back of my hand, which I see now as worked but not yet worn. Together we slip our hands under the dough and start working it out, carefully, toward the edges of Matilde's table.

"Now we move our hands with the motion of Liszt. He is coaxing us to take great care," says Molly with her nine-year-old take on her Tildie's accent. "His music is guiding us so we don't tear the dough."

We are in rhythm with Liszt and in touch with each other and holding Matilde.

And a thought enters that part of my heart that turns facts into feelings. . . .

■ ■ ■

I am me.

Allegra at thirty-eight, feeling more like you do when you're at every point between eleven and a hundred and two.

I'm not split in two, but made by two, who were made by two, who were made by two, who were made by two. . . .

And I in turn have given life to one, who is the sum of all the couplings and the divisions. The love, fate and lived decisions. The DNA that programs her cells but is not her destiny. The DNA that nourishes that part of her heart that holds hands with the body and the soul of Joy and Matilde, from where she can lift off and expand.

My daughter is of me and of all before me.

But greater than the truths of any of these lives lived before her, will be the freed heart and opened opportunities that beat her story . . . her story . . . her story.

And so continues mine.

I tore myself away from the safe comfort of
certainties through my love for truth—
and truth rewarded me.

—Simone de Beauvoir

ACKNOWLEDGMENTS
AND THE STORY OF ALLEGRA

A *Girl in Three Parts* started with the thought . . . *I wonder if I could actually write a novel.* I whispered it years ago to my friend and now–literary agent, Catherine Drayton, who not only said, "Well, give it a go," but also recommended I read a book called *The First Five Pages* by Noah Lukeman. I did read that book, more than once, and highly recommend it to anyone who's ever had that same thought.

I wanted to combine my love of creative writing with my training in journalism, and for much of the time that I was writing Allegra, she was a hobby, something I felt might be found in my post-funeral cleanup. Something my kids would pick up and say, "Oh, Mum . . . look what she was up to here!" However, my cherished children—Bec, Jem, and Franny—got involved early and did so much more than that: they cheered me on every step of the way.

Allegra was conceived from a dual fascination:

What was happening for women in the 1970s during the second wave of the women's movement, from the street marches to the kitchens? And how does a child carve out their sense of self, especially when there are family-trait differences and when family-perspective differences lead to conflict?

Allegra took her first breaths when I was fortunate to travel to Florence as a participant in the hugely helpful Art of Writing retreat, run by my friend, accomplished author and excellent tutor Lisa Clifford.

She first crawled when I had contact with leading feminist Anne Summers, who put me in touch with Diana Beaton, who, in 1974, along with Anne and others, bravely established Elsie, the first refuge for women and children in Australia. Thank you to Diana for the long conversations, beachside lunch, and telephone calls when I rang with questions like: *What on earth did you feed all those thousands of women and children who came to you at Elsie urgently seeking refuge?* Thanks also to Kris Melmoth, who was there, too, the day that they kicked in the doors and changed the locks. She shared with me compelling stories of her life and the life of women's champion Bessie Guthrie, some of which inspired Whisky Wendy.

Allegra sat up when I sat down in discussion with feminist and heroic change agent for a civil society Eva Cox, who gave me, quite clearly, over a bowl of seafood chowder, direction with a certain aspect of my story line to help make it more credible. And, Eva, I'm going to dob you in . . . you fancy that you project "cranky," but you are actually kindhearted and definitely encouraging.

Allegra got on her feet when I traveled to Yass and spent many hours checking details against lived history with my aunt-in-law Ann Daniel, mother of ten, professor of sociology, businesswoman, shire councillor, feminist, and farmer. It was Ann who confirmed for me that "I Am Woman" was absolutely the anthem of the women's movement in the 1970s. I played that song, on repeat, into the early hours, to keep me focused on the drive back to Sydney.

Allegra really started to trot when, three-quarters through my draft manuscript, Catherine happened to call, on a rather grim day, to see how I was progressing and suggested I have a freelance editor, Alex Craig, look at it for a "reader's response." Alex warned me that she would be "brutally honest" and that in the past she had probably wounded some aspiring authors. I tried to

313

act cool but sweated out her response . . . for ten days . . . until she came back super-generously spurring me on with "Finish it! Just finish it!" Up until that point I hadn't dared ask Catherine to be my agent, nor had she offered, but then she did, and momentum kicked in. I spirited myself away to our farm in Berry and went into "okay, this is a job now" mode, writing night and day, with my husband, Mike, clearing his work so he could handle just about everything else. He made meals, endless cups of tea, concessions, and the time to listen to "readings" of my writing. This is but a skerrick of what Mike has done for me during our decades together. He is the love of my life.

Catherine magically got my manuscript under the noses of great people in publishing in Australia, and on a day that I was attending a School Governance Symposium, she juggled offers and achieved an outcome that, to borrow Allegra's words, had me "bowled over bloody astonished." How fortunate for me to sign with Pan Macmillan and be placed under the wing of publishing director extraordinaire Cate Paterson, my editor. Thank you, Cate, for taking me on, backing, supporting, and developing me. I feel I've known you my whole life, and I hope that I do for the rest of it.

And heartfelt thanks to the magnificent Danielle Walker, senior editor, who has worked closely with me and responds to everything with expertise and grace. My thanks go also to Brianne Collins for her outstanding copyediting skills and to Sammy Mason and Adrik Kemp.

And while I was recovering from all that excitement, in downward dog at a yoga retreat, Catherine called from a business trip to New York with the heart-racing news . . . Knopf Books for Young Readers had picked up Allegra with enthusiasm and was keen to publish her in the US and Canada. It was certainly hard to hold any poses after that! Special thanks to the fabulous Katherine Harrison for her excellent guidance and support and to Allegra's champions at Knopf, Melanie Nolan and Judith Haut. My gratitude goes also to copyeditors Janet Frick, Artie Bennett, and Alison Kolani; managing editor Jake Eldred; and Nathan Kinney in production. And the clever artists and designers Alison Impey and Liz Casal, who dressed Allegra brightly with the beautiful cover.

I had some early readers or listeners who gave me encouragement and valuable advice, especially my wonderful cousin Alanna Swanson, but also Julie King, Helen Moore, Deb McGill, Kylie Pickett, Bronwyn Delaney, Mary McGlinchey, Louise Humphreys, Bridget Walsh, Kate Perkins, Lella Pacetto, and Anita Belgiorno-Nettis. My nephew Paddy Leary, an avid reader and skilled surfer, reviewed the surfing scenes and waved me through. Paddy, I was in the room when you were born, and you were there as my adviser twenty-three years later. Alanna's daughter Molly Swanson was about twelve when I first sent her Allegra's thoughts, words, and feelings, and she provided an invaluable sounding board, letting me know if it was "real" for Allegra to think, speak, and feel this way. My friend Phil Macken put me in touch with surfing-culture legend Albe Falzon, director of the *Morning of the Earth* film in 1971, the first Australian film to receive a Gold Record for album sales. Albe was super helpful, and what wonderful, rounded, and long discussions we had. Thanks, Albe—and keep enjoying those pristine waves at Crezzo! Another friend, Tony Boutagy, rode the old Bulahdelah bends on his bike to check exactly where those "bloody good burgers" were once sold, and pointed out that it was because Liszt didn't have the usual webbing between his fingers that he had extra span on the piano keys. Léone Ziegler, a most talented violinist with the Sydney Symphony Orchestra, listened to my offbeat idea that Liszt's Hungarian Rhapsody no. 2 could provide the right tempo for Matilde to throw the dough when making her cherry strudel. Léone counted it out and confirmed that, yes, this could indeed be possible.

I'd like to thank *my sisterhood:* those who are dear to me from school, university, work, travels, and life. Those who have walked, talked, and laughed with me: bolstered, balanced, and expanded me. Within that group are some who have been particularly supportive of this project. Diana Mills and Mary Beatty read my manuscript, closely, and discussed it like it was one of our children. Allegra, it seems, became as real for them as she did for me. And my lifelong friends Claire Allen and Serena Sanderson: I'm blessed by their friendship because it truly is the color of sunshine. I'd like to acknowledge, too, Madeleine Pedersen, Annette Tynan, my cousin (more sister) Kate Melrose, Claire Tynan, Madeline Tynan, Jacinta Tynan, Maria Vladetta, Hilary Hannam, Caroline Furlong, Kerry Henville, Kathryn Cistulli, Helen Hamblin, Narelle Pye, Robyn and Hannah Silverton, Karen Barkl, Bin Farrell, Peta Daniel, Penny O'Meara, Sarah Buntine, Geraldine Kondilios, Lisa McSweeney, Deb McKeith, Maree Mangan, Kath Daniel, James Leary, Andrew Leary, Chris Manion, Peter Hall, and Mark Forstmann. Because, as Joy says, "Friendship is so fortifying for we girls" . . . and I'd like to add . . . for boys, too!

On the last day before I got my manuscript to Catherine, I had great help from Maureen Whirfler and my daughter Franny with proofreading, every-single-word. Franny's friend Ali Littlewood turned up in the evening thinking she was setting off for a night out with Franny, but instead she set to work with us, printing and collating. Ali, you became my friend, too, that day. Thank you.

I grew up in Yowie Bay with two very different grandmothers, Mollie and May, who lived on opposite sides of the Sydney Harbor Bridge. I was close to them both, but neither of them was much like Joy or Matilde. Although Nanny (Mollie) was about the most loving person I've ever known, and, in many ways, she was my harbor.

Finally, I'd like to remember with great love my mother-in-law, Cyndy, and my extraordinary mother, Colleen. My mother gave me the finest example of strength of character, steadfastness, intellectual curiosity, inclusiveness, enthusiasm, compassion, kindness, and great cooking, and even though she told me to "sit up like a lady," she was, in spirit and by action, a fabulous feminist.

Both of these women were educated by the same order of nuns who educated me, the Sisters of the Society of the Sacred Heart. And those strong, clever, kind, and life-loving sisters taught us all to pursue truth, social justice, and empowerment. They really were, and remain, an unsung yet important element of "the sisterhood."